Denise Sewell grew ... writer, she worked v... substitute teacher, hot-... ... office clerk. She now lives in County Monaghan with her husband and two children. *The Fall Girl* is her second novel.

15

The Fall Girl

DENISE SEWELL

PENGUIN BOOKS

PENGUIN BOOKS

Published by the Penguin Group
Penguin Books Ltd, 80 Strand, London WC2R ORL, England
Penguin Group (USA) Inc., 375 Hudson Street, New York, New York 10014, USA
Penguin Group (Canada), 90 Eglinton Avenue East, Suite 700, Toronto, Ontario, Canada M4P 2Y3
(a division of Pearson Penguin Canada Inc.)
Penguin Ireland, 25 St Stephen's Green, Dublin 2, Ireland (a division of Penguin Books Ltd)
Penguin Group (Australia), 250 Camberwell Road, Camberwell, Victoria 3124, Australia
(a division of Pearson Australia Group Pty Ltd)
Penguin Books India Pvt Ltd, 11 Community Centre, Panchsheel Park, New Delhi – 110 017, India
Penguin Group (NZ), 67 Apollo Drive, Rosedale, North Shore 0632, New Zealand
(a division of Pearson New Zealand Ltd)
Penguin Books (South Africa) (Pty) Ltd, 24 Sturdee Avenue, Rosebank, Johannesburg 2196, South Africa

Penguin Books Ltd, Registered Offices: 80 Strand, London WC2R ORL, England

www.penguin.com

First published by Penguin Ireland 2007
Published in Penguin Books 2008

1

Copyright © Denise Sewell, 2007
All rights reserved

The moral right of the author has been asserted

Set by Rowland Phototypesetting Ltd, Bury St Edmunds, Suffolk
Printed in England by Clays Ltd, St Ives plc

ISBN: 978-0-141-03515-4

www.greenpenguin.co.uk

Mixed Sources
Product group from well-managed
forests and other controlled sources
www.fsc.org Cert no. SA-COC-1592
© 1996 Forest Stewardship Council

Penguin Books is committed to a sustainable future
for our business, our readers and our planet.
The book in your hands is made from paper
certified by the Forest Stewardship Council.

For Leo and Nuala McGrath

(Mum and Dad)

15 September 1999 (sometime in the middle of the night)

There are no excuses for what I've done.

My daughter's eighteenth birthday

It's 24 August 1999: almost midnight. I've just spoken to my father on the phone. He's very upset; I've let him down again.

'It'll be the shock,' Sergeant Hennessy says. 'Give him time, he'll come round.'

I have to spend the night in a cell at the Garda Station, but I don't care; a bed is a bed and at this stage my body feels shaky with exhaustion. As soon as the bangharda opens the door leading to the cells, a vile smell fills my nostrils and my stomach churns.

'I'm not going in there,' I whimper, taking a panicky step back. 'It smells of piss and shit.'

'I'm sorry,' she shrugs. 'There's nowhere else to put you. This is it, I'm afraid.'

Someone lets out a string of obscenities from behind a cell door.

'Are there *men* in there?'

'Just one man so far: the night is young. But, don't worry, you've a cell to yourself. Now, come on,' she tugs my elbow, 'you'll be grand.'

'Can I stay in the interview room?'

'No, Frances, you can't. That room could be used several times before the night is out.'

'You can put her in beside me,' the gruff-tongued man shouts. 'I'll keep her company. Is she good-lookin'?'

'Shut up, Packie,' she tells him.

But he doesn't. 'Are you good-lookin'?' he shouts a little louder.

We're standing at a cell door now. The bangharda is turning the key. 'Don't mind him,' she says, 'he's a regular guest in here.'

As she opens the door, the smell thickens and my stomach retches.

'Toilet,' I cry, putting my hand over my mouth.

'OK, come on.' She leads me back to the Ladies, where I vomit several times.

Afterwards, she gets me a cup of water and I stand with my back against the cubicle wall, sipping and sobbing.

'It's only for one night, Frances,' she says.

'Why? Where will I be tomorrow night?'

'I don't know, but it won't be as dirty as this kip here, I can promise you that.'

'I can't go back in there. Can I not stay in the other room where I saw the doctor?'

She shakes her head.

'Please let me.'

'I can't.'

'If you take me back there, I'm going to throw up again.'

'Then you're going to have to do it inside the cell. You can't keep coming out to the toilet all night.'

'Is there no toilet in there?'

'No, but there is an alternative. Come on,' she sighs, taking the empty plastic cup from my hand, 'let's go. The eyes are hanging out of your head; you need to sleep.' She opens the door. 'After you.'

'Oh no, oh Jesus!' I groan, dragging myself down the corridor a reluctant pace ahead of her.

'If it's any consolation,' she says, 'I find the stink revolting too, and I'm in and out of here several times a week.'

'So where's the alternative?' I ask as soon as I step inside the cell.

'There.' She's pointing to what looks like a shallow sink built into the floor.

'You're joking.'

'I'm not.'

'But –'

The man in the next cell lets out an unmerciful belch.

'I need a drink, youse shower of fuckin' bastards,' he roars. 'If youse don't get me one now, I'll kick this fuckin' door down.'

'Sorry, I have to go,' the bangharda says. 'Just try to get some sleep, will you?'

Before I have time to draw breath, she's out the door and turning the key in the lock.

I'm alone now, heart banging inside my ribcage like a mad animal. I look around me. The walls and floor are grimy. There's a dirty blanket flung across a thin, stained mattress. The toilet is a dip in the ground with a plughole that is clogged with all sorts of grot.

My God! What have I done?

A buzzer goes off and I yelp, staggering as I take a step back. Within a few seconds, I hear whistling and a key turn in the outer door. It's not the bangharda this time.

'What do you want now, Packie?'

'A fuckin' drink.'

'Will water do you?'

'Water me arse. I want a real drink.'

'If you call me in here again to ask me for booze, I'm switching that buzzer off for the night, got it?'

'You can't do that; it's against the law. I'll report you.'

'Report whatever the fuck you like. If you don't stop wasting my time, the buzzer is going off, end of story.'

'Excuse me, Guard, excuse me, Guard,' I splutter, bolting towards the cell door and knocking frantically.

The hatch opens. 'Yes?' Two angry eyes are glaring at me.

'Eh, eh . . .' I swallow hard, fighting back the tears.

'What? Spit it out, I haven't got all night.'

'I don't want to stay in here,' I sob. 'Please.'

The man in the other cell starts shouting, 'This little piggy went to market, oink oink. This little piggy stayed at home . . .'

'That's it, Packie,' the Guard tells him, 'your buzzer's going off.' He looks back at me. 'What did you expect, the Hilton?'

'. . . and this poor piggy got none,' the man roars.

'No, but –'

'Look, it's a cell you're in, not a honeymoon suite, so get used to it, cos there's nothing I or anyone else can do for you.'

'Tom, Tom the piper's son, stole a pig and away did run. Yah-fuckin'-hoo,' the man howls.

'Christ, such a night!' the Guard groans, slamming the hatch shut.

As I back away from the door towards the bed, it begins to hit me – the depth of the trouble I'm in. I have committed a serious crime. It can't be undone. I'm a prisoner. My father doesn't want to know me. My life will never be the same again.

I lift the manky blanket and wrap it around my shoulders.

Surrendering to the dirt and the smell, I lie down on the mattress and curl up. My feet are swollen, my back aches. I'm still trembling.

Why did I listen to that woman in the jeweller's shop? Why do I always let other people's comments get to me? Why did I do it?

My head is swimming. When I shut my eyes, I see myself back in Dublin, chin up, all business. I'm happy, and why not? It's my daughter's eighteenth birthday – a milestone. I walk into a jeweller's shop in Henry Street and pick out a gold chain – a T-bar chain, eighteen inches. An inch for every year.

'Good choice,' the assistant says. 'Is it for yourself?'

'No,' I smile. 'It's for my daughter.'

'Lucky girl. How old?'

'Eighteen.'

'Same age as my own,' she says, fixing the chain in the velvet-lined gift box and holding it up for my approval.

I nod.

'I must say, I love gold myself, though you'd not see *my* young one wearing it. They're all into silver nowadays. Still, as far as I'm concerned . . .'

I run out the door and into the middle of the street, where I stop short. She calls out after me, 'Are you all right, missus?'

There are throngs of people walking in all directions. What's wrong with me? Why didn't *I* think of that? I should have known – silver, not gold. My cover's blown. I can't even fool myself any longer. She isn't eighteen. She hasn't grown up. I lost her. No! Stop! Don't think about it, not today. Don't go, Baby Fall. Be, for me. Get back in my head. Get back in my womb. And kick.

People brush past me, bump into me, tread on my toes. They've no manners. Can they not see me? Someone nearly knocks me down. I try to walk away, but I can't find a passage: I'm surrounded. A mother with a pram crosses the street in front of me: 'Excuse me, excuse me.' Everyone makes way. Like a disciple, I follow her, just to get out of the maze, to breathe. She stops outside a boutique, puts her foot down on the brake of the pram and walks in the door, a bag slung over her shoulder, high heels, lipstick. She has her hungry eyes on the merchandise, on the price tags. Never mind the baby.

When I peep inside the pram, I clamp my hand over my mouth and gasp. Although she's bigger than my baby was, she still looks new.

The security guard is watching the shapely mother flicking through the rails. Tight jeans, tight bum.

I could have been anyone – a nutter, a killer, one of those child-traffickers, just waiting for the right opportunity. You can't be careful enough these days.

'She was lucky it was me and not one of them.' That's what I tell Sergeant Hennessy.

'I suppose it's one way of looking at it, but you still did wrong.'

'I never meant to hurt anyone. I'm sorry.'

'I can see that.'

'Can I go home now?'

'It's not that simple, I'm afraid.'

'Why not?'

'There are procedures.'

'Procedures?'

'In cases like this.'

'How do you mean?'

'You kidnapped a baby, Frances.'

'You're making me out to be some sort of criminal.'

'Technically, you are.'

Can you believe that? Me, Mousy Fall – a criminal. Put that in your celestial pipe, Mother, and smoke it.

19 September 1999 (afternoon)

Mousy Fall was my nickname at school. I hated it. I used to feel grateful if someone called me by my name, especially Lesley. I was always Frances to Lesley.

Introducing Mousy Fall

It's my first day at secondary school. I'm waiting for the school bus. My mother's poking her head in and out of the front door, keeping an eye on me. I'm pretending not to see her. The twins – Angelina and Attracta Reilly – say she's like one of those ornamental storks on a pendulum, long pointy hooter and all. Hurry up, bus.

My uniform skirt is hanging inches below my gabardine to half-way down my calves. I'm wearing white knee-high socks, no flesh exposed. I look hideous. There are only two other girls from the village attending the Mercy Convent, but they're in third year and are wearing blazers and knee-length skirts.

My schoolbag feels a ton weight. The straps are digging into the tops of my shoulders. I'm too warm. I'd love to throw my bag down on the ground where the other students have thrown theirs and undo the belt and buttons of my gabardine, but my mother is probably still watching me. Best to leave it the way it is.

With all the pushing and shoving to get on the bus, I stand

back and wait. I don't mind being last. What about it? Blessèd are the meek and all that. I get the front seat. For they shall inherit the front seat. No one else wants it.

'Oi, look, Frances,' one of the boys shouts down the bus, 'your mother's waving at ya.'

Big laugh.

'Your man back there gave your mother the fingers,' Attracta tells me.

It's all right for the rest of them. They're used to it – the rowdiness, the slagging, the crude language.

Every time the bus stops to pick up more students, there's an uproar.

'Hurry up, Jones, ya huare ya.'

'Shut it, Four-eyes, or I'll bate the head off ya.'

And it isn't just the boys. When I hear someone strike a match, I turn and see Susan Scully, in the seat behind me, light a cigarette like a seasoned smoker.

'Want a drag, Mousy?' she says, sticking out her chin and blowing a thin line of smoke in my direction.

Mousy! Is she talking to me? She is!

'Here, Mousy Mousy, want a nibble of my cheese sandwich?'

'Where's your hole, Mousy?'

I don't react. If I ignore them, they'll get fed up and pick on someone else. But they don't.

By the time we arrive at the convent, I'm well and truly christened. Mousy Fall. It sticks. I think it's funny how my mother often turns out to be right about people, hard as I find her scornfulness to swallow.

I don't expect to see Lesley there. There was no sign of her at the enrolment months earlier, but it's her for sure. Apart from her height, she hasn't changed much. But there's something different about her. I can't put my finger on it.

A couple of days later, our eyes meet in the corridor, she walking in one direction, me walking in the other. There's a group of girls with her. I'm on my own. I smile at her, hopeful of rekindling our friendship. She smiles back, nostalgically I think. A that-was-then-this-is-now look on her face. The moment passes. There's definitely something different about her. What? An air of tragedy? Eyes that have seen darkness? I'm drawn to her again, but I can't go where I'm not invited. I wouldn't dare. Besides, she has her new friends, lots of them. Smitten just like I was. Am.

It isn't long before Lesley is earning a reputation for herself, and not a great one at that. She doesn't turn up to all her classes. One day she doesn't show up at all and she's not ill. Sister Marie-Therese, the principal, has phoned her mother, who has confirmed that she's not at home sick. We're not in the same class, though, so I only hear rumours.

I find a friend of my own in the end or, should I say, a companion. Kathleen Mulcahy, or Kat, as she becomes known, in order to satisfy their mocking tongues – Kat and Mousy.

She comes to me, one oddball sniffing out another. I don't really like her. In fact, she drives me mad the way she chews her egg and onion sandwiches with her mouth gaping or slurps her tea, while she scoffs up her sleeve and nudges me sneakily, whispering about this one and that one. She's cowardly – an onlooker.

Three years our companionship lasts; three dreary years. During that time Lesley and I never speak beyond the odd greeting, usually if I bump into her on her own, which isn't very often. It's only a *howaya, Frances*, but it means a lot to me. I appreciate it. She makes me feel normal, acceptable, un-mouselike.

25 September 1999 (evening)

I'll never forget the first time I met Lesley. She danced her way into my heart.

My best friend Lesley

It's 1971. I'm almost eight. I'm at my Irish dance class. My mother is sitting by my side on the bench at the back of the hall. It must be summer because the window is open behind me and I can feel the heat prickle the back of my neck. Miss Jackson, our teacher, is finishing up with the younger group and asks me to call in the other children from the car park. That's where they play while they're waiting their turn to dance. I'm not allowed to join them. My mother tells me to stay where I am and put on my pumps; she will call the others in.

As she's heading out the door, she stops suddenly and stands back, and a very tall, heavily built woman steps into the hall, with a striking, dark-haired girl of about my own age trailing behind her.

Taking hold of the girl's hand, the woman plods across the hall and plonks herself down beside me. She asks me my name. Her accent is strange. I can't see the girl; she's sitting on the far side of the woman.

'How old are you?' the woman then asks.

'Eight.'

'There you are, our Lesley. This young girl's the same age as yourself.'

The girl leans forward and stares into my face. She doesn't smile. She doesn't need to. She has the most beautiful face I've ever seen.

'A new girl,' Miss Jackson says.

'Yes,' the woman says, 'though she's been at the dancing back home in Manchester for a few years now.'

Miss Jackson asks the girl if she'll do a reel. The girl nods. My mother's sitting beside me again, giving the big woman the once-over. The girl stands in the centre of the hall, throws back her shoulders and puts her slender right leg forward, toes pointed. She's wearing a short, red, pleated kilt, a white polo, white knee socks and well-worn, wrinkly pumps without laces. They remind me of ballet shoes.

Before she lowers the stylus on to the vinyl, Miss Jackson says, 'Quiet, please.'

No further requests for silence are necessary. Lesley's like a pixie in the wind, circling and twirling around the hall, barely skimming the floorboards. I've never seen anyone leap so high and land so softly. I can feel my skin tingling. Tapping my mother's sleeve, I tell her, 'I want to dance like that,' but she ignores me, her cold eyes fixed firmly on Lesley, who has just finished her reel and is taking a well-rehearsed bow.

'I think the music needs Lesley more than Lesley needs the music,' Miss Jackson says.

My mother's jaw is stiff, as her chin withdraws into the folds of her neck. I wonder what it is that Lesley has done to earn this instant disapproval.

An hour later I'm on the swing in Aunty Lily's garden. I love that swing. She bought it especially for me, having no children of her own. My mother and she are sitting out in deckchairs, drinking tea.

'You should have seen her,' my mother says about Lesley, 'kicking her legs up higher than a French tart doing the cancan.'

I drag my soles along the grass and stop the swing. 'What's a French tart?'

'Quit earwigging, you,' my mother says.

Aunty Lily is bent over coughing, laughing and struggling for breath.

'Take it easy there, Lily.' My mother rubs her sister's back. 'Don't you know you shouldn't be getting yourself all worked up like that?'

'Ah Jesus,' Aunty Lily gasps, 'if I can't have a laugh now and again, what's the point?'

A couple of weeks later, my mother drops me off at my dance class and says my father will collect me at midday. She's going to spend the whole morning with Aunty Lily.

'Go on outside and play with the others, child of grace,' Miss Jackson says, 'and don't be sitting there all on your owney-o.'

I can't believe she's letting me go out. She knows very well my mother wouldn't approve. I keep looking back at her as I edge my way over to the door, half expecting her to change her mind. But she's busy showing a young lad how to point his toes. When I open the door, I can hear the other children playing. I walk down the steps, unsure of what I'm going to do with myself when I get to the bottom.

Lesley has everyone lined up against the back wall. She's skipping in front of them and singing:

My sister Jane was far too young
to marry a man of a hundred and one . . .

I sidle over to the adjacent wall and sit on an empty beer keg from the pub next door. Lesley is the only one who notices me. She smiles, gesturing me over to her line. I can feel my face turning red as I walk across to join the others. Lesley has to pick someone from the row to have a go and chooses me.

'I don't know how to play the game,' I tell her.

'It doesn't matter,' she says, taking my hand. 'Just follow my steps and I'll do the singing.'

25 September 1999 (bedtime)

I'm not sure about all this reminiscing. Where is it going to get me? It might do more harm than good. Earlier on today, when I was thinking about the first time I met Lesley, I almost felt normal. But I'm not normal. Normal people don't kidnap babies, do they?

Her eighteenth birthday

I stand beside the pram, facing the mannequins in the shop window. Inside I see the baby's mother rummaging through the bargain rail. She doesn't even look over her shoulder to check on her child. What the hell is wrong with her? Why is she being so irresponsible? How come she gets to be a mother and I don't? I would never have left my baby unattended. It's not fair. This shouldn't be happening. Everything's arseways. I could scream.

The security guard steps inside the shop and starts chatting with one of the assistants. The only eyes on the baby now are mine. It's a split-second decision – I stretch out my leg, release the brake with my foot and grab the handle.

'Excuse me,' I say, pushing the pram in front of me towards O'Connell Street.

A path opens up as pedestrians step out of my way. I don't feel crazy and I don't feel wrong. I just want to protect this child. *I* want to be . . . *should* be her mother.

I'm at the top of Henry Street in less than a minute. There's no hysteria; no screaming, delirious mother howling to the heavens, 'Where's my baby?'

Taking a left turn, I walk down to the traffic lights and around Parnell Square. When I see my car in the distance, I quicken my pace. The sooner we get away from the city, the better.

At the car, I try to remove the carrycot from the frame of the pram, but the blasted thing won't budge. I get down on my hunkers and start fumbling with the pram's undercarriage.

'Are you OK there, missus?' a man says. He has an inner city accent, black loafers and white socks.

'Fine,' I snap, without looking up at him.

'Bleedin' hell, keep your fuckin' wig on, will ya?' he says, stomping on his cigarette butt. 'Oi was only askin'.'

When I finally manage to release the four clamps that secure the carrycot to the frame of the pram, I lift it off, put it into the back seat and fasten the seatbelt around it. The baby's eyes are flickering underneath her spongy eyelids. Aching to kiss her, I bend down to pick her up, but then think better of it: I don't want to waken her. Besides, there'll be plenty of time for kisses later. I take the baby bag from the carrier basket and put it on the passenger seat. Then I fold down the frame and shove it into the boot.

I turn the key in the ignition. Gerry Ryan is still on the radio, so I know it's not yet twelve o'clock. At the first red light I turn to check on the baby. All I can see is the back of her head – wisps of downy white hair – and I remember how my father once told me that when I was born my hair was as white as snow.

Several minutes later, I find myself on a roundabout. I drive around it three times wondering where to go, before taking the exit for the Naas dual carriageway: the farther away from Crosslea, the better. There's no way I can bring her home yet: maybe in a week or two. Then I could tell my father that she's mine. Women do it from time to time – disappear for a couple of weeks and arrive back home with their babies.

She begins to stir and moan.

'Ssh, little baby, ssh, ssh.'

When she quietens, I'm sure she's comforted by the sound of my voice and I'm chuffed.

On hearing the news come on, I bless myself and turn up the volume. I can't believe it's one o'clock. How did I manage to miss the twelve o'clock news? There is no mention of a missing baby in the headlines. It doesn't make sense. I can't understand it. Why aren't they looking for her? I should be relieved, and part of me is, but I'm angry too, because if it hadn't been me who had taken her, she could've ended up in the arms of some nutter; in danger, dead even. Thank God it was me, I think, my eyes filling up at the thought of what might have happened to her otherwise.

She begins to stir again. This time she makes little kissy sounds that tell me she's hungry. When she starts to cry, I sing to her:

Hush little baby don't say a word
Mama's gonna buy you a mockingbird . . .

It's getting hot inside the car. I roll down the window.

And if that mockingbird won't sing
Mama's gonna buy you a diamond ring . . .

A couple of miles outside Naas, I get stuck in a traffic jam. The baby is wailing now, stopping only to draw breath. Afraid that someone in the surrounding cars might hear her cry and become suspicious, I roll up the window again.

'Oh God, please help me.'

I can see a service station about a hundred yards away, but at the rate we're moving, it could take me another ten minutes to get there. I cannot wait. Indicating, I pull over on to the hard shoulder and drive up into the courtyard. My hands are trembling as I lift the baby out of the carrycot and hold her close to my chest. She nestles into me, urgently searching with her mouth. Her impatient lips try to latch on to my breast. She's moving back and forth on me, as if she's blowing on a mouth organ. I want to rip open my blouse and feel the softness of her head on my naked breast. If only I could quench her thirst.

A bottle, I think, puffing and panting to keep myself calm. I put my free hand into the baby bag, pulling out nappies, a bib, a bottle. The flipping thing is empty! I root around the inside of the bag again, this time finding a soother. When I put it in her mouth, she sucks furiously. I turn the baby bag upside down and shake out the rest of its contents on to the passenger seat, but there's no formula, just a packet of baby wipes and a baby-gro. As I lift the bag to throw it into the back seat, I feel something rectangular and solid in the front pocket. Undoing the zip, I pull it out. Yes! Thank you, God. It's a carton of Cow and Gate milk.

'It's OK, baby,' I pant, wiping my brow. 'It's OK.'

She cries and kicks, banging her feet on the steering wheel. I try to open the carton of formula, but my nails are too short to make a slit: I have to use my teeth. Outside, people are getting in and out of cars, I can hear doors slamming, but I don't look out. The baby spits out the soother and throws back her head, flexing her limbs and squalling as if she's in terrible pain. She's frightening me now. Pushing back my seat, I lay her down on my knees. I need to fill her bottle quickly. As I loosen the top, I become aware of two children staring in the window. The baby jolts again, this time kicking my elbow. Milk spills over the side of the bottle and soaks my skirt. I don't care as long as I can manage to get enough into the bottle to satisfy her, to shut her up.

'OK, baby, here it comes,' I say, screwing on the top. 'Ssh ssh ssh.'

Holding her in the crook of my arm, I put the teat to her mouth.

There. There. There.

She's drinking now, fast and furious. I sense her relief in the sound of her breathing. Beads of sweat are trickling down the small of my back, making me itchy. I haven't time to scratch myself. I don't have a free hand either.

Looking down at her, I find it impossible not to feel moved by her big, blue, dependent eyes gazing back up at me and scanning my face.

I listen to the one-thirty news headlines. There's still no mention of a missing baby. It doesn't make sense. It must be two hours now since I found her. Unless, of course, she'd been abandoned. It's not beyond the realms of possibility. I've heard of several cases of mothers abandoning their babies in Ireland. And this child's mother did look very young: too young. Perhaps she couldn't cope. She could be on her own, without a man, without support, without money. She could be depressed, on drugs; at the end of her tether. Who knows?

'Did your mother abandon you, sweetheart?' I look at her helpless face. 'Don't worry, I'll look after you.'

Maybe it's fate. I've never really believed in fate, not since . . . not for eighteen years. But why me? And why now? Today on her eighteenth birthday. Fate – it's the only explanation.

26 September 1999 (middle of the night)

Fate is only an explanation, a watery excuse. And, as I've said, there are no excuses for what I've done.

27 September 1999 (afternoon)

Fate reminds me of that song: 'Que sera sera'. My Aunty Lily used to sing it. I can still see her sitting in the armchair, singing and swaying, her eyes dancing in her head, her face flushed from brandy. Oblivious to her fate. Not a worry in the world that I could see.

'Come on, Frances, sing along with your Aunty Lily,' she'd say, taking me on her knee. 'You have a lovely sweet voice just like me.'

Aunty who?

We're having a visitor – my Aunty Lily. She's from London, no less. I can hardly wait. I look at the clock for the hundredth time since morning. Though I can't yet read the time, I can tell it's after two o'clock, but not yet three.

'A watched kettle never boils,' my mother says.

'I'm not watching the kettle,' I tell her. 'I'm watching the clock.'

'Here, make yourself useful.' She hands me a plate, a doily and a packet of assorted biscuits.

'What's she like?' I ask, as I arrange the biscuits around the plate – plain, fancy, plain, fancy, plain, fancy.

'You'll see for yourself,' she says with a sigh.

Tearing off wads of tinfoil, she covers the plate of sandwiches, the biscuits and the apple tart. Then she checks her watch.

'They should be leaving the airport about now,' she says, wringing her hands nervously. 'Run upstairs and get my beads from under my pillow. We'll say a decade of the rosary that your father and Aunty Lily will have a safe journey home.'

Prayers said, I kneel up on the armchair next to the window in the front room to watch out for them. The Reilly twins, who are in my class, are playing out on the street. I lean across the back of the armchair, knock on the windowpane and shout out to them that I'm waiting for my aunty who's coming over from London. When I realize that they can't hear me, I climb across the top of the armchair and on to the windowsill. As I reach up to open the top window, my mother comes in and scolds me for being so noisy. I don't think she quite understands how excited I'm feeling. Up until this day, apart, of course, from my parents, I haven't met any of the few relatives I have. Both my grandmothers and my maternal grandfather are dead. My paternal grandfather lives in Australia with my father's sister, Aunty Philomena. I didn't even know Aunty Lily existed until last week. My mother never said she had a younger sister.

'Aunty who?' I asked her, when she'd told me about our visitor.

'Your Aunty Lily. From London.'

'I didn't know about her.'

My mother said of course I did, but that I must have forgotten, and that she's not surprised because I've a head like a sieve.

Everyone else at school has sisters, brothers, grandmothers, grandfathers, aunties, uncles, first cousins, second cousins, third cousins once removed. They're all part of big families, local families. They all have the usual surnames – Maguire, Reilly, Cusack, Kelly. No one ever asks – Which of the Falls would that be?

Through the net curtain, I see the car coming and I call out to my mother. She shoos me away from the window and reminds me once again to be on my best behaviour. The key turns in the front door.

'Stay where you are,' my mother says, patting her hair as she steps into the hall.

'Rita!' my aunty whoops. 'Ah Jesus, it's great to see you.'

'Hello, Lily,' my mother says. 'It's good to see you too. Eh . . . and who have we here?'

'That's my old man,' my aunty tells her.

'Your . . . pardon me?'

'My husband.'

'Good God!'

'Rita, Xavier. Xavier, Rita.'

'It's very nice to meet you,' the man says.

'Holy Immaculate Mother, when did all this happen?' my mother asks.

'Arragh, I'll tell you all about that later,' my aunty says. 'First things first. Where's Frances?'

The door swings open and a lady, whom I can't believe to be my mother's sister, throws open her arms to me. I'm standing facing her, staring at her tangerine blouse, her brown bell-bottoms and her crocodile boots, not quite knowing what I'm supposed to do.

'Hello,' I say.

'Come 'ere and give me a hug, love,' she says, her arms still outstretched.

I try to catch my mother's eye for her approval, but I can't see her face; she's standing behind my aunty's husband, who has the cut of a grandfather about him. As I walk towards Aunty Lily, I see tears in her eyes. She bends down and squeezes me so tight my ribs hurt. For a moment, everyone is silent.

'Sit down, why don't ye,' my father says, and I'm relieved to be released from my aunty's embrace.

My mother shows her sister round the house. My father and my new uncle, Xavier, have a drink. I like the whiskey smell and the crystal glasses. Xavier tells my father about meeting Lily two years after his first wife had passed away. He has two daughters – Madeleine and Linda – in their late teens, working lassies, one a nurse, the other a telephonist.

'Nice steady jobs,' my father says. 'I'm in the post office myself – a postman.'

'A good, honest job,' Xavier says.

'Aye.'

'The women have a lot of catching up to do.'

'They have indeed. It's been a while.'

'Almost seven years, I take it.'

'Aye, that'd be about right.'

'I think Lily misses having family around her.'

'I suppose she would,' my father says, shifting in his seat like he's sitting on something lumpy.

'Twenty-five years I've been in London and I still don't call it home.'

'Do you not?'

'No. Armagh is still home to me, and will be till the day I die.'

'But your girls are settled in London, aren't they?'

'Oh aye; they were born and reared in it.'

'Sure, they're the most important family you have now. And Lily, of course.'

'The girls will move on, get married and set up homes of their own. That's the way it goes,' Xavier says, pulling a pipe and a box of matches from his sports-jacket pocket.

Aunty Lily peeps in the door and tells her husband that she needs help to take the luggage up to their room.

'Will you let the man finish his drink first?' my father says.

But my uncle is already on his feet.

'She keeps me on my toes, does this one,' he says, putting down his pipe on the mantelpiece. There's something about the way he says it that makes me think he could stay on his toes for ever.

While they're upstairs, my mother slips back into the room and says in a loud whisper, 'Has that girl lost leave of her senses altogether?'

'As far as I can gather,' my father says, 'she's just the same old Lily – full of surprises.'

'I think I'd class marrying a white-haired publican as more of a shock than a surprise. And did you know he's a widower and has two daughters in their late teens?'

'Aye, so he was telling me.'

'What in God's name possessed her? Why couldn't she have just waited? A fine-looking woman like her – she could've had her pick of husbands if she'd played her cards right.'

'They seem right happy to me.'

'Yeah, but for how long? That man will be collecting the pension before Lily hits thirty.' She lifts back the fire screen and pokes the coals. 'And she'll be spoon-feeding him before she hits forty. If my poor mother could see her now, she'd turn in her grave, God rest her.' She hangs the poker back on its hook and blesses herself.

'Will you not be worrying about Lily, Rita? She'll be grand.'

'Living in the upstairs of a public house! I can't see them getting a rosary said of an evening in that kind of seedy atmosphere, can you?'

As if in response to my mother's remarks, we hear an outburst of laughter from upstairs.

'See,' my father says. 'Happy as the day is long.'

I don't think my father realizes that it's not her sister's happiness my mother is worried about: it's her soul. If she's not getting a rosary in every day, she could find herself on what my mother calls the slippery slope.

When Lily and Xavier come downstairs, my mother goes quiet, but I know she's thinking and worrying, and wondering what she can do, if anything.

'I'll make the tea,' she says at the first lull in conversation.

'I'll have coffee, Rita, if it's not too much trouble,' Aunty Lily says. 'You just can't get the same kick out of a cuppa tea.'

'Oh you can't, can't you?' my mother mutters on her way out the door, signalling for me to follow her.

'Here,' she sighs, handing me a pound note in the kitchen. 'Run up to Scully's for a jar of coffee. Madam must have her kicks, God help us!'

After we've eaten, Aunty Lily tells me to follow her and leads me upstairs to her room.

'For you, love,' she says, handing me a black-haired doll in a yellow dress.

'Listen,' she says, pulling a string on the doll's back.

My name is Rosie, it squeaks.

'You do it,' Aunty Lily says.

I pull the string. *Will you play with me?*

'You'll be looking forward to having your friends round to show her off, won't you?' she says.

'I don't have any friends.'

'Of course you do,' my mother titters, coming into the room. 'Though living in Crosslea, she's hardly spoiled for choice.'

For the first time since she's arrived, Aunty Lily isn't smiling.

At seven o'clock, my mother announces that it's time for the rosary and offers a set of beads to her sister.

'Ye go on ahead,' my aunty says, dragging on her cigarette. 'Xavier and I say ours together in bed at night. Isn't that right, darling?'

'Oh God, aye,' he says and either sneezes or sniggers, I'm not sure which.

'How long do you intend staying?' my mother asks her sister over breakfast the following morning. My father and Xavier aren't up yet.

'Just the week. Why? Are you getting tired of us already?'

'No, no, it's not that. I was just wondering.'

'Sure, I have to spend a few days with my long-lost niece,' she says, ruffling my hair. 'You wouldn't begrudge me that, would you?'

My mother lifts the teapot. 'I'd better fill the kettle again,' she says. 'It's nearly empty.'

'Who do you think she looks like, Rita?'

'I really don't know.'

'I think she's the down stamp of Mammy.'

'Good morning, ladies,' my father says, coming into the kitchen.

My mother looks up at the clock. 'About time.'

'She's as bossy as ever, I see,' Aunty Lily says, pulling out a chair for my father.

My mother's cheeks flush.

'I was just saying to Rita, Joe, I think Frances is the image of our mother. Would you agree?'

'You needn't be asking him,' my mother says. 'When it comes to family resemblances, he wouldn't have a notion who's like whom. Would you, Joe?'

'Nah,' my father says, looking at the floor and scratching his head, 'Rita's right. You're asking the wrong man.'

'Take it from me, love,' Aunty Lily smiles at me, 'you're the picture of your grandmother. *Bee-autiful* she was. Everyone thought so. Didn't they, Rita?'

'They did.'

'I'm supposed to be like her too.'

'That's the first I heard of it,' my mother says, placing a clean cup and saucer in front of my father.

'Oh yeah,' Lily says, pulling a cigarette from her packet, 'people were always telling me that.'

*

When the visitors take the bus into town on the Monday afternoon to go shopping, my mother sprays air-freshener all over the house and tells my father that she's counting the hours. I'm not quite able to count the hours, but I am counting the days. I'm going to miss them. In fact, I'm already missing them and they've only gone into Castleowen for a few hours. What I notice most is that I can hear the clocks tick again and somehow that makes me feel lonely.

The night before they leave, my mother invites her friend Nancy, the district nurse, and Nancy's brother, Father Vincent, the parish priest in Castleowen, to join us for the evening. They're all from the same town in County Cork. When Father Vincent asks about London, Aunty Lily talks about the underground trains, Buckingham Palace, Piccadilly, Hyde Park, Chinese restaurants and its huge department stores.

'Some day I'll take you to London, love,' she says, winking at me. 'You'll absolutely love it.'

'With all its attractions,' Xavier says, and takes two quick puffs of his pipe, 'it can't hold a candle to Ireland.'

'I'd say not,' Father Vincent says.

'To be quite frank with you, Father, London's going to the dogs.'

'Is that right?'

'Och aye. Between the hippies and the junkies and the nig ... the blacks, you don't know who you're going to run into when you step outside your front door.'

'Are there a lot of blacks?' Father Vincent asks.

'They're coming in their shiploads.'

'From where?'

'Africa, Jamaica, Timbuktu, I don't know. Sure they all look the same to me. And I'll tell you something else –'

'What's that?'

'I'd sooner have an English Protestant for a next-door neighbour than one of them fellas. And coming from a deep-rooted republican family, that's saying something.'

My father unscrews the top of the whiskey bottle and refills the glasses. My mother pours more tea for Nancy and herself.

'Are you sure,' she says to Lily, 'you'll not have a cup of coffee instead?'

'Thanks, but no thanks. I'm on my holidays. I'll enjoy my wee drink, if it's all the same to you.'

Aunty Lily's legs are crossed: the upper one is swinging. She forgets she has a cigarette resting in the ashtray and lights another.

'I don't mind the blacks,' she says, and everyone looks at her as if she's lost her marbles. 'Well, I don't. There's a black woman working in the laundromat up our street and I'm telling ye straight, a nicer woman you wouldn't meet.'

'Well, isn't that something,' Nancy says. 'And would ye have a chat, you and this black lady?'

'We would surely. We have a bit of a natter every time I'm in doing my laundry. She's a great oul character.'

'And where does this woman hail from?' Father Vincent asks.

'Jamaica.'

'Is she a Catholic?' Nancy asks.

'I couldn't tell you what religion she is; I've never bothered to ask her. Sure, what difference does it make to me who she prays to?'

'Talk to the divil, would my wee Lily,' Xavier says, reaching over and touching her cheek with the blunt tips of his fingers.

When he looks into her eyes, Xavier's face reminds me of

a sleepy moon and I think that he must really like her, even though she does talk to blacks.

'Tell me this, Rita,' Father Vincent says. 'Now that you and Lily are back in touch, would you consider taking a trip over to London yourself?'

'Indeed, I would not. I've no desire to go chasing excitement, Father. A couple of days on the Donegal coast is more than enough for me.'

'Not to worry,' Xavier says, and straightens himself up in the armchair, 'because Lily and I –'

'No, no. Not yet, Xavier,' Aunty Lily says.

'Sure, why not, love? Isn't now as good a time as any?'

Aunty Lily tips the last of her whiskey into her mouth. Then she nudges her husband. 'OK, go on so. Tell them.'

'That trip into Castleowen the other day – well, it wasn't just a shopping excursion. Lily and I have put a deposit on a house in Sycamore Street. I'm selling the bar beyond, and we're moving back.'

Father Vincent says it's great news and won't it be ideal for both of them to be so close to their families. Isn't Xavier's hometown of Armagh just a stone's throw from Castleowen and yet they'll be south of the border and not stuck in the middle of all the troubles. From what he's heard, it'll get worse before it gets better.

'That's right,' Nancy says. 'He has a good point there, right enough.'

'Well, isn't that a good one,' my father says. 'Castleowen, begod.'

Both himself and Aunty Lily are looking across at my mother. Her eyes are downcast. She's picking off specks of wool from the bottom of her sleeve.

'Here's to your health and happiness,' Father Vincent says,

raising his glass. 'And to coming back to your home country. Lily and Xavier.'

The men hold out their arms and chink their glasses.

'To Ireland,' Xavier says. 'All thirty-two counties.'

'Come on,' my mother whispers, taking my hand. 'Time for bed.'

We're just at the door when Aunty Lily says, 'And what do *you* think, Rita?'

My mother half turns her head but looks no farther back than the door handle. 'You become very accustomed to a way of life after seven years. Woolworths is a far cry from Harrods, isn't it? Just don't expect too much.'

1 October 1999 (middle of the night)

I've been thinking a lot about Aunty Lily and my mother. In fact, they've been keeping me awake tonight. What I cannot fathom is how two sisters could turn out to be so different from one another. Aunty Lily was everything my mother was not – funny, exciting, modern, but, most of all, tender. She was motherly; the kind of woman who nearly couldn't stop herself from reaching out and stroking my head if I was walking by her, or putting her arm around me if I was sitting next to her. It felt strange to me at first because I wasn't used to being touched. But I got to like it. It made me feel loved: mothered. That's all I wanted to do the day I took the baby. To mother.

Her eighteenth birthday

I've just finished feeding the baby. The side of her face is resting on my shoulder. I'm touching the back of her head with the tip of my nose and inhaling her infant smell. I can hear the wind gurgling in her tummy as I caress her back in a circular motion. I love her softness, her vulnerability, the harmless huff of her breath. Our breathing becomes synchronized, slow, sleepy. I feel so tired.

Just forty winks, I think, closing my eyes.

The baby hiccups, and a warm mouthful of milky froth soaks through my blouse. Cradling her in my arm, I wipe my shoulder with an old J-cloth. When I look down at her again, she's fast asleep. I wish I could lie down beside her cheek to cheek, but I can't. It's time to move on.

Before I go anywhere, I need to use the toilet: I'm bursting. But how will I manage? I can't leave her alone in the car; someone might take her. If only I had one of those things like a rucksack, I could strap her to my back. Or one of those car seats with a handle. I need things, so many things: a car seat, more bottles, more milk, more nappies, baby clothes. A place to live, a bed to lie on, a night's sleep. A clear head. A sign. Some sort of sign, so I'll know that I'm doing the right thing. A toilet: most of all a toilet.

I'm out of the car, baby in my arms. The back of my skirt is clinging to my legs. Someone's cackling. What's the joke? What's so bloody funny? Stop laughing at me.

'Excuse me, where's the toilet?' I ask a teenage boy who's passing. He shrugs.

A woman who is walking a couple of steps behind him points to a door and says, 'Over there, love.'

'Thanks.'

'A wee boy, is it?' she asks, smiling down at the baby.

'No, a girl.'

'Ah, she's lovely. How old?'

'What?'

'How old is she?'

'Three months.'

'Isn't she tiny?' she says, craning her neck to take a closer look at the child.

Why is she being so friendly? So nosy? She's making me nervous.

'She was premature,' I say, hurrying into the Ladies.

It's a dingy room with no window. It takes a few seconds for my eyes to adjust to the darkness. With one hand, I wipe the toilet seat, struggle with my underwear and sit down. My heart is pounding. That sweetie-pie woman has shaken me. What if she suspects something? I check my watch: it's after two o'clock. I've missed the latest news. What if she's heard about the baby's disappearance? She could be on her mobile phone right now, dialling 999 and telling them that there's a weird woman in the toilet with the missing child. Jesus!

The baby shudders in my arms as if she's having a bad dream. When I kiss her forehead, her button nose twitches and she relaxes again.

There's so much noise outside: cars revving, people shouting, doors slamming. Footsteps. Someone bangs on the toilet door.

What if it's the Guards? Oh God! What'll I do?

'Just a second,' I say, jumping up.

I'm sure they're going to knock down the door and barge in on top of me. My legs go weak at the thought of it.

'I'm nearly finished,' I squeak, flushing the toilet.

I give my hands a quick rinse under the tap, one at a time, changing the baby from one arm to the other. She stirs but doesn't waken. I put her up on my shoulder and kiss her: maybe for the last time. I kiss her again just in case. Reaching out to unlock the door, I take three short sharp breaths. God help me, I pray, pulling back the bolt and opening the door. As I step out, the brightness hits me and for a moment I cannot see clearly. I'm waiting for someone to swipe the baby from my arms and pounce on me, but no one does. A teenage girl brushes past me and into the toilet, slamming the door behind her.

Move, I think. Put one foot in front of the other and walk over to the car. No one's watching. They're all too busy.

As I lay her down again in the carrycot, I notice that her baby-gro is damp at her bottom, but it's too late to start changing her now. I don't feel safe. I've got to get out of here.

3 October 1999 (evening)

I thought that once I got away from the city, I'd be able to relax, but I couldn't. I was terrified of getting caught. Of the day being ruined. It was her anniversary. My day. I couldn't let anyone take it away from me. It's all I have to hang on to, you see.

My day

It's half past nine in the morning on 24 August 1982: my daughter's first anniversary. I'm standing barefoot in the middle of the living-room, still in my nightdress. I don't know what to do with myself.

Neither of my parents has mentioned what day it is. The bloody bastards. In the kitchen, my father is slumped over in his chair, polishing his shoes. As if having shining fecking shoes mattered. My mother is tiptoeing round the house gathering her holy things – her prayer book, her beads, her mantilla – eyes downcast, lips sealed. Solemn. Giving the occasion the reverence it deserves. The unspoken words are stifling me. I want to open my mouth and fill the room with angry, ugly noises. Rage: that's what this occasion deserves.

Without even looking in my direction, they walk by me and into the hall to put on their jackets. They're off to Mass, to pray for my baby's lost soul, dutiful to the last.

I start singing:

Happy Birthday to you (quietly)

Happy Birthday to you (getting louder)

Happy Birthday, Baby Fall (and louder)

Happy Birthday to you. (shouting)

My mother bounds back into the room and orders me to pull myself together.

'How?' I cry, as she storms out of the room. 'For God's sake, how?'

The front door slams shut. They're gone.

I don't know how to live this day. I'm not sure if I can. How am I to remember her? As the baby who kept me awake at night dancing in my womb? Or as the still and silent baby I cradled in my arms? Or neither? Maybe I should be thinking about where she is now, a year after her death? Limbo – that's where the Pope says her soul is. But I refuse to believe that. She can't be in Limbo. If she is, I'll never see her again, and that would be unbearable. To hell with what he says, I will see her again, even if I have to denounce Jesus and become a lost soul myself.

I don't want to be around when my parents return from Mass, her playing the martyr, him paying homage to her martyrdom, so I hurry upstairs, get dressed and splash water on my face. I've no plans other than to get out of the house. As I rummage through my top drawer in search of my baby's white bootees, I stumble upon Aunty Lily's wedding ring and try it on. It's a perfect fit. I find the bootees in a small brown paper bag, stuff them into my jeans pocket and run downstairs.

I hitch a lift into Castleowen, where I head for the bus depot and join the queue for the Dublin bus. In order to discourage anyone from sitting next to me, I sit on the aisle side of an empty pair of seats. I'm in no humour for idle chit-chat. As the bus crawls through the town traffic, I find myself twiddling the ring on my finger and thinking about my baby – what she might look like if she'd lived, and what we might be doing right now. I'm enjoying the fantasy. I need it: today of all days.

After a few stops, an old woman gets on and starts making her way down the aisle in search of a seat. Closing my eyes, I pretend not to notice her.

'Can you shove over there, love?' she says, tapping my shoulder.

Without looking at her, I move in and close my eyes again. Every so often she turns and looks at me: I can tell by the warm tickle of her breath on my face. She keeps shifting about in the seat, and opening and closing her handbag, and blowing her nose, and making silly, pointless remarks like 'Ah now' and 'Sure, that's how it goes'. She's distracting me from my dreams.

'Excuse me, girshe,' she says, digging my ribs, 'but would you mind opening that window, before I die of suffocation?'

'OK.' I open it and sit down again.

'Oh, that's much better,' she says, taking a deep grateful breath and inspecting my left hand at the same time. 'You're not married, are you?'

'Yes,' I say, touching Aunty Lily's ring. Even to me, there's no hint of a lie.

'But, sure, you're only a slip of a lassie.' She leans towards me and whispers, 'A shotgun wedding, was it?'

I nod.

'Same as me own,' she says, giving me a wink. 'Is it just the one babby you have?'

'Yeah.'

'How old?'

'It's her first birthday today.'

'Ah, they're little dotes at that age, aren't they?'

'Mmm,' I say, imagining her podgy cheeks, big eyes, soft curls. 'I'm going to Dublin to buy her birthday present.'

'It's a long way to go just to get a birthday present.'

'I don't care; I want to get her something special.'

A couple of miles farther, the driver pulls in at a crossroads bus shelter.

'This is me now,' the woman says, holding on to the headrest in front of her and hoisting herself up off the seat. 'Enjoy your shopping trip.'

'Thanks.'

As she totters down the aisle, I settle back down to my dreams.

Once I step off the bus in Dublin, I can pretend to be whomever I want to be. And on this day, I want nothing more than to be the mother of my one-year-old daughter. So I am.

I spend the day wandering from one department store to

the next, picking up baby clothes and toys, checking sizes and prices. I'm in no hurry. I have all day to browse, to consider, to indulge the fantasy.

'Have you this dress in pink?' I ask one of the shop assistants, making sure she sees Aunty Lily's ring.

I stop for coffee; pay the waitress; flash the ring.

They notice: young mother, young wife.

I'm somebody. And somebody's.

In the end, I buy her a pink rabbit. It's soft and floppy, beany on the inside, nice to hold.

On my return home, I find my parents sitting watching TV. *The Late Late Show* is just starting, an owl flying across the screen.

'You're back,' my father says.

'I am.'

He doesn't ask me where I've been.

My mother hasn't turned her head. She's busy clicking her knitting needles, one eye on her stitches, the other on Gay Byrne. She's knitting a matinee coat for one of the village wives, who's entitled to have a baby.

Click click click.

Upstairs, I put my baby's bunny into a box in the bottom of my wardrobe and go to bed.

4 October 1999 (after tea)

I've started smoking again. I had to; my head is all over the place. Raking up the past does that to you. The cigarettes help me to focus. Besides, it gives me something to do, something to look forward to. There isn't much else. I'd forgotten how satisfying cigarettes can be. I love the way they catch my chest. I've just stubbed one out, but I think I'll have another one. They're so addictive, so damaging. I've always been drawn to what's bad for me. Like Lesley. I still say she was worth the trouble.

Worth the trouble

As I skip through the car park towards the dancing hall, I hear singing coming from somewhere behind.

> Aunty Mary had a canary
> Up the leg of her drawers.
> She pulled a string and made it sing
> Up the leg of her drawers.

'Who's that?' a red-faced woman says, emerging from the open side doors of Brady's pub, with a mop in her hand. 'Was that you?' she shouts across at me, giving me the evil eye.

'No,' I say. 'Honest.'

'Well, it better not have been, or I'll stick this where the sun don't shine,' she says, threatening me with her mop, then disappearing back through the doors.

As I look around me wondering where the singing had come from, it starts again. This time I recognize the voice.

> Aunty Mary had a canary
> Up the leg of her drawers.
> While she was sleeping, I was peeping
> Up the leg of her –

Just as I catch sight of Lesley and Stephen Taylor crouched behind a couple of beer kegs, the mop woman comes charging across the car park holding her mop like a rifle and screeching at the top of her voice, 'You're in for it now, ya scut ya.'

I bolt up the steps, screaming all the way.

Miss Jackson meets me in the doorway with a 'Jesus, Mary and Joseph, what's going on?'

'Keep them brats out of my sight,' the mop woman roars.

'What are you on about, Mary?' Miss Jackson says, taking me by the hand.

'Why don't you ask her?' the woman points at me.

Before I have the chance to defend myself, Lesley appears, pushing a reluctant Stephen Taylor a step ahead of her.

'Yis little bas—'

'Now, hang on there a second, Mary,' Miss Jackson says. 'Keep the bad language out of it.'

Lesley whispers something in Stephen's ear.

'They were singing a filthy song at me,' the mop woman says. 'Weren't yis, yis scuts yis?'

Miss Jackson looks at the culprits.

'Go on, tell her,' Lesley says, nudging Stephen.

'It was me,' he mumbles. 'Lesley didn't do nothing. I'm sorry.'

I know he's lying. It was Lesley's voice I heard.

'It's Mary here you should be apologizing to,' Miss Jackson says. 'Not me.'

Mary's eyeballing him, one hand on her hip, the other holding the mop at a very intimidating angle.

'Sorry,' Stephen says, hanging his head and legging it up the steps.

As Mary walks away grumbling to herself, I notice she has a limp.

'One leg longer than the other,' Miss Jackson says.

Stephen is huffy with Lesley afterwards; sits in the corner and turns his back to her. She's on her knees, walking her Cindy up and down the bench. She makes the doll pirouette, stand on one leg, even do the splits, all the time edging closer to Stephen, trying to get his attention.

'Are you still friends with me?' she asks when she catches him looking at her.

'Feck off,' he says and turns away.

'Look,' she says, pulling the blouse off the doll, 'she's got tits.'

I can feel myself blushing. I can't help it.

'You can kiss them if you like,' she says, offering Stephen the doll.

'Do you dare me?' he chuckles, taking the doll from her.

'Yeah, go on,' Lesley giggles, nudging me.

He gives the doll a quick peck on her lips and looks at Lesley. She rolls her eyes and sighs. He kisses her again, a quick peck on each boob, and then throws her back to Lesley.

'Is that it?' she says.

'Watch this,' he says, snatching the doll back out of her hand and licking her boobs until Lesley and I are in stitches.

5 October 1999 (afternoon)

During my first three years in secondary school, all I could do was watch Lesley from a distance laughing with her friends, the way we used to laugh. I began to resent my mundane life, my mundane friend.

Summer of 1979 (a summer of discontent)

The days are long. There's so much time to kill.

'The devil finds work for idle hands, Frances,' my mother says.

I want to tell her that he's welcome to. Digging my nails into something dirty is exactly what I need.

Where's it coming from, this madness? Why am I feeling this way?

The piano – my fingers can no longer hack it. They're too angry. They hate the discipline. They're heavy and disgruntled, hammering out each note as if they are indeed hammers, and the keys nails.

'What's wrong with you?' my mother asks.

'Nothing.'

My father seems baffled by my dourness. Although I don't look at him, I sometimes sense him staring at me after I give him a snappy one-word reply to a question.

'Did ye two have a row, Rita?' he asks my mother one evening when he arrives home from work and I don't bother responding to his greeting.

'No, indeed we did not,' she says. 'But if she doesn't buck up her ideas sharpish, we just might have one.'

Oh, fuck off and leave me alone. Stop talking about me. Quit sizing me up. Drop dead.

I wish I had a friend, a real one. Like Lesley was.

I lie on my bed, stare at the ceiling, touch my body – the private bits. That's the devil at work. Dirty pleasure. I feel guilty afterwards, but I do it again. Then I pray for myself. You can't hide from God, my mother reckons. Fat chance of that, when I'm down on bended knee beseeching Him every night at seven. Another Joyful Mystery. I feel no joy, just misery.

My father takes his summer leave, rents a house in Mullaghmore for a fortnight. Powerful weather.

'Aren't we fierce lucky?' he says each morning as we walk down the steep hill towards the beach, rugs, towels and bathing suits tucked under our oxters. 'Look at that – not a cloud in the sky.'

We haven't been to a beach for several years, so my mother has bought me a new bathing suit. It has the cups of a bra inside it and I don't like it. We spread out the rugs, peel off our clothes underneath our towels, slip into our bathing suits and rub suncream on ourselves and on each other. It's the most naked we've ever seen each other and I'm mortified by the fact that my father can see the shape of my breasts. As soon as my mother finishes suncreaming my back, I slip on my T-shirt over my bathing suit before doing hers. I hate the gritty texture of her skin and the folds of flesh that sag from underneath her armpits down to her waist, like two puckered hems. The thought of leaving a patch unprotected and exposed to the burning rays crosses my vicious mind. In the shape of a cross. Suffer, suffer.

I hurry when I do my father's back because it makes me uncomfortable to touch his bare flesh.

My mother and I share one rug; my father stretches out on the other. He relaxes and sighs with pleasure, despite the moodiness of his wife and daughter. Sunhat on her head and wearing the sunglasses she's borrowed from her friend Nancy, my mother flicks absent-mindedly through the newspaper, raising her head every so often to stare out at the sea. Gathering handfuls of sand and letting it slip through my slack fingers, I pass the time watching people. I feel sad, lost, disconnected. I don't know how to be one of them.

When my father suggests a stroll along the beach, my mother reluctantly agrees. I volunteer to stay and keep an eye on our stuff. I watch them wading through the shallow water, my mother always a deliberate step behind, chin up defiantly. I can't understand why she doesn't love him any more. Ever since Aunty Lily's death, she's been really mean to him. No matter how hard he tries, she won't let him get close to her. He said once that the loss of her sister drove her to distraction. But I reckon there's more to it than that. After Aunty Lily's funeral, Xavier had a row with my parents, a row that seemed to suck the compassion out of my mother and leave her cold. Whatever the argument was about, you'd think after all these years she'd have got over it. Looking behind him, my father holds out his hand to her, but she refuses to take it and I wonder how he can still love her. I think to myself that she's a bitch and I'd love to tell him that I'm on his side, but there's no point, because he's on hers.

By noon, the beach is bustling with little ones tottering to the water's edge with their buckets, parents calling them back when they wander too far, and teenagers chatting out loud to be heard over the blare of their radios. I envy them all looking so comfortable in their skin, while all I want is to crawl out from under mine.

Towards the end of the week, Nancy arrives out of the blue.

'I'm just up for the day,' she says.

But my mother insists she stay the night. Cornering me in the kitchen, she tells me to hurry down to the bedroom my father has been sleeping in and to move his belongings into her own room.

That evening, my father insists on treating us all to dinner in the village hotel. Everyone's in a better mood and my mother doesn't bat an eyelid when my father orders a second brandy for himself after the meal. They talk about their home county and the coincidence it was that my parents ended up living in the same small village as Nancy, a whole two hundred miles from their home town in County Cork. They toast friendship, clinking two coffee cups and a brandy snifter. They don't notice that I haven't raised my glass and they don't invite me to. I'm sipping my cola and thinking that the only one I would raise my glass and toast friendship with is Lesley. If only I could get close to her again.

A few weeks into the school term, I'm on my way over to the toilets during French class when, at the other end of the corridor, I see Lesley standing outside her classroom door, pirouetting: skirt above her knees, blouse untucked, permed hair, black loafers.

I don't need to pass her by, so I just wave and carry on.

'Frances,' she calls in a loud whisper. She's the only one at school, teachers aside, who calls me by my name. 'Where ya going?'

'Loo.'

'Hang on,' she says, catching up with me. 'Flanagon, the stupid cunt, threw me out of class for yawning. What the fuck does she expect, yammering on about *Stony Grey Soil*? I mean, even the gobshite who wrote it couldn't fucking stand it. Hated it so much, he left the fucking county to get away from it.'

'And she threw you out for yawning?'

'Well, it wasn't the first yawn. And I stretched too. You know the way a hungover man does when he wakes up in the morning?'

'No.'

'No, I suppose not. Anyway, want a fag?'

'OK.'

She follows me into the cubicle.

'I need to pee,' I say to her apologetically.

'Fire away.'

That's what I love about Lesley: no barriers.

She blathers on while I pee, saying it was just as well that it was me who came along and not PMT, the oul hoor.

'Who's PMT?'

'Principal Marie-Therese,' she says, 'who's in a permanent fucking state of PMT, crazy bitch, or haven't you noticed? Jesus!'

'Oh right,' I say, pulling up my pants in a hurry, no clue at all as to what PMT stands for.

'Here.' She hands me a cigarette.

'What if we're caught?'

'Just bung your fag into the bog. If they don't see ya at it, they can't prove anything.' She pulls a packet of ten Carrolls from her pocket.

'Maybe I shouldn't. I've never smoked before.'

'Loosen up, will you, for fuck sake. It's a fag, not a joint . . . more's the bloody pity.'

'Hah?'

'Just shut up,' she giggles, squeezing the fag up against my reluctant lips. 'Hey, will you ever forget yon *Feis*?' she asks, holding her flaming lighter between her face and mine.

'How could I?'

'You won the gold, you bitch. Beat me to it.' She puts the flame on the end of my cigarette.

I suck in, splutter and swallow smoke.

Lesley taps my back and says, 'Never mind; it just takes practice.'

That was exactly what she'd said the first time I'd tried to pirouette.

7 October 1999 (evening)

What use is winning the gold when you're beaten by your own glory?

The Feis

I'm eight and a half. It's not long since Aunty Lily's death, weeks rather than months. I miss her. My parents are sad; they seem tense too. Since that row with Xavier, there's a lot of silence hanging about, but it's not a calm silence. I don't like it.

I've been looking forward to the *Feis*. I haven't stopped practising. Lesley's been teaching me new steps; they're complicated. I haven't told my mother about the steps. She still doesn't like Lesley. That's why I've been practising behind her back. In my bedroom, the bathroom, the back yard; anywhere out of her sight.

I know I'm in with a chance. Even Miss Jackson says so. She says I'm flying.

I love all the dances – reels, jigs, hornpipes, four-hand reels, 'The Sweets of May'. That's what I'm lilting in the kitchen as I tap on my knees and clap – one two three four clap clap . . .

My mother shouts at me to stay quiet.

'Sorry.'

'Sorry,' she squawks, mimicking me, I think. She's staring at me with queer eyes.

Careful not to make any more noise, I pull out a stool from underneath the kitchen table, sit down and pour some cornflakes into a bowl. My mother is sitting opposite me polishing my dancing pumps with short, swift swipes of the brush. I do my best to eat in silence, allowing the flakes to go soggy in the milk before spooning them into my mouth. All the while, I'm wondering where my father is.

'Don't forget,' she says, putting the shoebrush and tin of polish back into the cupboard. 'Shoulders back, chin up, toes out-turned and no raising the foot above the knee.'

'Yeah, OK.'

'Yes, OK, not yeah –'

'Yes, OK.'

'The traditional way is the best way. That's why it's called Traditional Irish Dancing. I don't like that modern version of it that they're at nowadays. All that kicking and leaping about like jinnets. It ill-becomes any young lassie to be throwing her legs in the air like . . . like . . . like a good-time girl. Without a modicum of modesty.'

My father arrives back from wherever he's been, whistling. It's not a tuneful happy whistle.

We drive to Moynehill, where the *Feis* is taking place, only my mother's odd cutting remark perforating the brutal silence.

'I told you we should have left earlier,' she says when we arrive at the car park and find it full.

I'm sitting directly behind her, staring at the back of her head, her lacquered mesh of mousy strands glistening and prickly. The tips of my fingers are tingling with vicious desire. The only thing stopping me from digging my nails into her brambly scalp is that damned Fourth Commandment and the serious consequences of breaking it.

My father turns around and looks out of the back window to reverse the car. He hasn't responded to her niggling remarks, but his face bears all the signs of exasperation.

'Don't worry, Daddy,' I say, 'we've loads of time.'

'Indeed I know that, love,' he says. 'It's just that some people like to make a mountain out of a molehill.'

'While others,' my mother screeches, 'insist on making a molehill out of a mountain.'

I hate their angry tones and the way they can't look at each other.

Inside the hall, my mother takes a tight, bossy grip of my hand and hurries me through the audience towards the side of the stage. I can hear a musician tuning his fiddle from behind the moss-coloured velvet curtains.

'I'm afraid,' Miss Jackson says, 'I can't allow the parents backstage, Rita. It's chock-a-block back there.'

Unimpressed, my mother mumbles something about poor organization, then stands stubbornly and intrusively at the top of the stage steps, straightening my Celtic brooches and flicking specks of dust off my shawl. No one can pass up or down the steps.

Eventually, one of several women jammed in the queue cranes her neck over the other heads and yells, 'Oh, take your time, why don't you, missus?'

'Honestly, the ignorance of some people,' my mother retorts before *excuse me, excuse me*-ing her way back down the steps with stiff-necked loftiness.

Lesley is already in the back room when I get there. My God, her dress! It's dark red, with a full skirt that hangs just above her knees. There's a white crocheted band around the neck and cuffs. Intricate Celtic designs of green, white and gold adorn the bodice, skirt and matching shawl. Both dress and shawl have a golden lining.

'What do you think?' she asks, twirling.

'I love it.'

'You can have a lend of it, if you like.'

'But you're wearing it.'

'I'll tell you what,' she says. 'When Miss Jackson lines us up to give us our competitor numbers, you go first and I'll go last. That way, we won't be dancing on stage together and I'll have time to change back into this,' she touches her dress, 'whenever you're finished.'

I look down at my own dress. Its long, pleated skirt is hanging around my waist like a heavy curtain.

'Oh God!'

'I know,' Lesley says. 'It's desperate hicky.'

After we swap dresses in the toilets, I stand in front of the mirror staring at my reflection, feeling just about as startled as the ugly duckling had when he saw the image of a swan looking back at him from the shimmering water.

Lesley starts pulling down her gold-coloured panties.

'What are you doing?'

'Look,' she says, holding up the heavy pleats over her waist. 'I've two pairs on. You'll need to wear these gold ones so that the audience won't be able to see your other knickers.' She hands them to me. 'Arse of gold, that's what my brother Keith calls me when I wear them.'

'Janey Mac, knickers and all; my mother's gonna kill me.'

'Why?'

'I don't know. I just think she will.'

'Sure, she'll not even twig it's you.'

'What if she does?'

'Here,' she says, standing behind me and undoing my plaits,

'I'll put your hair in a bun and she'll surely not know you . . . silly old bag.'

Girls who pass in and out to go to the toilet giggle and point at us as Lesley bunches my hair into a ponytail and starts twirling it around and tying it down with hairclips she's pulling one by one from her own bun.

'There,' she says. 'Now shake your head to make sure the bun won't fall out while you're dancing. Like this.' She shakes her head wildly, laughing.

Even in my dress, Lesley looks happy.

When I shake my head, I hear clips falling on to the floor. And when I stop, Lesley tells me the bun looks like a daddy-long-legs.

Miss Jackson comes in, complaining that she's been looking all over for me.

'What in the name of God are ye at?' she says. 'Why aren't you wearing your own costume? And what kind of hairstyle is that?'

'Will you fix her bun?' Lesley asks. 'Pleeease.'

'There isn't enough time. She's on in a minute.'

'Ah, go on. It'll only take a minute.'

She calls Lesley a pushy article and tells her to pick the clips off the floor. Quickly.

Fixing a bun is no problem for Miss Jackson. I've never seen her own hair styled any other way.

'Doesn't she look lovely?' Lesley says about me.

'A picture,' Miss Jackson says, talking out through the clips she's holding between her puckered lips, 'though I dread to think how her mother's going to react.'

Bun in place, I hurry out to the stage and stand facing the audience, two other dancers to my right. The compère is calling for silence.

'Thank you, thank you,' she says. 'Next we have the first three competitors of the under-ten reel, as you can see, from three different schools of dancing – the Jackson . . .'

My right calf is wobbling. I try to steady it by standing with my legs together, flat-footed. But I can't stay like that. In a few moments, the music will start and I will have to dance. My heart is battering against my chest, the rapid rhythm throbbing in my ears, like the beat of the bodhrán. Inside my head, I pray for the stage floor to melt underneath my feet and swallow me, like quicksand.

'Good luck, Frances.'

I turn and see Lesley waving at me from the wings, hands up, fingers crossed, egging me on. And then the music plays and somehow my right leg is stretched out in front of me, straight as a fiddler's bow.

The memory I have of performing the reel is not of how I dance, but of how I feel.

Nothing exists but me and the reel – a whistling wind at my back, chasing me, pushing me forward, encircling me, trying playfully to trap me. And no matter how much I try to sidestep it, or hop out of its way, or unravel myself from it, or stamp my feet in mocking defiance, it is still at my tail, controlling me, charming me. As I skip and pirouette, my skirt rises and falls, like flapping wings, lifting me. Yes! That's how I feel – lifted . . . unreachable . . . free.

And then the music stops and I'm conscious again of the solid floor beneath my feet, the stage, the other dancers, the musicians, the adjudicators, Lesley in the wings, Aunty Lily watching over me and, somewhere among the applauding audience, my fuming mother.

Or perhaps not, I think, when I see the look of pride on Miss Jackson's face.

'Terrific, Frances,' she says. 'Absolutely terrific.'

Then she starts lining up the next three competitors.

Lesley and I hurry back to the toilets to swap costumes. As we stand facing each other, giggling our way back into our rightful dresses, our slender limbs covered in goose-pimples, I feel warmer than I've ever felt before.

'Frances. Frances, love,' Miss Jackson says, coming in the door. 'Your mother wants you. She's not very happy, I'm afraid. She's taking you home.' Her voice is trembling, the way my father's does when he's arguing with my mother.

'Why? What did she do?' Lesley asks.

'She didn't say. But she's probably annoyed over ye swapping your costumes. You'd better hurry, love,' she says touching my shoulder, 'before she causes a scene out there.'

'My dress was lovely on her,' Lesley says.

'I know that, Lesley. But obviously that's not how she sees it.'

I'm standing in front of the mirror, back in my own dress. Raising my eyes, I look up at my reflection and think how much I hate being me. Lesley is almost in tears, saying that they need me for the set dancing, that I can't go home. Miss Jackson tells her to keep quiet. I have to go and that's that.

'But she's done nothing bad,' Lesley says, resting her head on my shoulder.

'I was a good-time girl,' I say, now deeply regretting my foolhardiness.

'What do you mean by a good-time girl?' Miss Jackson is looking at me anxiously.

'I had a good time . . . danced my own way, not *her* way. She's gonna kill me.'

'However your mother feels, love, you're a good child. The best. You –'

A girl shouts in the door that Frances Fall's mother wants her RIGHT NOW.

'Look,' Miss Jackson says, hand on my shoulder, 'go home and I'll give your mother a ring tomorrow. There'll be plenty of other *Feiseanna*.'

When I say goodbye to Lesley, she throws her arms around my neck and kisses my cheek. Then she hurries out on to the stage, where her number is being called for the third and final time.

My dress feels like a heavy sack as I trudge my way out to the side steps, where I find my mother standing at the bottom with a face like thunder.

'Home,' she says. 'Now.'

Stepping out in front of her, I hurry down the hall towards the exit, her menacing footsteps catching up behind me.

My father is already in the car, weary-faced, with the engine running. Not a word is spoken until we reach Castleowen and head out the Crosslea road. Suddenly I feel terrified.

'I'm sorry, Daddy,' I whimper, hoping to find refuge in his parental desire to protect me. 'I'm really sorry.'

'You shouldn't have disobeyed your –'

'You stay out of it,' my mother shrieks.

'Between youse be it so,' my father says resignedly, and now I want to cry.

He doesn't even come into the house. He needs a walk, he says, to clear his head.

'Upstairs and into your bedroom.' The horrible, flat tone of her voice unnerves me.

Inside my bedroom, she orders me out of my costume and into my nightie. I feel quite sick but just do what I'm told.

Standing in my underwear, I reach over and lift the pillow to get my nightie. That's when she grabs me. Before I know it, I'm across her knee, panties down, the patterned carpet beneath me becoming more blurred with every blow of her hand across my bottom. I try to wriggle away at first, but her left hand is pressing down firmly on my back, while her right hand does the punishing, smack after smack after smack, until the pain has numbed me and the shock has dazed me into submission. There are words coming out of her mouth – 'Ever . . . ever . . . dare . . . bad . . . disobedient . . . betrayal . . . Judas . . . cheap . . . slut . . .'

Other words too. I can't hear them all with the ringing in my ears.

It's not the flesh-stinging pain that bothers me, as I lie curled up and shivering on my bed afterwards. Had I landed on my bottom in a bunch of nettles, I'd understand that the soreness would pass. It's the inner pain that lingers, like a hole in my soul.

I hear the tap running in the bathroom – my mother washing her hands of me, the dirty sinner. I feel so small, so ashamed.

There's something wrong with me; there has to be because I don't understand why what I've done is so bad, such a terrible sin. But it must be. Otherwise I wouldn't have been beaten. It's not as if she's ever hit me before. There's badness in me and my mother can see it. She's good at sniffing out badness. And why wouldn't she be, her being such a holy woman? Stations of the Cross . . . rosaries galore . . . novenas . . . Mass three times a week. A better woman to pray you wouldn't meet. Oh, she can sniff out the sinners all right. And maybe she's right about Lesley too, the way she showed Stephen Taylor her Cindy doll's tits and the way she sang that dirty song to Mary, the woman with the mop. And then lied about it. How can I love a girl like that? Why do I?

I don't want to get beaten again. I'll be a good girl from now on.

When it comes down to it – obedience or humiliation – obedience wins, hands down.

7 October 1999 (middle of the night)

It's chilly tonight. I cannot sleep. Behinds my curtains, the icy moon is casting a silver beam on the front lawns. The trees that swish their golden arms during the day are still now and silent. It's a lonely picture.

All those sayings – *spare the rod, spoil the child*; *be cruel to be kind*; *for your own good*; *tough love* – was that my mother's mindset on the day of the *Feis*? Did she believe that she was doing the right thing? Was it really about discipline? Did she love me underneath it all?

No matter how hard I try to make sense of it, I'm not able to accept it. I still resent her for it; hate her even. She's been dead almost fourteen months now, and although I've shed many tears over her, I haven't yet shed one for her. What's more, I don't intend to.

After the Feis

For days afterwards, I cry at the drop of a hat. It's the shock of it that hits me hardest and lingers longest. I don't think I'll ever feel happy again. I'm scared that I've turned bad. But why or how? When I close my eyes, I see my soul with a big, dark, mortal sin spot on it, like a splat of black ink. It's weighing me down. I don't talk much, in case I say the wrong thing. Of course I deserved to be punished for breaking the Fourth Commandment, but I wish my mother had given me a tongue-lashing, or extra chores, or no supper – anything but being pinned down and slapped stupid.

The frightening part is that I'm no longer sure that I know the difference between right and wrong. I don't trust my own judgement. I'll have to play it safe, stay out of harm's way . . . Lesley's way. I think it's sad how all the things that make me feel good turn out to be bad. I'm sure it's Satan trying to trick me. My mother has warned me about that fella, how he's always working on us, putting temptation in our way – poaching souls. He must have chosen me because I'm weak. What if he does it again? And succeeds? I'll need to be on constant guard. Because if I take the bait, she'll do it again – slap the badness out of me. The thought of it makes me quiver. I'll never be able to look at or touch my mother's hands again without hating them.

By the time my father comes home, the evening of the *Feis*, I'm in bed and on the verge of sleep; crying is so draining. My bedroom door creaks open and I know he's looking in on me, but I don't stir.

He's not himself over the next few days; he walks in and out of rooms with a puzzled expression, as if he's trapped in a maze and is searching for a way out. When he sits down, he hones in on the TV, and I think he looks like one of the rabbits that come into our garden from the back field and sit motionless for hours. I hope I'm not the cause of his peculiar mood, but suspect that I am. Still, he hasn't shown any anger towards me and I love him for that.

About a week later, my mother goes to visit Nancy, leaving me and my father alone in the house. It's a Sunday evening. We're watching *The Black and White Minstrel Show*, he on an armchair, me on the sofa. Between the performances, he pops out to the kitchen, returns with two apples, sits down beside me and hands me one.

A minute later, I'm watching the show again, this time through a fog of tears, and now I can't tell the black from the white; everything seems grey. Leaning my head on my father's arm, I squeeze my eyes shut and tears slide down my cheeks.

'I know, I know,' he whispers, caressing my head. 'She isn't the easiest of women, your mother. But what can we do?'

It isn't a question. He's simply letting me know that there's nothing he can do. That's all right – he understands. That's all I need to know.

As the seasons pass, the beatings continue. Some are more severe than others, but all occur when my father is out of the house. Once she wallops the back of my legs as I climb the stairs ahead of her.

'That's for interrupting me yesterday while I was talking to Missus Scully in the post office,' she says.

No matter how well I behave, I can't stop the beatings. I feel so stupid. I should know how to stay out of trouble, but I don't.

I'm sure my mother hates me, feels ashamed of me. That is, until one evening when Nancy and Father Vincent are at our house for tea. I'm ten or eleven at the time. We're in the sitting-room. We've all finished eating except for Father Vincent, who keeps stretching across to the coffee table and restacking his side plate with sandwiches.

As he munches his way through the egg and onion, and the ham and tomato, he starts quizzing me about what I'm learning in catechism. My mother tells me to go and get my copybook; that way he'll be able to see for himself.

'You'll be fit to tell us,' she says to him, 'whether or not you think she'll be adequately prepared for her Confirmation.'

Handing him my copybook, I sit back down on the sheepskin mat by the fire. He fingers the embossed wallpaper covering and says, 'Isn't that very snazzy?'

Flicking through the pages, he stops at random and throws questions at me. I twiddle tufts of wool from the mat between my thumb and index finger and rattle off the answers; I have them off by heart by now.

'So, what do you think, Father?' my mother asks when he finally closes my copybook.

'Oh, she's well versed.' He looks at me. 'I doubt the Bishop will be able to catch *you* out.'

'Well, as I keep telling her,' my mother says, 'there's no point in her making her Confirmation if she doesn't know what it's about.'

'It's a woeful pity, Rita Fall, there aren't more parents like you,' he says, eyeing the Victoria sponge.

'Do you fancy a slice, Father?' my mother simpers. 'You may as well; it'll only go to waste otherwise.'

'In that case, it'd be a sin to say no.'

I'm not sure that I should ask a question that's been worrying me for ages now, but with everyone looking so pleased, I decide to chance it.

'Is it true,' I look up at our revered guest, 'that if someone gives the Bishop the wrong answer, he'll slap them across the face?'

'I suppose it all depends on the mood he's in,' the priest says, and my parents and Nancy laugh.

My father reaches over, pats my head and says, 'Don't worry, Frances, that'll not happen to you.'

After a while, Nancy asks my mother if she's heard the latest.

'What's that?'

'About a certain young lady who doesn't live a hundred miles from your front doorstep.'

'Who?'

Nancy glances at me, winks and says, 'I'll fill you in later.'

But later isn't soon enough and my mother tells me to be a good girl and make a start on the dishes. I leave the room without a grumble, delighted with the opportunity to make her proud of me twice in the one day.

When I've finished the dishes, I go into the living-room to watch TV.

'Ah now, that's a living dread, the poor unfortunate lassie,' I hear my father say as he leaves the sitting-room a few minutes later.

'Well, you know what they say,' my mother says, 'If you lie down with dogs, you can expect to get up with fleas.'

Dying to know who has fleas, I stand like a spy by the living-room door and listen. I hear my father climbing the stairs and muttering something about my mother always having to throw in her twopence-ha' penny's worth. I wait until he returns to the sitting-room before I turn off the TV and ease the door open. I don't manage to get the whole story, but apparently a girl in the village is in some sort of trouble and, judging by their tone, there's not too much sympathy going to waste. It's the parents Nancy feels sorry for, though; according to my mother, they're far too lenient. I don't catch the next bit.

Then, as if he has somehow sensed my sneaky presence

lurking behind the living-room door, Father Vincent says in a booming voice, 'Frances is a fortunate lassie to have parents like ye, to keep her on the straight and narrow throughout her teenage years.'

I can almost hear my mother's lungs fill with pride. I am, according to Nancy, a credit to her.

'Poor Missus Mooney,' my father says. 'I'd say now, in fairness, she does her best by those kids. It's no picnic, having a family that size.'

'She keeps no dick on them at all, Joe,' Nancy says. 'They've been running the roads since they were knee-high to grass-hoppers, every last one of them. She's far too soft for her own good.'

'I think she's a grand wee woman myself,' my father says, 'very warm.'

'A bit more of the cane, a lot earlier on, wouldn't have gone amiss in that house,' my mother says.

'Wise words, Rita,' Father Vincent says. 'I've no time for the softly softly approach myself. It'll get parents nowhere in the long run.'

So that's why my mother does it – to keep me on what Father Vincent calls the straight and narrow. All that lying across her knee submissively and taking the scorch, it's going to pay off. I'm well trained. Thanks to my mother, I'll sail through my teenage years unscathed by sin.

Perhaps I should be grateful.

12 *October* 1999 *(evening)*

When I returned from a walk this morning, I noticed that Aunty Lily's wedding ring had slipped off my finger. Three times I retraced my steps down the path that cuts the front lawn in two. I got down on my hunkers several times and rummaged through the leaves with teary eyes. A shower of rain urged me back inside to the warmth of my room, where I lay down on my bed and wept.

A couple of hours later, I found it under my bedside table. It must have fallen off while I was dressing the bed. I'm going to wear it on the chain around my neck now, like she did when she lost all the weight before she died. How I miss her.

Rest in peace, Aunty Lily

My mother is pacing the living-room floor, hands deep in her apron pockets. Her cheeks are pulled back tight and her mouth looks like the opening of a letter box. Aunty Lily and Xavier aren't long gone. They're living in Sycamore Street now.

'That man,' my mother says, 'sang one too many rebel songs for my liking; he could be an IRA man for all we know. And as for Lily, she can't even pass an afternoon without resorting to alcohol.'

My father is trying to watch the six o'clock news to see how the Catholics are getting on in Derry. I know all about the North, how the Catholics are out marching because the Protestants are treating them badly. I'm sitting beside my father and taking it all in. There are girls as young as myself out on the street with their parents, who are shouting at the police and throwing things at them. I wonder which is worse: being a persecuted Catholic or having the wrong religion.

My mother paces in front of the TV, obscuring our view, while my father sways his upper body so he can keep his eye on the screen.

'I blame London,' my mother says.

'I couldn't agree with you more; they give them Unionists far too much clout.'

'No, not for that hooliganism! For Lily. London's changed her.'

'Lily was Lily,' my father says, 'before she set her sights on London at all.'

'Maybe so,' my mother says, coming to a halt and standing directly between my father and the evening news, 'but she wasn't always an atheist, was she?'

My father sighs, gives up on the Derry Catholics, and looks at my mother. 'And who says she is?'

'I do. She's not seen the inside of a chapel since she came home from that godless metropolis.'

'Isn't she on her way into evening Mass as we speak?'

'She is my eye. Wait till you see. Come morning, she'll not be fit to tell me one thing about the readings or the homily. The girl is lying through her teeth.'

'Well, whether she is or not, it's not up to you to get involved. Be careful what you say. She's a married woman now, with a husband to look after her.'

'I told you before, Joe Fall, that I promised my mother I'd take care of her, and I'll be damned if I let her down now.'

An hour later I'm on my knees, hands joined and leaning into the sofa where Aunty Lily had been sitting all afternoon. I can smell the dregs of cigarette smoke off the cushion. My mother offers up a decade of the rosary for those misguided people who have foolishly turned their backs on God, that they may see the error of their ways and ask for His forgiveness. I think that Father Vincent couldn't have put it better himself. With my eyes shut and my face scrunched in serious contemplation, I pray for my aunty's redemption.

The next time Aunty Lily visits us, my mother fires questions at her.

'Still going to evening Mass?'

'Yeah.'

'Does there be many at it?'

'A fair crowd.'

'Any choir?'

'Sometimes.'

The three of us are playing Ludo at the kitchen table. After a few minutes, my mother has dropped out to make the tea. I'm taking her turns for her.

She lifts the saucepan of custard off the hob. 'Who did you tell me says it?'

'Says what?'

'Evening Mass.'

'Oh. Father eh . . . what do you call him, Xavier?' Aunty Lily shouts out to her husband, who's in the living-room chatting with my father.

'Who?'

'The priest that says evening Mass.'

'Isn't he Higgins?'

'That's right, Higgins.'

'God, isn't that odd?' my mother twitters, placing a plate of steaming apple tart and custard on the table in front of her sister. 'Nancy was just telling me the other day how Father

Vincent has been saying the evening Mass in Castleowen this past month.'

'Are you calling me a liar?' Aunty Lily reddens and reaches into her handbag for her cigarettes.

'And why would I do the like of that?' my mother asks, turning to cut another slice of the tart. 'Sure, you know as well as I do that Mammy'd turn in her grave if either of us strayed from our Christian duties. Said so herself, on her deathbed, if I remember rightly. I hardly think that you're denying the good woman her final wishes.'

'Of course I'm not.'

'There you are, then; it's just a bit of a mix-up. Maybe Father Vincent is the concelebrant.'

Aunty Lily tightens her grip on the cigarette with her lips and sucks on it so hard, the entire tip disappears into her mouth. When she inhales, a curly whiff of smoke escapes and disappears up her nostrils.

'Here, love,' she says, pushing her plate over to me, 'you can have that. And will you take my turn for me too, till I smoke my fag in peace?'

'Not hungry?' my mother asks.

'Not any more.'

'I'll wrap a couple of slices in tinfoil. You might feel like having it for your supper.'

Licking the custard-coated spoon, I shake the die in the cup and throw it on to the Ludo board – two. I move the yellow counter – that's Lily – two spaces.

'Who's winning now?' Aunty Lily asks.

'Still Mammy,' I sigh.

Then I take my mother's turn.

*

The following Sunday morning, my mother and I are clearing up after the breakfast when the doorbell rings. It's Aunty Lily and she says she's coming to Mass with my parents and me in Crosslea chapel.

My mother sweeps her eye over her sister's outfit. 'Is that all you're wearing?'

'Yeah.'

'You'll be skinned alive. There's fierce cross-winds up at that chapel. It's a day for a coat and scarf.'

'It's April, Rita.'

'April or not, you'll catch your death in that flimsy get-up.'

'It's a trouser-suit.'

'Oh, is that what you call it?'

My father comes in from the shed with a full basket of briquettes.

'What do you think, Joe?' Aunty Lily asks, twirling in the middle of the kitchen floor.

'Oh, very swish, Lily, very swish,' he splutters, looking over his shoulder at her as he slams the back door shut with his foot.

'See, Rita – even Joe approves,' she says, lifting a slice of leftover buttered toast from my side plate and taking a bite.

'Spit that out,' my mother shrieks. 'What about Holy Communion?'

'Arragh, it'll be all right; it's only a scrap of toast. Besides, I'm starving.'

'Well, you've broken your fast now. You won't be able to receive the Host.'

After leaving the basket of briquettes by the living-room fire, my father comes back into the kitchen to wash his hands.

'It's time we were making tracks,' he says.

In the hall, my mother, tying her headscarf in a knot under her chin, looks down at Aunty Lily's feet. 'Them narrow heels will make an awful clatter going up the aisle.'

'Isn't it a good job I'll not be traipsing up to the altar for Holy Communion so?'

Sometimes when my father is busy gardening, my mother and I get the bus into Castleowen.

'No Joe today?' Xavier asks, and I know by the way his voice drops on 'today' that he's disappointed.

'Arragh,' my mother says, 'I don't like to disturb him when he's half-way through a job. It's as well let him get a good run at it while the weather lasts.'

One afternoon, early in autumn 1971, Xavier doesn't ask about my father and Aunty Lily isn't calling me into the kitchen to give me my usual bar of chocolate. Instead, Xavier tells my mother that her sister wants to have a private word with her upstairs. I don't mind because Xavier gives me a glass of orange and a plate of biscuits and my mother isn't there to say 'You've had enough' after two. Then he lets me help him with the 'Spot the Ball' competition in the *Sunday Press* and promises to split the winnings with me.

There are two pink spots on my mother's cheeks when she comes back down to the kitchen and her eyes are swollen. Aunty Lily looks just the same. But then I don't see her again for several weeks and I don't win 'Spot the Ball'.

I'm not sure what exactly is wrong with Aunty Lily, only that she's sick. And because my mother is helping Xavier nurse her, she can't always stay with me during my Irish dancing lesson. But that's good, because I get to play with Lesley. When I tell her that my aunty's sick, Lesley says that she's probably up the pole.

'Don't forget your night prayers,' my father says when I bid him goodnight. 'And offer one up for Lily.'

'Is that because she's up the pole, Daddy?'

He shouts at me not to be so impertinent and threatens to give me a clip on the ear if I don't get out of his sight.

At school on the Monday morning, I tell Attracta Reilly that I think my aunty is up the pole and she tells Master Fitzgibbon in front of the rest of the class.

'My mammy said her aunty has cancer and had one of her tits cut off,' a sixth-class girl says from the back of the classroom.

When I burst into tears, Master Fitzgibbon takes me out into the corridor and says that, as far as he knows, my mother's sister has had an operation and is recovering well, but why don't I talk to my parents about it? But I don't because if I say 'tit', I'll surely get a telling off. Besides, my mother says that as soon as Aunty Lily is out of hospital, we'll go to see her together, so I'll know myself soon enough if the tit thing is true or not.

My legs feel like mush as I climb the stairs on my way up to see her. She's propped up in her bed, her hair combed back and tied in a ponytail. Her knees are bent and the blankets are pulled up under her armpits so I can't see her shape. When I sit down beside her, she holds my hand and I play with her rings the way I always do when she comes to Mass with us in Crosslea chapel. She asks me how I'm getting on with my dancing and I offer to do a reel for her.

'Not today, Frances,' my mother says from the bedside chair.

'Let her dance away,' Aunty Lily says, waving a dismissive hand at my mother, so I slide down off the eiderdown and start one two three-ing around the bed. The floorboards are creaking underneath the carpet and my mother insists that I stop before I knock the chandelier off the sitting-room ceiling below.

'I couldn't care less if the stupid thing smashed to smithereens,' Aunty Lily hops off her. 'I'd rather see her dance.'

From Christmas on, I see less of my mother and more of her friend Nancy, who looks after me until my father comes home from work. There's talk of doctors' visits, hospital appointments, holy water from Lourdes, miraculous medals and green scapulars. But, despite it all, they're still frowning, whispering or pulling handkerchiefs from their pockets. And it's those quiet things that bother me most.

I don't ask if Aunty Lily is dying. Instead, I think of reasons why she couldn't be. She's way too young for starters. All the people I know who've died are old. Hasn't my mother dragged me to all their funerals? She rarely misses a local funeral. We have a drawer full of in memoriam cards in the dresser to prove it.

I take them out and examine them one by one – *Aged 72 RIP* and a horrible wrinkly face to prove it, *Aged 79 RIP* and looks like a skeleton, *Aged 82* and not a hair on his head, *who died on 3 February 1970*; no age given here, just a face that tells you – I have all my living done. Then I think of Aunty Lily's face and smile.

After I go to bed, I hear my father make a call to Australia to tell my grandfather that Lily's suffering will be all over in a matter of weeks.

Better in weeks! Sure that's no time at all.

*

It's a Saturday. I'm surprised to see my mother coming in the hall door to collect me after my dancing lesson. I'd been expecting my father. She sits at the end of a bench and doesn't speak to Miss Jackson. I take down my coat from its hanger and walk over to her.

'Where's Daddy?' I ask, sitting next to her.

'At Aunty Lily's house,' she says. 'Stand up till I button up your coat; it's very blowy out.'

When she's finished, she loops my hair behind my ears, pulls my hat out of my coat pocket and puts it on me.

'There,' she says quietly, 'we're all set.'

Hand in hand, we walk down to Main Street and through the town. A pair of nuns from the Mercy Convent greet us with a nod as they pass and I nod back twice, once for myself and once for my mother because she's looking at the ground and doesn't see them. When we turn the corner into Sycamore Street, the wind catches my breath and makes me cough. My mother lets go of my hand to push back a strand of hair that's escaped from under her headscarf and is flapping across her face. I take off down the footpath, dancing through the wind with an empty brown paper bag that has blown out of a dustbin. I stop at the yellow door, but don't ring the doorbell because Aunty Lily might be sleeping and, anyway, my mother has a key.

'Here she is now, pet,' Xavier calls out to his wife when he hears us enter the hall.

I like the way they always make a fuss of me.

'Frances,' Aunty Lily says, holding out her arms.

She's sitting in an armchair by the fire with a blanket over her lap and her feet resting on a pouffe, but even with all that cosiness, she still looks uncomfortable. When I bend down to give her a hug, she grabs my wrists and pushes me down on her knee, and I think her strength must be coming from her head and not her arms because they're as thin as sausages. There's panic in her eyes as she pulls off my hat, scans every inch of my face and combs my hair back with her fingers. I can hear my parents and Xavier talking in the kitchen.

'You're up today,' I say.

'I am.'

'Are you better?'

'I always feel better when you're here.'

We talk for a while about ordinary things: school, homework, dancing.

As soon as I mention dancing, she asks, 'How's the girl who dances like the French tart doing the cancan?'

'Fine.' I'm not sure if I should say any more. What if she tells my mother?

'Do ye have fun?'

I nod.

'What kind of divilment do the pair of ye get up to?'

I hesitate.

'Go on,' she nudges me, 'tell me. I'll not breathe a word to your mother. Don't forget: I know her better than anyone; the woman wouldn't know a good time if it came up and bit her on the arse.'

After we share a conspiratorial smirk, I tell her that Lesley is teaching me a new reel for the *Feis* at Easter, and about how sometimes the two of us stay out in the car park and dance in the rain.

'Oh, how I'd love to see that.' She cups her hands around my face and plants a kiss on my forehead. 'I love you,' she whispers.

'I love you too.'

'Do you?'

'Yeah.'

'How much?'

'Loads and loads.'

'That's good. Cos I love you more than . . . more than anyone could love anyone. Remember that, won't you?'

I nod, because I don't think my voice will work.

Lowering my head to hide my teary eyes, I lean in on her bosom and now I know that the tit thing is true after all.

I look up at her when I feel her chest shudder beneath my cheek. There are tears in her eyes too, but they don't fall. I hear a moaning sound. It's coming from within Aunty Lily, barely audible at first, like the drone of a faraway ship. Her lips are closed, but quivering. I touch them, run my forefinger over them, trying to comfort her. She begins to rock, slowly at first. Rock and moan. Slowly and quietly. Getting faster, getting louder. I feel frightened, sad. She's squeezing me so hard, my bones are sore.

'Oh God, oh God,' she cries out, resting her head on mine. Whatever she was going to ask God for, she's changed her mind because she knows that there's no point and I know it too, just like I know that this is our last goodbye.

Years later my father tells me that while my mother went to collect me at my dance class, Xavier and he carried Aunty Lily downstairs to the armchair in the sitting-room specially for my visit.

'She said she didn't want you to remember her as the woman who was always sick in bed,' he says. 'I swear she'd have done a jig with you if she'd had the strength. As soon as you left, we carried her back upstairs to bed. She was exhausted. Not a single word did she utter for the rest of that day.'

16 October 1999 (evening)

Aunty Lily is gone but not forgotten.

The row

It's Saturday, a bustling day in the village. My mother has allowed me to go out the front with my skipping-rope. These days she seems anxious to get me out from under her feet. I'm sticking to the rules and staying between the butcher's shop, which is fifty yards or so to one side of our house, and Scully's shop and post office, which is roughly the same distance to the other. I like watching the comings and goings. People stop to chat with me, especially the older women. Some days they buy me sweets or, if it's sunny, an ice cream. So far today, I haven't got anything, even though I've smiled and said hello to everyone. Nuddy Neary's bike is parked outside the butcher's. He's a nosy old bachelor who lives alone out the back of beyond, wherever that is: I've never been. He cycles into the village at least twice a day to catch up on the latest gossip and then spreads it round like a heap of manure.

The butcher's shop door is open. Nuddy is inside spinning a yarn and making tracks in the sawdust with his wellies. The other customers are laughing.

'Jaysus, you're a gas man, Nuddy,' the butcher says. 'If you hung around for the day, I could charge the customers an extra few bob for the entertainment.'

'At least I'd give them val-ya for their money,' Nuddy says, 'not like you, ya dear cunt ya.'

They're all in stitches, even the man he has insulted. He

has to step away from the meat-slicer to regain his composure.

Everyone says Nuddy is harmless, except for my mother, who claims he's dead fly and not half as simple as he looks.

I turn round to look up the street when I hear a car coming. It's Xavier's. He's driving much faster than usual. Madeleine, his daughter who's been over from London since the funeral, is in the passenger seat. My mother isn't expecting them. When I think they can see me, I start waving. I don't bother speaking to the man who's passing by. With the visitors arriving, I'm sure to get my sweets now. Madeleine is waving back, but Xavier isn't. It's as if he doesn't see me. He looks odd. His hair is untidy and his eyes are glassy, like marbles. When he goes to get out of the car, Madeleine puts her hand on his shoulder. She's trying to tell him something, but he won't listen: he can't get out quickly enough.

I take a few paces back and it's just as well, because he slams the car door shut and starts banging on our front door, shouting at my parents to open up.

My father comes round the side of the house with a spade in his hand.

'What the . . . Xavier!' He stops in his tracks. He seems as baffled as I am by his brother-in-law's behaviour.

'Look at him.' Xavier staggers and points an accusatory finger at my father. 'Honest Joe himself.'

My mother opens the front door. 'What in God's name is going on?'

'Come on, Dad,' Madeleine pleads, 'this isn't the right time. We can come back when you're sober.'

Xavier shrugs her off. 'I'm not drunk. I'm angry.'

'What's wrong with him?' My father looks at Madeleine.

'He's upset,' she says, 'and not without cause.'

My mother's head is darting right and left. 'Will you get

him in off the street,' she scolds my father, 'before he makes a holy show of us?'

'Hah!' Xavier snorts. 'We wouldn't want that now, Rita, would we?'

'Dad!' Madeleine says. 'Please.'

Nuddy Neary comes out of the butcher's and walks his bike along the footpath to the house two doors from ours, where he stops to light his pipe.

'Joe.' My mother nods towards Nuddy. 'Do something, will you?'

Xavier is rooting in his pocket. 'It's all in here,' he says, 'the proof.'

'Xavier,' my father says softly, 'whatever it is, we can sort it out. Why don't you come inside?'

'And sit with youse two, youse pair of thieves.'

'Dad!' Madeleine shouts, and points at me. 'For God's sake!'

For a few moments no one speaks, and Nuddy grabs his handlebars and walks past us, tipping his hat three or four times as he goes.

I look up at my uncle. His mouth is hanging open. He looks so sad, like Pierrot. My chin is wobbling. I start to cry.

'Now look what you've done.' My mother looks daggers at Xavier. 'We'll be the talk of the village, thanks to you.'

Xavier takes his empty hand from his pocket.

'Leave the man alone, will you, Rita?' my father yells. 'Can't you see how distraught he is?'

My mother gasps.

'Frances.' Xavier teeters towards me with open arms. 'I didn't know . . . I'm sorry, sweetheart.'

Madeleine pulls him back. 'Dad, leave her. You've frightened her. I'll take her for a walk. You go inside and speak with Rita and Joe.' She looks at my parents. 'I'll be back in a while.'

Madeleine tells me not to worry; that the row has nothing to do with me or her and that it's best to let them at it. They'll sort it out among themselves.

We're barely at the end of the street before the heavens open and we have to dash into Jimmy's pub to take shelter. If my mother knew, she'd be raging, her having no time whatsoever for pubs or anyone who frequents them.

Inside, the lounge is dark and gloomy. It reeks of stale smoke and furniture polish. There's a man in a suit having tea and a sandwich at a small round table. At the counter, three men in wellies are sitting on high stools and chatting. When we take a table near the door, the barman walks over to us with a notepad.

'What can I get for ye, ladies?' he asks, lifting a pencil from behind his ear.

Madeleine orders coffee with cream for herself and cola and crisps for me.

A couple of minutes later, Nuddy Neary swings open the door and tramps across the lounge to the counter.

'The bould Nuddy,' one of the men says. 'What's the crack with you today?'

'Oh, how the mighty have fallen,' Nuddy says, rubbing his hands.

One man nudges another. 'It must be a good one. Would you look at the smug gob of him?'

'Come on, Nuddy,' the barman says, 'spill the beans.'

'Boys,' Nuddy takes off his cap and pulls out a stool, 'I regret to tell yis that yis missed a very interesting fracas down the street.'

'Jaysus, who's fighting, Nuddy?'

'Ah now, that'd be telling yis,' he says, sitting down and pulling out his pipe.

'For fuck's sake, Nuddy, you can't come in here tantalizing us with the makings of a nice bit of gossip and then refuse to spin the tale,' one of the men says.

'Aye,' says another, 'that's like giving a child a sweet and not allowing him to take the wrapper off.'

'Yis are overlooking one very important matter, boys,' Nuddy says.

'What's that?'

'It's wild thirsty work, this tale-spinning.'

The men laugh.

'Get the wee bollocks a pint, young fella,' one of them tells the barman, who's on his way out from behind the counter with our order on a tray.

'Well, seeing as yis are so nosy, I'll tell yis,' Nuddy says. 'There's something wild fishy going on at the Falls'.'

'Keep it down there, will you, Nuddy?' the barman says, taking a second glance at me and realizing who I am.

Nuddy looks behind him and sees Madeleine and me.

'Wasn't that a shockin' shower?' he says, turning back to the men, and they all start going on about the weather.

'Crosslea is a very pretty village,' Madeleine says. 'Do you like living here?'

'Not really.'

'Why not?'

'I don't know.'

'Where would you like to live?'

'London. Aunty Lily said I'd love it.'

'Then maybe you will live there some day.'

'Do you like it?'

'Yeah, I guess I do. It's home. It's where I work.'

'Are you the nurse or the telephonist?'

'Guess.'

'The nurse.'

'You're right. How did you know?'

'I just did.'

'So, what do you want to be when you grow up?'

'A mammy.'

'Yeah! Me too,' she says. 'That's every girl's dream, isn't it?'

When we get back, Xavier has left.

'He said he'd park up at the chapel gates and wait for you there,' my father tells Madeleine.

'OK.'

'And will you tell him,' my father falters, 'I'm sorry.'

'I will.'

He lays a weary hand on my shoulder. 'I think it might be best if you went to your room for a while, Frances,' he says. 'Your mother is horrid upset.'

16 October 1999 *(middle of the night)*

I've been awake half the night. I can't say for sure that it was the row that tipped my mother over the edge. She'd been in very bad form since the funeral, the death, the illness . . . I'm not sure how far back. And what about that man at the funeral? Whoever he was, he wasn't welcome. Had the row something to do with him? And if so, what?

The man at Aunty Lily's funeral

At the graveside, I slip my hand into my mother's and rest my head on her arm. I want to comfort her the way Xavier's daughters are comforting him, but her hand stays limp and she won't look down at me, so I let go of her and back away.

'Are you OK?' Nancy asks, touching my shoulder.

Father Vincent is finishing the rosary. The undertakers are catching hold of the ropes underneath the coffin. Xavier is looking down at it and crying, 'Lily, ah no, Lily.'

'I don't like this bit,' I tell Nancy. 'Can I go now?'

She takes my hand and we weave our way through the mourners. A short distance away, an elderly woman from the village is holding on to a headstone.

'Are you OK, Sadie?' Nancy asks her.

'Och, I'm grand. It's just me oul chest. I got a bit breathless on my way up and decided to rest here.'

'You poor thing. Come on with me and I'll give you a lift home.'

'You don't mind?'

'Not at all. Hold on to me,' she says, offering the woman her arm. 'Take your time.'

I hear the scraping sound of a shovel.

'I'll wait for ye at the car,' I say, hurrying down the gravel path. I don't want to think about what's happening.

Just outside the gates, a man is leaning on the bonnet of a car, smoking a cigar. It's one of those thin ones with a white tip. The car looks familiar but the man doesn't, and I think he must be one of Xavier's relatives from the North.

'Hello,' he says, smiling.

'Hello.'

'Did you know Lily – the lady who died?'

Now I think there *is* something familiar about him, but I'm not sure what.

'Yes, she's my aunty.'

'Your aunty. I see. So you must be Rita and Joe's daughter?'

'Yes.' It's his accent. He speaks just like my parents, Nancy and Father Vincent.

'How old are you?'

'Eight and a half.'

'That old?' He broadens his eyes as though he's impressed and then takes a long contemplative drag off his cigar.

'Is your grandfather here today?'

'He lives in Australia.'

'What about the other one?'

'He's dead.'

'Dead?'

'Mmm.' I nod.

'I see.'

He rubs a piece of fallen ash off the sleeve of his tweed jacket. I can hear Nancy and Sadie's footsteps approaching and I don't want to be caught talking to a stranger, so I say goodbye and walk away.

'You didn't tell me your name.'

I stop and look back over my shoulder. 'Frances.'

'Frances,' he says theatrically. 'A good, strong Christian name. Well, nice meeting you, Frances.'

'Nice meeting –'

'Oh my God! What are *you* doing here?' Nancy says, glaring at the man.

'Paying my respects, of course.'

'You shouldn't be here. If Rita gets wind of you turning up, she'll do her nut.'

'I'm not here to cause trouble, Nancy,' the man says, holding up his hands in surrender. 'I came, like the rest of ye, to bid farewell to Lily.'

'Well, now that you have, away with you. They'll be leaving the graveside any minute.'

'I'm going, I'm going,' he says, standing up straight. 'Goodbye, Frances,' he says, turning to me and bowing his head.

'Bye.'

'Take these,' Nancy says, handing me her car keys. 'Run on down to the car and wait for us there.'

Hurrying along the bank behind the line of parked cars, I wonder who the man is and how he knows my parents, my aunty and Nancy. Before I get into the car, I look back and see that the two women are still standing at the gate. They're looking down the road in the opposite direction. Even on my tippytoes, I don't manage to get a final glimpse of the friendly man. When I hear a car door slam and an engine purring, I know it's him.

Nancy seems bothered as we drive back to Crosslea. She doesn't talk.

'A relative, is he?' Sadie asks, breaking the awkward silence.

'No. No relation at all.'

'Must be an oul flame then,' she coughs, tapping her bosom.

I haven't a clue what she means and obviously Nancy doesn't either because she says, 'Don't talk rubbish.'

Sadie ignores her, saying that they all come out of the woodwork for a funeral, and now I'm convinced that her mind must be packing up as well as her chest.

A couple of days later, I let it slip to my parents about the man. They keep giving each other funny looks and my mother's face turns puce.

'Did Nancy not tell ye?' I ask.

'She did surely.' I catch my father giving my mother a wink. 'He's just an old neighbour from Glendarragh.'

'Why do ye not like him?'

'Because,' my mother says with tight lips, 'he's an undesirable. And anyway, what were you thinking about talking to a stranger?'

'He wasn't a stranger. He knew ye and Aunty Lily and Nancy.'

'But *you* didn't know him, did you?'

'Arragh, no harm done,' my father says. 'Just don't allow yourself to get dragged into conversation with a stranger again.'

My mother stands up and heads for the hall.

'Where are you off to?' my father asks.

'I told Nancy after Mass this morning that I'd call in to her later for a cup of tea. She should be home from work by now.'

19 October 1999 (evening)

I haven't washed my hair for several days. A glimpse at my reflection in the mirror brought a smile to my face when I saw it was standing on end at peculiar angles.

That's never you, Frances Fall? Well, fuck me pink!

A new hairstyle

After our chat in the school toilets, Lesley and I meet up every day at lunchtime. When Kat tries to tag along, Lesley says, 'Who are you, her fucking shadow?'

Kat looks at me for support, but I don't want her company

any more than Lesley does, so I say, 'Well, what are you waiting for?' without the slightest twinge of guilt.

The following day, we see Kat walking around the grounds of the school alone and Lesley wonders how I stomached hanging around with that pig's melt for so long.

'At least,' she says, 'you live in a village and not on a poxy pig farm.'

All Lesley's friends are townies and I can't believe my luck at being accepted by her cool clique. She tells the others how we used to do Irish dancing together when we were kids and that they should see the po-face of my mother; PMT wouldn't have a look in.

When I ask her if she still dances, she laughs and says, 'Oh aye, every Saturday night out in the Ulster Arms.'

'You mean a céilí?'

'Céilí! Where do you think we are, Conne-fucking-mara?' No, not a céilí. A disco, ya eejit ya. Why don't you come with us some night?'

'I might,' I say, but, after a few weeks of making lame excuses, she cajoles me into admitting that I'm not allowed to go to dances, or any other nocturnal social gathering for that matter.

I can't get the thought of going dancing with Lesley out of my mind. The niggling anger that's been brewing up inside me since the summer is coming to a head. My mother and I have been needling each other for months now.

She thinks I'm lazy, doesn't like my tone of voice, the way my hair hangs over my eyes, how I slouch in the armchair. I get her back by answering her questions in monosyllables.

'How was school today?' 'Fine.'

'Any news?' 'No.'

'Did you get your essay back?' 'Yes.'

'How did you do?' 'Fine.'

'What grade did you get?' 'C.'

'That's no great shakes, is it?' I shrug.

Sometimes, for pure badness, I pretend not to hear her.

'Are you deaf?' she screeches, red face, red neck. I'm getting on her nerves.

The showdown – it's only a matter of time.

'What you need to do,' Lesley says, 'is to make one, big, bold statement. Leave your mother in no doubt as to who's in control of your life.'

'But how?'

'Your hair,' she says decisively. 'It says everything about a person.'

Lesley's older sister Sandra is training to be a hairdresser. She's always looking for models to practise on. I'll get a new hairstyle, free of charge.

'But when and where?'

'Just come to my house after school tomorrow; it's Sandra's day off.'

'What will I tell my mother?'

'Nothing. That's the whole point, Frances. Just do what you want to do. No explanations.'

'Oh God! I can just see her standing at the front door waiting to see me arrive home off the school bus and me not on it. She'll have a scabby babby.'

'Let her.'

Lesley's other two friends agree with her – my mother is in for one fucking rude awakening.

'How will I get home?'

'My brother will give you a lift on his motorbike.'

'Oh Jesus, Lesley –'

'Ah, come on, Frances. Do you want to be a pushover all your life? Or do you want to show your sad freak of a mother who's boss?'

'Yeah, you're right; I'll do it.'

All I can face the following morning is a cup of tea. My mother asks me if there's something wrong with the porridge and I assure her that it's fine; it's just that I have a queasy stomach.

'Do you want to stay at home from school?'

Of all the bloody days to show some compassion.

I think of my bed, how I could crawl in under the blankets and forget the whole daft idea. That would be so easy, so defeatist, so typical me.

'No, it's OK. I'll be grand.'

After school, on the way up the hill to the housing estate where Lesley lives, the boys behind us hurry to catch up with her. They flock around her like kids around a magician. Although it's mid-October, her legs are still sallow from the summer. They don't go blue and blotchy in the cold like mine would were they not hidden under my calf-length skirt.

At Lesley's house, we drop our school bags inside the kitchen door. I get only a glimpse of her mother, who is standing with her back to us leaning over the sink, making choking sounds as if she's trying to catch her breath.

'Is she all right?' I ask Lesley, following her upstairs.

'Who?'

'Your mother.'

'Why? What's wrong with her?'

'She's gagging.'

'Ah, it's just her asthma; she'll be grand.'

I don't know if her mother even realizes that Lesley is home with a friend in tow; they haven't spoken. If only my mother would pay me so little attention. An unshaven man emerges from the bathroom at the top of the stairs, doing up his fly. There are others in the house too; I can hear a TV on downstairs and chatter coming from behind one of the bedroom doors.

'Lesley, get your arse down here and pick up your school bag before I break me friggin' neck on it,' her mother roars hoarsely.

'No such fucking luck,' the man mutters.

'Coming, Mammy.' Lesley runs downstairs, leaving me alone on the landing with the man. There's a smell of drink off him. When he leers at me, I say hello, looking down at my feet. I'm glad my legs are covered now. He staggers and holds on to the top of the banister.

'Who's your one?' he asks Lesley, who's on her way back up the stairs.

'Get lost, Daddy.' She brushes past him and pushes me ahead of her into a bedroom.

Fifteen minutes later, I'm sitting on a chair in front of a cluttered dressing-table – wet hair, puce face. Compared to Sandra, Lesley's eighteen-year-old sister, who is combing out my hair, I feel like a drip. Her jeans are so tight, her bum looks like a pear-shaped balloon on stilts. Her purple T-shirt is ripped in several places, showing a black string vest underneath. My stomach tightens at the thought of my hair ending up anything like hers – short, black and spiky with a plum-coloured, slanted fringe covering one eye. I don't know if I love it or hate it; only that it scares me. She rolls up a stick of gum and pops it into her mouth. After trying out a left, a right, a centre and a zigzag parting in my hair, she combs it all back, stares at my reflection in the mirror and sighs, as if to say that it doesn't matter what she does, I'll still end up with the same unfortunate face.

Lesley is sitting on the windowsill, feet resting on the bed, singing along to Queen's 'Bohemian Rhapsody' and playing drums with two rulers, battering them off the windowpane, the wooden sill, her knees, her loafers. I recognize the song because I've heard some of my classmates sing it between lessons. An older boy sticks his head in the door and asks the girls if they have any spare smokes.

'Fuck off, Keith,' Lesley shouts.

I can't believe a house can be so noisy and so rude. It's worse than the school bus.

'Can you perm her hair like mine?'

'I haven't the right gear with me, Lesley.'

'So what are you going to try out?'

'I was thinking maybe . . . Suzie Quatro. What do *you* think?' Sandra asks, tapping my shoulder.

'Me?'

'No, the cat's mother. Yes, of course you; it's *your* hair.'

'Go for it, Frances, definitely; it'll be cool.'

'OK.' I haven't a clue what I'm going for, or who Suzie Quatro is, but I do know that if she impresses Sandra and Lesley, then she'll do for me.

When I see big chunks of hair falling to the floor, I close my eyes and visualize my mother sitting at the kitchen table staring into a crystal ball like the witch in *The Wizard of Oz*, her fingernails scratching the smooth glass and her squawking 'No, no, no.'

Go scissors go: snip snip snip.

I hear Lesley jumping off the bed and changing the tape. The sisters sing along to a song I haven't heard before. At the end of every line the male singer shouts, in a husky voice, *cocaine*. Although I still have my eyes shut, I'm aware that Sandra is dancing to the beat – I'm getting sporadic digs in the shoulder from her jerking hips.

When Lesley tells me to, I open my eyes to find that she has her nightdress draped across the dressing-table mirror. It's blue, with a big Bugs Bunny on it. 'Bugs will unveil the new you,' she says, 'whenever Sandra's finished.'

'I hear your mother's a bit of a fucking fruit-cake,' Sandra says, pushing the chewing-gum out with her tongue and blowing a bubble that touches the tip of her nose before it cracks and splatters on her lips like glue.

'Yeah.'

'So how do you think she'll react when you arrive home two hours late and looking like Suzie Quatro?'

'She'll go spare.'

'Here, Lesley.' Sandra hands her a plastic bowlful of gold-coloured powder. 'Mix that with a cupful of water.' Then she looks at me. 'So what's your mother's fucking problem?'

'Dunno.'

'Lesley says she won't even let you watch *Top of the Pops*.'

'No.'

'The bitch. She sounds like a right pain in the hole. Why don't you just tell her to fuck off?'

'I couldn't. She'd make my life hell.'

'Are you allowed out to discos?'

'No.'

'You poor cow. The youth club?'

'No.'

She shakes her head. I'm enjoying the sympathy.

'What about the pictures?'

'No.'

'Bloody 'ell! You're living like a flamin' prisoner. I don't know how you stick it; I'd go mental, me.'

I love her accent. It's more English than Lesley's. She sounds like someone from *Coronation Street*.

All the attention is making me feel like a true teenager, a victim of injustice, with comrades who support my cause.

'See me and my mother,' she says, snapping her middle finger down on her index finger, 'we're like that.'

'It's well for you.'

'Mmm, I suppose. I couldn't imagine it being any other way.' She lowers her compressed bum on the edge of the bed, stares at my reflection with her black-lined, exposed eye and sighs. 'I feel kinda sorry for you.'

'Thanks.'

'Our Lesley's right: you do need rescuing. She's always been a sucker for a sad case has our kid.'

Lesley returns with the plastic bowl, and Sandra, who has now finished cutting, picks up lumps of the gooey mixture and starts massaging it into my scalp. It looks and smells like cow dung.

'Don't look so worried,' Lesley says, 'it's only henna. It'll make your hair red. Not carrot red; sexy red.'

I have to sit with a towel on my head for twenty minutes until the colour takes. Sandra goes downstairs for the cup of tea she says she's gasping for. Lesley and I share a cigarette. She's not at all bothered about the fact that her mother is padding across the landing and could easily walk in on us. We use the cap of the hairspray can for an ashtray. When we're finished, she grabs my hand, pulls me up off the chair and climbs on to the bed, dragging me after her.

'I just love this song,' she says, bouncing on the mattress. 'It's this one's hairstyle you're gonna have.'

'Which one's?'

'Her singing – Suzie Quarto.'

'Oh.'

She bends down to the tape-recorder on the bedside locker and turns up the volume. Shaking her head, she pretends to be playing a guitar as she sings along to 'If You Can't Give Me Love'.

I try to pick up the lyrics: the chorus is easy.

'Dance.'

'I can't.'

She bumps into me and makes me stagger. 'Go on.'

I start leaping about on the bed, the towel unravelling and falling on to the bedspread. Lesley thrusts herself in front of a poster above the headboard of a man with make-up called Bowie, pushing her breasts into his face and wiggling her bum. I turn my blushing face to the door and carry on dancing. The next thing I know, she pounces on me, knocking me down and falling on top of me in a fit of giggling. Raising her head, she looks into my eyes, her curly strands dangling and tickling my face. For a second I think that she might kiss me and I'm not quite sure if I want her to or not.

'You can rinse out her hair now, Lesley,' Sandra roars up the stairs, and it's just as well she does, because my face feels hot and sweaty and, anyway, I don't know how to kiss.

In the bathroom, I kneel down and hang my head over the side of the bath. I'm thinking about what Lesley told me shortly after I'd started palling around with her again – that the other girls in our year reckoned that myself and Kat Mulcahy were a pair of lezzies. Then she explained to me what lezzies were and I thought it was disgusting and said, 'No way.'

I felt gutted that anyone would say that about me and Kat Mulcahy. But me and Lesley?

I can't deny, even to myself, that I love her. I think about her first thing in the morning and last thing at night. During school, I count the minutes to the lunch breaks when I can spend some time with her, and after lunch I count them again until I can meet up with her at four o'clock. Sometimes she sits on the wall outside the main doors and waits for me, her legs swinging. Secretly, I'm prouder than a pop star's girlfriend that she has chosen me over all her other fans, and I can't help wondering if they envy me, hoping that they do. Jesus, what if I am a lezzy? What would Lesley say?

She pours jugs of cool water over my head, her nimble fingers working their way through the strands until the water runs clear. Towel-drying my hair, she reassures me that the colour is nothing short of fucking gorgeous.

Sandra's hands have no mercy as she blow-dries my hair, lifting, tugging and back-combing until my eyes sting from the sheer effort of trying not to cry. She finishes off by massaging a handful of gel into the roots, then sprays my entire head, face included, until I can taste the hair lacquer on the tip of my tongue.

'I'd give my right tit,' Lesley says, 'to be a fly on the wall when you get home.'

'I'd give my left one,' Sandra says, resting her hip on the dressing-table and pointing her comb at me, 'to give your loola mother a piece of my mind.'

'And I . . .' I start but change my mind.

'What?' Lesley says.

'Ah, nothing.'

'Go on, spit it out,' Sandra says.

'And I'd give both of mine to swap mothers, watch *Top of the Pops* and go dancing in the Ulster Arms.'

There's silence as I look from Sandra to Lesley to Sandra,

and smile. Then, one after another, our jaws balloon like toads' throats and we burst out laughing.

Sandra is trying to say something, but she isn't able to get the words out. 'At least . . .' she says several times but can't get any further.

I laugh so hard, my stomach hurts. I wish that every pain could feel this good. We pull tissue after tissue from the box on the dressing-table and when the box is empty, we wipe our tears on our sleeves.

'At least . . .'

I have to stop looking at them and pretend that I'm on my way home and about to face my horrified mother.

'At least . . .'

Lesley rips a page from one of her copybooks and hands it to Sandra with an eyeliner pencil. Sandra starts writing, snorting and gasping for breath.

She gives the note to Lesley first, and when she's finished, Lesley giggles louder, clutching her side, and passes it to me. I can just about make it out through my glazed eyes: *At least we'll still have one lopsided pair of tits between the three of us.*

Lesley says she has a feeling of déjà vu.

'That's because it's like the day of the *Feis* all over again,' I tell her as she swipes her nightdress off the mirror.

'There you are, Frances,' Sandra says, 'from Nana Mouskouri to Suzie Quatro all in the space of an hour.'

'Shite!'

'What's wrong with it?' There's a threat in the manner in which Sandra asks the question.

'I look like him,' I tell her, pointing at the poster on the wall.

'David Bowie? Oh, that's cool – so does Suzie Quatro.'

I touch my feathery hair. 'Jesus!'

'What?' Lesley asks.

'It's stiff and sticky.'

'Like a big mickey,' Sandra shouts, and whoops like a mad banshee.

'What's like a big mickey?' Keith asks, barging into the bedroom.

'Her hair,' Sandra laughs. 'Stiff and sticky.'

'It's looks wild,' Keith says, smiling at me. 'Can I leave you home now?'

'She's not going yet,' Lesley says. 'Sure you're not?'

I check my watch; it's ten past six. I wonder what my parents are doing at this moment and how they're going to react when I get home.

'Your mother's gonna kill you now one way or another,' Sandra says, pulling a cigarette from the box. 'Here, have one of these; it'll calm your nerves.'

Keith says he'll wait for me downstairs. I'm mortified at the thought of being alone with him. He must be at least twenty. I light the cigarette and take a couple of pulls.

'Would your mother be able to leave me home?' I ask Lesley.

'Daddy's away in the car,' Sandra says, 'but don't worry, Keith won't bite you.'

'OK.' I pull my gabardine from the knob on the wardrobe door. 'I'd better go.'

'Scared?' Lesley puts her arm around me.

'It's Daddy I dread facing the most.'

'Why, is he a bollocks too?' Sandra asks.

'No, he's lovely. But he'll be worried sick about me by now.'

'Just tell him you're fed up of being treated like a two-year-old,' Sandra says. 'Fuck it, he was young himself once upon a time.'

'And if your mother as much as lays a finger on you,' Lesley says, 'clock her.'

It's cold and dark outside. My knees are knocking off one another – more the fear of riding on a motorbike with a fella than the chill. With the helmet on, I feel like an astronaut. I don't know where to rest my feet.

'Put your arms around my waist and hang on,' Keith shouts back at me as he revs up the bike.

I don't dare. Lesley is standing at the front door shivering and jigging about to keep herself warm.

'If you don't hang on, you'll fall off,' Keith says, taking my hands and wrapping them around his leathered body.

When he sees my feet dangling, he looks back at me, his eyes smiling through the gap in the helmet.

'There,' he shouts, pointing to the footrest.

At first, it's like being on a merry-go-round – a gentle breeze in my face. But, once we're out of the town, we're tearing out the road so fast, I'm swallowing great big pockets of air. And although it's almost choking me, I don't want the journey to end: I've never felt so high.

When Keith pulls up on the outskirts of the village, I step off the bike, remove the helmet and hand it to him. He hangs it on the handlebar and says, 'Come here.'

I think he's expecting a kiss. Why else would he want me to stand close to him? But I don't know how he's going to manage; he still has his helmet on. I step towards him, my lips and tongue suddenly draining of their juices. He pulls off his right glove and tousles my hair.

'That's better,' he says, 'the helmet flattened it on you.'

'Thanks.'

He smirks. 'You'd better go.'

'Yeah,' I say, without budging. I'm standing next to him, gawping into his face, still waiting for the kiss.

'See ya,' he says, turning on the engine and revving up the bike.

'Bye.'

I walk wobbly-legged down the street, feeling both relieved and disappointed about the kiss that didn't happen.

'Hello, Mister Scully.' He's closing up the shop.

'Young Fall, be the hokey!'

I'm glad I've shocked him.

Billy Brady, the village flirt from my class in primary school, is walking towards me.

'Evening, Red,' he says, and winks.

'Hiya, Billy.'

'That's never you, Frances Fall?'

'Yip,' I say, striding on.

'Well, fuck me pink.'

He stands looking after me. I throw back my shoulders and toss back my hair.

'Oh, by the way,' he shouts, 'your father's been looking for you. I've just seen him driving out the Castleowen road.'

My heart sinks.

'Shite shite shite,' I whisper, slowing my pace.

If only I had thought of ringing him from Lesley's house and asking him to collect me. I could have talked to him on the way home and explained to him why I've done what I've done.

20 October 1999 (the early hours)

I've just woken up in a sweat. I thought I heard a baby crying, but there are no babies in here. I must have been dreaming.

Her eighteenth birthday

My vision is blurred. Indicating, I pull over on to the hard shoulder to dry my eyes and compose myself. I need to keep my wits about me.

When I turn to look at the baby, I find her lying on her back, hands facing upwards, fingers curled like petals on the verge of blooming. As I run my forefinger down her cheek, her lips quiver into what looks like a smile, then purse again into their little bud shape. Such beauty.

I turn off the engine just to gaze at her.

No, Frances, I think, not now. You've no time to brood, you must move on. You've stuff to buy, a hotel to find. Then you'll have time and you can lay her down and brood all night.

As I go to turn the key again, she lets out a sigh, soft as fleece, and I wish I could climb inside her dreams and dissolve.

I let the engine idle, lean back, shut my eyes and listen to her breathing. My face is warm and smiling. Flickering sunrays penetrate my eyelids, splashing yellow streaks across the blackness. I feel weary, but calm. Cars are whizzing by. The whirring sound of the traffic ebbs until it becomes a distant hum and seems like it's oceans away.

I drift off into a warm, easy sleep and sink to the bottom of the ocean. I'm lying on the seabed, watching tiny fish swim above me, circling me like a baby's mobile. Each fish is either baby-pink or powder-blue. They're blowing bubbles. I reach up and touch a pink one with the tip of my index finger. It falls, flopping on to my stomach like jelly and wriggling about as if it's out of the water and struggling for breath. Frantically, I try to put it back on the revolving mobile, but when I scoop it up, I realize that's it's not a fish at all, but a tiny baby, cold and slimy and slipping from my grasp.

The traffic roars and the fish dart through the water and disappear. I can hear the sharp, shrill cry of a baby, but when I look down, she's no longer in my arms. The water is draining away and the sun is blasting down on me like angry steam.

I wake with a jolt, look behind me and see that the baby's blanket is draped over her erect legs. Inside her mouth is as red as cherries and her lips are vibrating like plucked harp strings. What in God's name is wrong with her now?

I stagger out of the front seat and climb into the back beside her. My hands are shaking. My throat feels dry and acidy. Picking her up out of the carrycot, I see that her baby-gro and the sheet are drenched. After rummaging through the baby bag, I find a clean vest and baby-gro, a nappy and her soother.

'Good girl, good girl,' I wheeze, my head spinning so fast, I think I'm going to faint.

The soother pacifies her as I cradle her in one arm and pull the wet sheet off the mattress with the other. Then I turn the mattress over, take off my cardigan, spread it across the mattress and lay her down. Bending her limbs very carefully, I strip her down to her nappy. When I lay my hand on her stomach, I notice that her skin is clammy . . . or is it mine? I don't know, so I blow on her skin anyway to cool her down. She gurgles and shivers, her eyes widening with the cold sensation. I lean over her and blow again, this time on her chest and neck. She shudders and gasps in amazement. A lorry rattles past, causing the car to shake. The fright urges me to hurry up and move on. Her nappy is heavy and sodden and feels like warm dough. As I peel back the sticky strips to open it, she smiles at me and for a moment I breathe easy.

'What the – Jesus Christ! You're a boy,' I cry. 'A boy.'

My face is tingling from perspiration. What have I done? Who is this child? And where is his mother? When I lift the nappy out from under him, his legs flap like socks on a line on a blustery day. I hold his feet in my hands and put them to my damp cheeks.

'I'm sorry,' I cry over and over, but all he does is smile and gurgle.

If only I could turn back the clock and start the day all over again, I'd choose the silver necklace and not the gold. Then I'd go home, place the necklace in the box at the bottom of my wardrobe, lie down on my bed and watch her dancing in my dreams. I'd see her on a stage, in the spotlight, smiling down at me, sure of my admiration. And I'd smile back, the proud mother in the audience, until sleep would come along and draw the curtains on me.

I don't know what to do next. I dare not think about the trouble I'm in. If I turn on the news, I'll hear all about it, but I don't want to. Not yet, not in the car; not while I'm driving.

Come on, I think, pull yourself together, don't crack up.

I give myself orders and follow them.

Put on his clean nappy. Give him his soother. Get back into the front seat. Dry your tears.

I open the front pocket to get a tissue and find a half-drunk bottle of Ballygowan water. A drink at last; warm but wet. My grateful lips, tongue, throat. Small mercies.

Put on some music, something mellow: *A Woman's Heart* – perfect. Drive to the next town. I'm on the road again.

22 October 1999 (evening)

I walked across the grounds to the chapel today, lit a candle and sat in the back pew. There was an old man doing the Stations of the Cross, rosary beads dangling from his fragile hands. I held my hand to the corner of my left eye. I couldn't say a prayer.

The showdown

It's just a new hairstyle, I think, walking round the side of the house; no big bloody deal. My footsteps seem louder than usual.

'Is that you, Frances?' my mother shouts from another room as I step in through the back door.

'Yeah.'

She comes thundering down the stairs. Straightening my back, I take a deep breath. The kitchen door swings open.

My mother yelps when she sees me and, as if it's a reflexive reaction, whips my face with her rosary beads. She gets me in the corner of my left eye with the crucifix, and now my back's not straight any more and I want to kneel down on the floor and cry.

Hand on my face and bleary-eyed, I try to push past her, but she grabs my sleeve and jostles me, screaming into my face about my father scouring the village for me and ringing the Guards, and her on bended knee praying that I had come to no harm, and then me turning up, bold as brass, looking like a cheap whore.

My courage has deserted me. I don't know what to do. She

won't stop shaking me and screeching in my ear. It's been a few years since she's hit me, but at this moment it feels as though it's the very first time. The fear is back. I try to pull away from her, but ferocity is giving her the upper hand. She sneers at my feeble attempt to push her arm away and again lashes out at me with her beads, this time striking my neck. The sting makes me jolt backwards and I knock my head off the doorframe. Pain pierces through my skull. She's standing in front of me, her hot, red face like a ball of rage. I cannot breathe. I have to put a stop to it – her madness, her yelling, the pain.

'Fucking bitch,' I howl, grabbing her by her hair and pushing her through to the living-room and up against the back of the sofa. She struggles and tries to unleash herself, dropping her beads in the tussle. When she goes to pick them up, I kick them away. Only when I have to let go of my scream to draw breath do I realize that she is now silent. Her face is white; her eyes are pinched, glistening, like two gashes.

'How dare you?' she says through constricted lips.

I loosen my grip on her hair and smile, although my face and neck are still burning with pain. I think it's the relief; I've finally done it – stood up to her. And won.

As I head out the living-room door to go up to my bedroom, I step over her rosary beads, stop, turn, and start stamping on them, looking into her face as the beads fall apart beneath my feet. She doesn't move; she's still backed up against the sofa, her bottom lip clenched between her teeth. I don't stop until I see a tear rolling down her cheek. Then I turn and walk out.

About twenty minutes later the phone rings in the hall and I hear my mother tell my father that I'm home, and to hurry back because I've gone berserk and God only knows what I'll do next.

I'm lying on the bed wishing that I'd been born into a

different family, with brothers and sisters who'd do my hair and play their records and fill up the house with noise. The key turns in the front door and before my father even steps inside, my mother is out in the hall crying and saying, 'Oh, Joe, thank God you're back.'

I think it's a pity that she's not always so grateful to see him when he arrives home after a hard day's work. She's not humming her way through the house now, pretending that she hasn't noticed his presence and waiting for him to break the silence, which he always does in the end.

I want to listen to what they're saying about me, but my ears feel clogged up from crying. I'm holding a tissue to the side of my eye to stop the tears from stinging the abrasion. The Blessed Virgin is staring down at me from a picture on the wall, her hands upturned like someone who's checking to see if it's still raining, or simply asking – What can you do?

Lesley says the only thing standing between me and my freedom is a yellow belly. If only I could ring her now and tell her what I've done! I know she'd be proud of me.

After a long session of listening to my mother, my father is climbing the stairs; I can hear his knees cracking. He knocks on the door and comes in before I get the chance to tell him that he *can* come in. I'm dreading this confrontation more than the one I had with my mother. He glances at me sideways and drags my dressing-table stool across the floor. I sit up on the side of the bed and lean my elbows on my knees, keeping my eyes downcast. There's a pots and pans orchestra being conducted in the kitchen just so my father won't forget who's most upset over this row and whose side he should be on. Letting out a laboured sigh, he sits down in front of me.

'What's got into you at all at all, Frances? And what sort of ludicrous hairdo is that?'

I look up at him, finger my gluey hair and snigger.

'Sorry,' I say, trying to sound as serious as he looks. 'For laughing, I mean; I just couldn't help it.'

He's staring at me as though I'm someone else and not his daughter, as if he has a whole lot of questions to ask, but now that he sees my face, the words won't pass his lips, because I couldn't possibly be the same girl he'd said goodnight to on the landing only the night before. He sighs again, scratches his head, then swallows hard, his Adam's apple bouncing inside his neck like a ping-pong ball. I imagine a string of question-marks sliding down his oesophagus and into his stomach, where they are broken down by enzymes and no longer form questions at all.

He reaches into his pocket, pulls out the broken rosary beads, holds them out in his hand and says, 'This is hardly a laughing matter.'

'Neither is this,' I say, wincing as I touch the cut on the corner of my eye.

'She told me about that and explained that it was an accident.'

'And you believe her?'

'She's never lied to me before.'

'It was no accident, Daddy, believe me. I swear, *she* lashed out at *me*.'

'The poor woman was in a state of shock. She was climbing the walls all evening worrying about you; both of us were. What you did was cruel. For all we knew, you could have been attacked and left lying dead in a ditch.'

There are tears welling up in his eyes and he has to pull out his handkerchief and blow his dry nose into it, just so that he can wipe them away before they roll down his cheeks and make him look weak.

'Wait till you have children of your own,' he says. 'Then you'll understand how distressed we were.'

'I didn't mean to hurt *you*, Daddy.'

'But you did.'

'I'm sorry.'

'And what about your mother?'

'She banged my skull off the doorframe, you know. My flipping head is still throbbing.'

'Because you pushed her.'

'No, I was trying to get past her.'

'She says you pushed her up against the sofa.'

'Daddy, will you lis —'

'Well, did you, or did you not?'

'Yes, but –'

'God Almighty, Frances, that's no way to treat your mother.'

'Oh.' I let my head flop back, grit my teeth and make fists of my hands. 'I hate her guts,' I say, looking at the ceiling.

'Don't say that.'

'Why not?' I level my face with his. 'It's the truth.'

'There's a thin line between love and hate, you know,' he says, his droopy eyes pleading for my surrender.

'Well, she crossed it first.'

I cannot hide the tear that stings my cut and runs down the side of my face. Now I look weak.

'Your mother doesn't hate you. I've never met a woman more dedicated to her family.'

'Is that why ye sleep in separate bedrooms?'

'That's a matter for your mother and me, young lady,' he snaps, 'and quite frankly none of your business.'

'I know, I'm sorry. It's just that she's trying to make out that it's all my fault, so that you'll be on her side.'

'Well, to be fair, Frances, in this instance, it *is* your fault. You took it upon yourself to go off and get your hair done without telling either of us where you were going, what you were doing or how you were getting home. How *did* you get home, by the way?'

'Lesley's mother.'

'Lesley who?'

'A friend from school. It was her sister who did my hair.'

'And a right muck she made of it too. What on earth possessed you to do all this without getting permission from your mother?'

'Because there was no fecking point in asking her, was there? She wouldn't have let me go.'

'If you needed a haircut, you should have told your mother and she'd have taken you into town for it on Saturday afternoon . . . and don't you say "feck" when you're talking to me.'

'I'm sorry, but I'm fed up with my poxy life. I feel like a right moron being escorted by Mammy everywhere I go. I'm sixteen years old, Daddy, and I'm not even allowed into town on my own. There's ten-year-old kids in this village with more freedom than I have.'

'Yeah, and a cheeky bunch of corner boys they are too.'

'Ah, for God's sake, Daddy.'

'What?'

I thought of what Sandra said about him being young once too. 'What were you doing at sixteen?'

'Working in my father's barber shop.'

'And did you have friends?'

'Of course I did.'

'And where did you go with your friends?'

'Football matches, the pictures . . .'.

'And did your father tag along to keep an eye on you?'

He slaps his hands down on his knees, stands up and starts pacing the room with long strides. My mother has sent him up to sort me out, and sort me out he must, because there'll be a price to pay for letting her down. She won't be satisfied unless he drags me puffy-eyed into the kitchen, begging for mercy and promising never to step out of line again.

But I know he's thinking now, and considering both points of view, because he's frowning and his lips look like they've been pulled together by a drawstring.

'I didn't really need a haircut, Daddy; I needed a friend.'

'I thought you were friendly with that young Mulcahy lassie from out beyond Corfinn,' he says, stopping and leaning his elbow on the chest of drawers.

'Not any more. I'm friends with Lesley Kelly – remember her from Irish dancing?'

'Oh yeah, the English lassie – a gobby wee one.'

'That's her.'

'They're a wild bunch, them Kellys, according to your mother.'

'And what would she know about them?'

'Ah now, you'd be surprised what goes about. People talk. Anyway, what's wrong with young Mulcahy? Now there's a lassie from decent stock; I believe they're a highly respectable family.'

'She's a twit . . . and a lezzie.'

'What?'

'She's a lesbian, Daddy.'

'Good God Almighty!'

'Yeah, well, it's the truth, if you must know.'

'Good bless us and save us. Keep well away from that one, whatever you do.'

'I fully intend to. The last thing I need is everyone thinking that me and her are . . . you know.'

'Don't even talk like that.'

He buries his hands in his pockets and starts pacing again. The pots and the pans have stopped fighting and the smell of dinner is floating up the stairs and in under the bedroom door.

'I think, begod, I'd better have a chat with your mother about this Mulcahy lassie.'

'And while you're at it, you can tell her that the only true friend I have is Lesley. You know, I'm not popular, Daddy. The other girls look at me like I'm a freak. If they have to sit beside me in class, they moan and roll their eyes to heaven, as if sitting next to me is some sort of punishment.'

'Why didn't you . . .' He sits on the stool again and looks at me with watery eyes.

'They call me *Mousy*, all of them except Lesley. She treats me with respect. She *likes* me, Daddy; Lesley Kelly *likes* me. And I don't care what you or Mammy say, I'm staying friends with her and that's that.'

Reaching across, he squeezes my hand gently, nodding his OK. Tears start brimming in my eyes again, but I don't care if I look weak any more because my father's on my side and wants to make things better for me, just like I did for him many years ago when I found him crying in the middle of the night.

'I'm tired of being lonely,' I sob.

'I didn't know,' he says, handing me his handkerchief.

'I know.'

'I'll talk to your mother and see if she'll cut you some slack.'

'OK.'

'Honestly, I didn't know how difficult –'

'It's all right.'

'But you'll let us know from now on where you're going and what you're doing?'

'Yeah.'

'Good lassie.'

'Dinner's ready,' my mother shouts up the stairs.

'Do you think she'll listen?'

'Maybe if you apologized to her, she'd be in a better mood for listening.'

'Do I have to?'

'Well, it'll make it a lot easier for me to persuade her to allow you more freedom, if you assure her that you're sorry and that you'll not disrespect her again.'

'OK, but I'll do it for you, Daddy, not for her.'

'I dare say it doesn't matter whom you do it for, love, so long as you do it,' he says, heading towards the bedroom door. 'Are you not coming down?'

'I'm not hungry. I'll just do my homework and go to bed.'

'Your hair, I –'

'What about it?'

'Arragh,' he says, half smiling.

'So you really don't like it, then?'

'I'll put it to you this way, love – don't be one bit surprised if you're greeted at the bus stop in the morning with a cock-a-doodle-doo.'

After he closes the door, I bring the stool back over to the dressing-table and sit looking into the mirror. Leaning my face towards the glass, I open my mouth, exhale a big puff of breath on its surface, making a cloud of condensation, and write with the tip of my nail, *Mousy Fall RIP 10/10/1979*.

A couple of hours later, not having eaten since lunchtime, I tiptoe downstairs for a glass of milk and some biscuits. Neither of my parents passes any remark as I scuttle through the living-room, where they're watching the nine o'clock news. I've no idea what, if any, conversation has taken place between them since dinnertime, only that, so far, no one has raised a voice.

Around ten o'clock, I'm sitting up in bed reading the second chapter of *Silas Marner* for my homework, when I hear the first rumblings of an argument coming from downstairs. I can't catch what they're saying; all I know is that my mother is doing most of the haranguing. I'm waiting to hear my father storm through the hall and out the front door, like he usually does when my mother verbally slaughters him, but he doesn't leave the room. He continues to respond to her in a low and patient tone.

When I wake up the following morning, I think that the row must have gone on into the small hours. The last thing I remember from the night before is checking the clock: it was half eleven. On my way downstairs, I notice that my mother's humming is chirpier than usual and I don't know what to make of it.

'By the way, I'm sorry,' I mumble, entering the kitchen and heading straight for the cutlery drawer to get a spoon.

She doesn't answer. She has a dishcloth in her hand and is wiping everything in sight – the draining-board, the counter-top, the cupboard doors, the cooker. I sit at the table and pour out my cornflakes. Just in case she hasn't heard my apology, I say it again. 'I'm sorry.'

Leering at me with a tight-lipped grin, she leans her hands flat on the table and narrows her eyes. 'Oh, you will be, madam,' she says, nodding her certainty. 'You will be.'

The spoon slips out of my hand and into the cereal, splashing milk over the side of the bowl.

'But Daddy . . .'

'But Daddy what?' she sneers, wiping up the milk around the bowl, her mocking face threateningly close to mine.

I push my chair back and dash into the hall where I pull my coat from its hanger and grab my schoolbag. Finding it still open, I get down on my hunkers to fasten the buckles. I don't cop, until I stand up again, that she has crept up behind me.

'If you think that hideous hairdo is going to do wonders for your popularity,' she says, 'then you're a bigger gulpin than I thought. That Lesley Kelly was out to make a laughing-stock of you, and you'll see for yourself when you get to the bus stop that that's exactly what she's done.'

Daunted by her remarks, I walk out the front door and slam it shut. What if she's right? What if they do laugh at me? My mother, not in the habit of making unlikely predictions, would never risk being proved wrong, would she? The thought of being ridiculed fills me with dread. As I approach the bus stop, I look back and see her standing outside the front door staring down the street after me, arms folded across her chest.

Attracta and Angelina Reilly are crossing the street and smiling.

'Love your hair,' Attracta says, and Angelina agrees.

Susan Scully looks me up and down and says, 'Since when did you go all funky?'

One of the lads says he thinks it makes me look tarty, but I don't mind because that's better than looking mousy.

The bus pulls up. The driver asks to see my ticket because he thinks I'm new and wants to check that I have paid up for the term like everyone else. The boys at the back whistle as I step over bags that are strewn all down the aisle. I find an empty seat and sit down. Susan Scully sits next to me and says, 'Who did your hair anyway?'

'Sandra Kelly.'

The bus pulls back out on to the street.

'The colour's rockin'.'

'Thanks.'

My mother is eyeballing me as we approach the house. Do it, I think, my heart skipping a beat.

Vroom vroom. She's gone.

'Am I fucking seeing things,' Susan says, nudging me, 'or did you just give your mother the fingers?'

22 October 1999 (evening)

I gave her the fingers all right; just like I did the day I took the baby.

You didn't think I'd be a good mother – fuck you!

Her eighteenth birthday

I pull in at a shopping centre. I need stuff – a car seat, bottles, nappies, formula, clothes. That will do until I have time to sort myself out and decide what to do. The baby is awake again and moaning. I must be doing something wrong. I didn't know a child could be so restless.

After attaching the carrycot back on to the pram-frame, I wheel him into the centre and head straight for a store where I see baby accessories in the window.

'Can I help you?' a young woman asks.

'I'd like to buy a car seat for my baby.'

She escorts me down to the aisle and shows me the range. There are so many, I can't decide.

'A boy?' she says.

'Yes.' How does she know?

'That eliminates these so,' she says, pointing to two that are pink and purple. 'How about this green one? It's suitable for newborn to nine months. And it has a padded handle, which makes it easier for you to carry.'

'Yeah, fine.' It's the blue teddies on his baby-gro; that's how she knows.

The baby starts to cry.

'Sounds like he's ready for a feed.'

'He is. Where's the nearest coffee shop?'

'Next door.'

She offers to hold on to the car seat for me until I've fed the baby and had my coffee.

'I know what it's like,' she says, swiping my credit card, 'having to lug a load of stuff around when you have a baby in tow. I've a four-month-old daughter myself. Just back to work after maternity leave, worse luck. Is your baby sleeping the night yet?'

'Yes,' I say, signing the receipt.

'You're lucky. I'm still getting up twice a night with my little monkey.'

As she hands me back my credit card, I notice that she's not wearing a wedding ring and wonder if she's raising the child on her own.

'Do you do all the night feeds?'

'I have to. I'm a single mum.'

Well, then, if she can do it, so can I.

'Me too.'

She cranes her neck and looks in at the wailing baby in the pram. 'Oh, poor babba.'

First I go into the Ladies to rinse out the bottle with hot water.

'Ssh ssh.' I can't pacify him. My feet are slippery in my sandals. I can smell the perspiration from under my arms.

'Ssh ssh.' I could just leave him, walk away, get in the car, drive off. Someone would take care of him.

But I can't. I cannot fail. I must succeed. I can and I will take care of this child. Do you hear me, Mother? Are you listening? You didn't think I'd be a good mother; fuck you! Just you wait and see. He's hungry, that's all.

Everyone turns and stares as we enter the coffee shop. A waitress says I can leave the pram in the corner.

'Can I get you anything?' she asks, pulling out a chair for me.

'White coffee, please,' I say, sitting down and trying to settle the baby in my arms.

Two old ladies smile at me sympathetically as I struggle to open the second carton of Cow and Gate milk.

'Will I hold him for ya, sweetheart?' one of them says, tottering over to me and taking him anyway. 'What's his name?'

'Joseph,' I say, thinking of my father.

'Ah, you could steal him, couldn't you?' she says, looking back at her friend.

I did. I did steal him, but I didn't mean to; it just happened.

I become tearful again as I pour in the milk and tighten the cap on the bottle.

'God bless him,' the woman says, handing him back to me. 'The old baby blues, is it, love?'

I nod.

'We've all been through it, sweetheart; it'll pass.' She pulls a tissue from up her sleeve, leaves it on the table and joins her friend again. I can't pick it up, my hands are busy, so I dab my cheek on my sleeve.

The baby is glugging back the milk, his curious eyes sweeping over every inch of my face.

'Who's a happy baby now?' the waitress cheeps, smiling at him and putting the coffee down in front of me. 'Would you like anything to eat with that?'

'No, thanks; I'm grand.'

The two old ladies natter, smiling over at me every so often and nodding their encouragement. I like the attention, how nice everyone is being to me, the automatic respect I'm getting just because I'm a mother. For the first time in years, I'm visible. I'm inside the circle, not skulking around the outside, afraid to cross the line.

'Thanks,' I whisper, kissing the baby's forehead. 'Thanks, Joseph.'

And if he's a boy, so what? Why should I have assumed that he was a girl? I didn't think he was Baby Fall, did I? I just came to the wrong conclusion. But there's no reason why him being a boy should change the situation, is there? He could still have been abandoned. This could still be fate, right?

'Take care of yourself, sweetheart,' the old woman says as she gets up to leave.

'Aye, and look after that wee babby,' her friend croaks, leaning on her walking stick.

'Thanks. I will.' I smile without telling myself to do so.

I check the time; it's ten to five.

Joseph is resting his head on my shoulder now. I'm rubbing his back to relieve his wind. There's a smell of new life off him; it's like breathing in hope.

By the time his bottle is empty, I'm the only customer left and he's falling asleep. As I gather my things to leave, the waitress wheels the pram over to me and I lay Joseph on my cardigan.

'The bottle spilled on the sheet.'

'One of those days, is it? Don't worry, we all have them,' she says, holding the door open for me.

'What time does the supermarket close at?'

'Seven o'clock; you've loads of time yet.'

It's a quick, easy scoot around the aisles as I fill the basket on the bottom of the pram with all the things I need. At the checkout, I pack five bags and place them in the basket.

When I go in to collect the car seat, the girl who'd served me earlier tells a young male employee to carry it out to the car for me. He helps me to fold the pram and to secure the car seat with the safety belt. I strap Joseph in. He doesn't stir.

It's the first hotel I come across.

'A double room with a cot,' I tell the receptionist. 'My husband will be joining me tomorrow.'

'Certainly. How many nights?'

'Just two.'

It's only now I realize that I'm in Kilkenny. There are several leaflets stacked in stands advertising nearby tourist attractions. Casually, I pick up a few and put them in my handbag. Joseph is sleeping in his new seat at my feet. Phones are ringing. Keys are dangling from hooks. A digital clock tells the time in cities all over the world – 13.13 in New York. Lucky numbers.

'Would you fill this in for me, please?' The receptionist hands me a clipboard and I write in my details on the check-in form.

'Would you like the porter to take your luggage up to your room?'

'Yes, thanks. I've a few bags in the boot of the car.'

The porter follows me to the car and carries my shopping and my overnight bag up to my room.

Settled at last, I put the car seat on the floor by the bed, draw the curtains, flop on to the mattress and close my eyes.

25 October 1999 (middle of the night)

In the visitors' room today, a man burst into tears when a young boy walked across the room and hugged him. It's like Mrs Scully said, there's nothing as sad as to see a grown man cry.

My father's tears

It's a year since Aunty Lily's death. Nancy and Mrs Scully, the local postmistress, call to the house one afternoon to talk to my mother about filing an official objection to the planning permission granted for the construction of twenty-four council houses on the outskirts of the village. I'm in the middle of making bread and butter pudding.

'If it goes ahead,' my mother says, 'we may kiss goodbye to village life as we know it.'

Mrs Scully suggests that the villagers sign a petition. She'll be able to nab them all when they call in for their pensions and children's allowances.

'And by the way, Rita,' she says, 'Herbert's retiring. Didn't you tell me at some stage that Joe had applied for the Crosslea post?'

'He did when we moved here first. But that's almost ten years ago now.'

'Well, it'll be up for grabs in August. Wouldn't that be a handy number for him? Sure he could tip home for his breakfast every morning and all.'

'There'll not be too many tears shed over Herbert's departure,' Nancy says. 'Talk about a contrary article.'

'You know, I'd swear he eats a bowl of wasps for his breakfast every morning,' Mrs Scully says. 'Oh, it'd be lovely to have an agreeable man like Joe about the place. I'm telling you, Rita,' she points her teaspoon at my mother, 'you got a good one there.'

'Joe's a brick,' Nancy says, 'there's no doubt about it. The way he took over the running of the house when you were looking after Lily; you'd not find another man in the country to fill his shoes.'

'You did as much and more yourself, Nancy,' my mother says, lifting the teapot. 'Anyone for a hot drop?'

'Aye, thanks,' Mrs Scully says, holding out her teacup. 'By the way, I'm very sorry I missed the anniversary Mass last week, Rita. I didn't hear a thing about it till it was all over.'

'Not to worry,' my mother says.

'Any word from Xavier at all?' Nancy asks.

'No.' My mother shakes her head. 'Not a dickybird.'

'I can't get over him not keeping in touch,' Nancy says. 'It maddens me when I think of how much support ye gave him in his hour of need.'

'Sure, there's not much point in him keeping in touch with us,' my mother says. 'We only knew each other a lock of months altogether.'

'All the same,' Nancy says, 'the odd phone call wouldn't go amiss.'

'Will you ever forget him the day of the funeral?' Mrs Scully looks from my mother to Nancy. 'Only for Joe, he'd have been in on top of poor Lily in her grave.' She sighs and blesses herself. 'He was a sorry sight.'

'It doesn't seem like a year ago, does it?' Nancy says, rubbing her knees in a circular motion and gazing at the floor. 'Where does the time go at all?'

Mrs Scully sips her tea. 'How are you bearing up yourself, Rita?'

'Arragh,' my mother says, picking up stray crumbs and flicking them on to her side plate, 'as well as can be expected, I suppose.'

'Daddy still cries in the middle of the night,' I say, scooping a handful of raisins from the bag and sprinkling them over a layer of bread soldiers. 'I heard him.'

Something about the way the three women swish their heads round and stare at me makes me think that they don't believe me.

'Honest, I did,' I cross my heart, 'loads of times.'

Mrs Scully pats her chest. 'God, but there's nothin' as sad as to see a grown man cry.'

The two visitors look into the distance, frowning and shaking their heads. My mother unsettles me with her stony, unwavering gaze.

In bed that night, the crying goes on for longer than usual. I sit at the edge of my bed shivering, my bare feet dangling inches above the floor. For warmth, I tuck my hands into the sleeves of my nightdress as I listen out for the sound of my mother's footsteps on the landing; she's bound to hear him.

After a few minutes, I tell myself that she must be asleep, but in my heart I know that she probably isn't. I tiptoe across my bedroom and stand with my hand on the doorknob. The curtains flicker and a streetlight winks at me as if for good luck. I don't want my mother to hear the door squeak open, so I pull it towards me inch by inch. My eyes are accustomed to the darkness now and I can see that my father's bedroom door is ajar and that his lamp is on. Feeling like a thief in the night, I skim across the landing and slip through the gap in the door. He's kneeling down, his upper body crouched across the bed, head in his hands, his shoulders shuddering. The blankets on one side of the bed are pulled back.

'What's wrong, Daddy?' I whisper, touching his shoulder.

He jolts and looks up at me, wiping his shiny face with the back of his hands. 'What are you doing out of bed at this hour of the night? You should be asleep.'

'I can't sleep.' I sit on the warm sheet where he'd been lying. 'I hate it when you cry. It makes me feel . . . worried.'

'I think, at nine years of age, you're a bit young to be worrying, love.'

'Nine and a half.'

He sighs.

'Are you crying because of Aunty Lily?'

'You're shaking with the cold, love.' He tugs at the bed-clothes and covers my legs. I lie back, resting my head on his pillow and tucking my feet under my bottom.

'To answer your question – yes, I suppose I am crying for your Aunty Lily . . . partly anyway,' he says, getting up and sitting on the edge of the bed. 'But for your mother as well.'

'Why? She's not sick too, is she?'

'No, no, love, not at all. Your mother's in perfect health, thank God. It's just that it's heartbreaking to see her so upset.'

'Oh.'

'They were very close, your mother and her sister. It's just terrible that things ended the way they did.'

'Mmm. I think so too, Daddy. I really liked Aunty Lily.'

'I know you did, and she was very fond of you too.'

'Yeah,' I say, feeling a little sad myself now.

'Your mother practically reared her, you know.'

'Because their mammy died?'

'Aye.'

'Who had to do all the cooking and cleaning and stuff?'

'Your mother.'

'*And* looked after Aunty Lily?'

'Yes.'

'Janey! What age was she?'

'Only fourteen. Lily was nine.'

'Did Mammy not have to go to school?'

'She stayed in school for a while, but she had to pack it in, in the end.'

'Why?'

'Her father's orders.'

'Did she not want to leave school?'

'No. She was a very clever girl, your mother. She could have made something of herself if she'd had half a chance.'

'Did Aunty Lily like school?'

My father smiles. 'No. She wasn't too fond of it.'

'Me neither.'

Enjoying our middle-of-the-night chat, I nestle down in the bed. 'How come Mammy never tells me about when she was small?'

'Some people don't like to talk about the past, love.'

'Why not?'

'All sorts of reasons.'

'Was she not happy?'

'She had a tough childhood.'

'Did Aunty Lily have a tough childhood too?'

'She did.'

'Their daddy wasn't very nice to them, was he?'

'Why do you say that?'

'Because when I asked Mammy about him once, she told me to stop annoying her head and her cheeks turned red.'

'I see.'

'I don't think she likes Aunty Lily any more either, Daddy, because she gets mad when I ask about her too.'

'The wound is still raw, love,' he says, looking down at his knees. 'She's still grieving. We have to be patient with her, you and me. She'll come round in the end,' he nods, 'you'll see.'

'So, when Mammy gets happy again, will you get happy too?'

'I am happy, love,' he says, turning to face me. 'I've got you, haven't I?'

With tousled hair and dressed in pyjamas, he looks soft and soppy and I wonder how my mother can stop herself from loving him.

'Yeah,' I smile, 'you do.'

He leans towards me and kisses my forehead. 'Now, how about some shut-eye?'

'I'm on my Easter holidays,' I say, tightening the sheets around me. 'I don't have to get up early.'

'Ah, but *I* do.'

'Can I sleep here, Daddy?' I don't want to leave him alone again. 'I'm lovely and cosy here.'

He hesitates, then smiles and says, 'Aye, OK. I don't see why not.'

After climbing into bed, he switches off the lamp and lies with his back to me.

'Daddy,' I whisper.

'What?'

'Sometimes, I try to remember Aunty Lily's face, but I can't. Does that ever happen to you?'

'Yes. I think it happens to everyone when they haven't seen someone for a long time.'

'But I can still remember Lesley's face and I haven't seen her for a whole year.'

'Go to sleep, will you?'

'Maybe that's because she's not dead.'

'Ssh.'

'Goodnight, Daddy.'

'Goodnight, love.'

Outside a gust of wind whirls and rattles the windowpane. I move towards the centre of the bed, nuzzling my knees into his back and wrapping my arm around his waist. I feel safe . . . perfectly happy.

The next thing I'm conscious of is the fierce fingers digging into my upper arms and dragging me away from the warmth of my father's bed.

'Stand up,' my mother screams, as my legs topple out on to the floor.

Still dazed from sleep and the unexpected bluntness of my awakening, I stumble to my feet and try to straighten up.

'Mammy.'

'Don't you dare speak to me,' she roars, walloping my arms, legs and back.

Then she pushes me ahead of her into my own bedroom, spitting obscenities at me through gritted teeth.

'You're nothing more than Mary Magdalene's bastard,' she snarls, levelling her rabid face with mine.

I don't understand what she's talking about and I'm too scared to ask.

Tightening her grip on me, she orders me to say an act of contrition.

'O my God,' I snivel.

'Louder,' she roars.

'I'm very sorry for –'

'From the beginning,' she says, shaking me.

'O my God, I'm very sorry for all my si-si-sins –'

'Si-si-si . . . start again.' The veins on her neck are bulging.

'O my God, I'm very sorry for all my sins because they offend Thee who art so good and and and . . .' My mind goes blank.

'And with Your help,' she yells.

'And with Your –'

'From the start. On your knees this time.'

I turn and kneel by my bed. Although my nightdress covers me down to my ankles, I feel naked. 'O my God, I'm –'

'Join your hands, you heathen,' she seethes, yanking my hair and striking me hard across the face.

The pain makes me gasp.

'Now,' she says with icy crispiness, 'say an act of contrition and say it properly this time.'

'OK,' I sob. I feel a hot dribble of urine trickling down the inside of my legs.

'Go on.' She's towering over me.

Joining my hands, I take a deep, quivering breath. 'O my God, I'm very sorry for all my sins because they offend Thee who art so good and with Your help I will not sin again.'

'Right,' she says, 'now get up and get dressed.'

I don't budge until I hear her footsteps on the stairs, at which point I flop down on the floor, let the piddle spill down my thighs and sob, my cotton nightdress seeping up the acidy fluid and clinging to my smarting flesh.

*

After lunch that afternoon, my mother tells me to put on my jacket. At the front door, she takes my hand, walks me down the street and out the Castleowen road about a half a mile. When she turns left down Quarry Lane, I tense up, knowing that there are two Alsatians at the third farmhouse in the lane and that they're never tied up.

'What about the dogs?' I ask, slowing down.

'We won't be going that far.'

In the garden of the first house, a boy whom I know as 'Tommy the ba' is playing in his garden. He's twelve, goes to a special school and lives alone with his mother, who says hello to everyone whether they bother to look at her or not. Angelina and Attracta told me once that Tommy's father was a Protestant and his mother wasn't allowed to marry him, and that that made him a bastard.

Tommy's jumping over imaginary hurdles now and shooting imaginary aeroplanes with an imaginary gun.

'Do you see that buck-eejit?' my mother says, pucking me with her elbow.

'Yeah.'

'Take a long, hard look at him.'

Tommy spots us and starts waving furiously with both arms. Although he's smiling, I can tell by his questioning eyes that he doesn't understand why we're not waving back.

I'm not brave enough to answer him or to wave back: I know my mother would cut the hands off me. All I can do is return a smile because my mother isn't looking at my face.

When two men emerge from the gap of a neighbouring field and start strolling towards us, my mother turns on her heels and marches me back home in silence.

In the living-room, she lifts her sewing basket from the top

of the dresser and perches herself on the fireside armchair. She
nods towards the sofa and tells me to sit down.

'Do you know what happens to girls who sleep with their
fathers?' she asks, rummaging through her sewing para-
phernalia.

From my neck up, my skin tingles, as if rows of ants are
criss-crossing my face. I'm terrified of giving her the wrong
answer, but I have no idea what she's getting at. Silence is my
only option. She pulls a handful of socks, some wool and a
darning needle from the sewing basket and then leaves it on
the mat by her feet.

'Of course you don't,' she says, showing no anger at my
ignorance. 'But I'm about to tell you. And when I do, you're
going to thank me. And that will be the end of it. Is that clear?'

'Yeah,' I say, as she settles herself in the armchair.

'All daddies are men,' she says, breaking off a length of
darning wool, 'and all men get strange urges in the middle of
the night.'

Feeling uneasy, I look down at my knees, hoping that this
chat isn't going to last too long.

'Look at me when I'm speaking to you,' she snaps. And
when I do, she adds, 'Oh, embarrassed, are you?'

'I –'

'Embarrassed as you may feel now, Frances Fall, it's nothing
in comparison to how you'd feel if you ended up being the
mother of a gombeen like that unfortunate Tommy boy down
the lane, who never asked to be born and, by right, should
never have been.'

I wish she'd stop saying such horrible things. She's making
no sense.

'I don't know what you're whingeing about,' she says, when
she sees my eyes bloating with tears. 'You'd have a sight lot

more to cry about if you ended up with your father's baby inside you. Oh yes,' she raises her voice when I turn my head and stare out the window, 'that's what happened to that Tommy boy's mother. You didn't know that, did you?'

I shake my head. 'Angelina and Attracta said –'

'That it was a Protestant man. Oh aye, that's the rumour all right. But I know better. I have my sources, and very reliable sources they are. There's not a Protestant in the county that'd touch yon one with a bargepole. Her father put that story about to save his own reputation, God forgive him . . . though I doubt He will, under the circumstances.'

I don't like hearing about strange, bad things that make sense only to adults. It frightens me to think that my father could get funny urges and do secretive things to me in the middle of the night, maybe even while I'd be sleeping. I don't want him to put me up the pole.

'Get yourself a tissue,' my mother says when she notices me wiping my nose on my sleeve.

For the rest of the afternoon, I wander from room to room looking for something to do. In my bedroom, I pick up my Tiny Tears doll, but as soon as I do, I drop her back into her pram; I don't want to be her mammy any more.

As I lurk behind the net curtains in the sitting-room, I see Nuddy Neary leaning on his bike across the street and blocking the footpath. He's talking out of the side of his mouth to Mrs Reilly. She's nodding, smiling, and at the same time trying to manoeuvre her way past him and his bike. Maybe he's telling her things she doesn't want to hear.

I walk my guilty body across the room and sit down on the piano stool to practise for my upcoming exam. Miss Piggott has been showing me how to use the pedals, but my feet keep slipping off them and, every time they do, I burst out crying.

I cry again when I play the scale of C minor and end up hitting the last note with the wrong finger.

Back in the living-room, my mother carries on darning her pile of socks. I take my colouring book and crayons from the dresser drawer, sit down on the sofa and start flicking through the pages.

By the time my father arrives home from work, my eyes are sore and my face feels as if it's been stretched from all the crying. I don't look up when he comes into the room.

'Evening, Rita, Frances,' he says, sitting next to me. 'Looks like there's rain on the way; it's got very cloudy out. Do you want me to take in the clothes from the line, Rita?'

'I'll do it myself when I finish this sock.'

I've found a picture of a ballet dancer and I'm taking my time colouring around the edges of her tutu: I don't want to make a mistake.

'You're very quiet this evening,' my father says, patting my knee.

I leap up, letting the colouring book and crayons drop and scatter around the floor.

'What's wrong?'

'Nothing.'

'Why are you so jumpy, love? Are you OK?'

I nod as I bend down and start gathering up the crayons. On my hunkers, I watch as he turns to my mother and stares at her with a dropped jaw. She's sitting with her legs outstretched and her eyes downcast, humming her obliviousness. As she weaves the darning needle in and out of the woollen strands and draws the thread through, her fingers are strangely graceful, uncharacteristically patient, slow and arcing, like a carefully drawn smile.

25 October 1999 (later in the night)

My head is addled. I've been thinking all sorts of queer stuff about my mother and Aunty Lily, and why they couldn't talk about my grandfather. And why my mother insinuated that my father might have a sexual interest in me. What if it happened to her? No! No! Stop thinking. It's not helping.

27 October 1999 (bedtime)

I've tried to put it out of my head, but I can't. The thought of my mother and her father at it makes me want to puke. Maybe that's why my parents left Glendarragh. And maybe he did it to Lily too and that's why she went to London. What if I'm *his* child? Jesus! That would explain the birth cert thing. No. No, I couldn't be. She was in her twenties when she had me. I'm so confused. Why won't my father put me out of my misery and just tell me the truth? He knows I don't buy the 'slip of the pen' explanation. I told him so the night I rang him from the hotel in Kilkenny.

Her eighteenth birthday

I'm lying on the bed in the hotel. Though I'm tired, I can't sleep; I'm too excited.

'Daddy,' I whisper, remembering that I'd promised to let him know if I decided to stay the night in Dublin.

I pick up the phone, dial 9 and our home phone number. I'm calm.

'Hello.' He's out of breath.

'Daddy, it's me. Are you all right?'

'Aye, I hurried in from the garden when I heard the phone. Where are you?'

'The Royal Dublin.'

'So you're staying the night?'

'Yeah.'

'What time should I expect you tomorrow?'

'I was thinking of staying a few nights, Daddy. I haven't had a summer holiday in years. So I thought, why not have a bit of a break before going back to work next week?'

'I see.'

'What's wrong?'

'Nothing.' A few seconds' silence.

'What is it, Daddy?'

'Well, it's your mother's anniversary on Monday. I thought maybe –'

'Don't, Daddy.'

'For *me*; come to the Mass for *me*.'

'I can't.'

'You mean you won't.'

'OK, then, I won't.'

'You got it all wrong, you know.'

'I know what I saw.'

'I told you; it was a slip of the pen, that's all. You've got to believe me.'

'Daddy, I don't want to argue about it. And I don't blame you for standing up for her, not any more. At this stage, I've come to expect it.'

'She was a good lassie, Frances. She'd never –'

'I'll ring you again in a couple of days, Daddy.'

'Right so.'

'And Daddy?'

'What?'

'Nancy will go to the anniversary Mass with you.'

'She will,' he says, his voice wobbling. 'Goodnight, Frances.'

'Good –'

The line goes dead.

'Feck you, Daddy,' I whisper, hanging up the receiver. 'Why can't you just tell me the truth? She can hardly tear strips off you now, with her rigor mortis tongue.'

Two weeks earlier he'd asked me to go through my mother's belongings. Neither of us had been in her room since her death. He was anxious to have the room cleared out before her first anniversary, but he couldn't face it himself.

One morning while he was in town, I brought my CD player into her bedroom and turned on Tina Turner. She hated the 'trollop'.

Her wardrobe was easy. I opened the doors, yanked her clothes off the hangers and stuffed them into a couple of large refuse sacks. It wasn't like you see in the movies. I didn't hold her garments to my face for comfort. There were no tears. I tied a knot in the top of the bag and left it by the bedroom door, intending to drop it off at the St Vincent de Paul shop later on in the day. Then I opened the top drawer of her dresser and emptied her jewellery into a small plastic bag, including her wedding, engagement and eternity rings. So what if they were worth a few pounds: I wanted nothing off her. There were four old, framed black-and-white photos in the next drawer. I sat on the bed and studied them. My grandmother, just her head and shoulders, fair and fragile. My mother and Aunty Lily at about ten and five, holding hands, Lily, one sock down and looking away from the camera; my mother, standing to attention like a little soldier and just as solemn. Aunty Lily, about sixteen, twinkling eyes, unashamedly happy. My parents and me, I'm no more than a few weeks old, both of them looking down on me, tense faces. I put the photos aside to give them to my father.

The next drawer was full of underwear. There were hats and scarves in the one underneath. I opened another refuse sack and binned the lot.

When I opened the bottom drawer, I found a brown A4 envelope. I picked it up and sat down again on the bed. As I leafed through the documents, Tina was singing my favourite song on the album, 'What's Love Got to Do with It?'

It was all the usual stuff – my grandmother's in memoriam card, her mother's and her own birth certificates, an old school report and her marriage certificate. The year 1963 catches my eye. I'm shoving the papers back into the envelope. Nineteen sixty-three! I pull the marriage certificate out again. Yes, 1963. Dated *4 June 1963.* How can that be? I was born on 7 September 1963. She couldn't have been . . .

I hurried to my room and started rooting through my own drawers to check my birth certificate. It was there somewhere. Eventually I found it.

Date of birth: *7 September 1963.*

Mother's maiden name: *Rita Murphy.*

Father's name: *Joseph Fall.*

Bastards! How could they?

'It must have been a slip of the pen,' my father said when I asked him about it later.

'Shut up, Daddy. She was pregnant. Mammy was pregnant. Admit it.'

'No, she wasn't like that.'

'Stop it, Daddy.'

'It's a mistake, that's all. I swear to you, your mother was not in the family way when we got married.'

'So how come between the pair of you, you never noticed this slip of the pen all over the years?'

'Come to think of it, your mother did mention it at some stage. But –'

'Come off it, Daddy; don't lie to me.'

All she put me through when I got pregnant – all the hurt, all the pain. And he stood by and let her.

Joseph stirs and I open my eyes, putting the ensuing argument to the back of my mind. There's no point going over it; my father will be loyal to my mother until his dying day.

'Hello, little Joseph,' I say, lifting him out of his seat.

A mouthful of milky froth gushes from his mouth. I wipe his baby-gro and nestle him close to me. As I walk towards the window, he lifts his arm and tickles my chin.

'Look,' I say, pulling back the curtains and looking out, 'the sun and the moon.'

Rocking him, I walk over to the television and turn it on.

There's a woman gazing into the camera. She looks disoriented. Her head is slightly tilted. Strands of lank hair hang over one side of her face. Two serious men sit on either side of her, eyes downcast. She talks, bites her lip, touches her chest with her hand and talks again. One of the men taps her shoulder and nods. There are cameras flashing.

What's wrong with the poor woman? Where's the remote?

I find it on the bedside locker and turn up the volume several notches.

'. . . this stage, all I want is my baby back. Please, please, bring him back to me. Please.'

'And that was the press conference broadcast earlier today by the

Gardaí – a plea from the mother of the missing two-month-old baby, Nathan Maxwell, abducted earlier today from outside a shop in Henry Street where his German child-minder left him in his pram . . .'

1 November (3 a.m.)

I've been in this place for seven weeks now. It feels more like seventeen. Maybe it's the ground I've covered that makes it seem longer than it is, or the sleepless nights. Nothing has changed, though. Except for the view from my bedroom window. The leaves have turned from green to gold.

But the past is still the same: untouchable. You can't rewrite history; isn't that what they say? Is that what I'm trying to do? And when I'm done, what will I have achieved? I'll still be the same person with the same past. I can't change who I am, no matter how much I'd like to. I've already tried that. Or, should I say, my dear friend Lesley did.

The new me

The Sunday morning after the new hairstyle incident, my mother's in a flap worrying about what the parish priest is going to make of my new image. She can't understand that no matter how many times I wash my hair, it won't fall flat. What she doesn't know is that Lesley has given me a jar of gel, and that it's shoved into an odd sock in the back of my underwear drawer.

I'm sitting at the breakfast table wearing the only outfit I possess that isn't totally humiliating – beige corduroy trousers with a rust and cream shirt, though my mother insists on calling it a blouse. I'd bought them that summer in Mullaghmore when Nancy came to stay with us. We'd taken a shopping trip into Ballyshannon, where I'd been hoping to buy my first pair of denims. The cords had been a compromise, negotiated by Nancy.

'You'll have to wear a headscarf to Mass,' my mother says, turning around from the sink where she's washing the dishes, and pointing her chin at me.

'You must be joking. I will not,' I say, getting up from the table and dropping my cereal bowl into the basin.

'Are you going to let her away with that, Joe Fall?'

My father is putting a pound note into the 'Dues' envelope. 'Leave me out of it, will you?' he says, licking the strip of gum. 'I'm tired of all this arguing. It's getting us nowhere.'

'Oh yeah, that's typical of you: ignore the problem and it might just go away.'

'You're the problem,' I mutter, leaving the kitchen and heading for the stairs.

'What was that?' She's on my tail.

'You're the bloody problem,' I roar, taking the stairs two at a time and hurrying into the bathroom, where I slam the door behind me.

'Time we were leaving,' my father shouts a couple of minutes later. 'It's ten to ten.'

My mother is standing on the bottom step of the stairs, holding out a green and cream silk scarf folded into a triangle. 'It's not a request,' she says, as I stomp downstairs; 'it's an order.'

I push past her, lift my jacket off the coat-stand and walk out the door. The village is at its busiest on a Sunday morning, with everyone in the parish making their way to Mass. A couple of bachelor farmers are rattling by in their tractors. Cars packed with children are pulling up around the village green. Women are clip-clopping down both sides of the street, finger-combing their hair and chatting to their men.

I think of how odd we must look – me hurrying along the edge of the footpath, trying to distance myself from my mother, her squeaking along on the inside in her rubber-heeled shoes, a carefully calculated few paces behind, and my father somewhere in the middle, with both of us and neither of us at the same time.

I stall at the steps of the chapel and wait for my father to catch up with me, and he, in turn, waits for my mother. Inside, she points to a pew and says to my father, 'We'll sit in here; I'm feeling a bit weak and I want to be by the door for a breath of air.'

During the Mass, she keeps her head bowed and fidgets with her rosary beads. While the priest is consecrating the Host, she checks her watch and nudges me.

'What?' I whisper.

'It's only half ten. You didn't finish your breakfast until twenty to. You may stay put.'

'Suits me.'

When Mass is over, the priest stands at the chapel door to greet the congregation on their way out. As we approach him, my mother grabs the hood of my jacket, pulls it up on my head and steps in ahead of me. I fall into line with my father.

'Good morning, Father,' my mother says. 'Lovely sermon . . . as usual.' She shakes his hand briefly.

'Thank you, Rita,' he says, looking at her curiously as she darts out the door. Then he turns to my father. 'How are you doing, Joe?'

'Not a bother, Father, thanks. That's a grand morning.'

'Powerful; long may it last. Hello, Frances.'

My mother's at the bottom of the chapel steps now, warning me with a threatening stare.

I pull my hood back down. 'Hello, Father.'

'Good Lord!' The priest tilts his head and considers my hair. 'Is that the latest fashion?'

'Oh, indeed it is, Father,' the woman behind me says, 'that's the whole go now.'

Nuddy Neary, who's creeping up behind the woman, shouts over her shoulder, 'You're gettin' very with it, Frances. You're like somethin' from *Top of the Pops* . . . one of them "Pan's People", or is it "Legs and Co." they call themselves nowadays?'

'Begod, Nuddy,' the priest says, 'you're the boy that knows a thing or two.'

My mother can't contain her rage when she gets home. She orders my father to peel the potatoes and, when he does, she gripes about him not having dug out the eyes.

'The only way you can get a job done properly in this house,' she says, 'is to do it yourself.'

As she lifts the roasting tray from the oven, hot fat sizzles and spits in her face. She bangs the tray down on the draining board and bulls out the kitchen door and up the stairs. My father finishes preparing the dinner while I set the table. We don't mention my mother's mood.

When my father calls my mother for her dinner, she picks up her plate, knife and fork from the table and brings them into the living-room.

'Ah, come on, Rita. Let's not spend our whole Sunday like this,' my father says, standing between the two rooms.

'Like what?'

'Not talking to each other.'

'What's the point of talking? No one listens to what I have to say any more. You and that cheeky brat in there have made that perfectly clear.'

After she's eaten, she goes out for a walk on her own and I take the opportunity to ring Lesley. When I tell her about the priest discussing my hairstyle, she says, 'The priest! Deadly. What did your mental mother say?'

'Nothing. She was too mortified to speak.'

'Good enough for her.'

'She just tore off down the street like she was being chased by a naked man,' I whisper, in case my father might hear me.

We both laugh down the phone.

'Are you coming into town for a while?' Lesley says.

'I've no lift.'

'Just get out on the road and stick out your thumb.'

'Yeah, OK, I will.'

'Call for me. I'll wait in for you.'

When I have my jacket on, I pop my head in the living-room door and tell my father that I'm off into town for a while.

'Have you told your mother?'

'No.'

'Don't you think you should let her know first?'

'She won't be back for ages. I told Lesley I'd call for her in a few minutes.'

'And how you do propose getting there?'

I hold up my thumb.

'You will not! God only knows who'd pick you up. I'll run you in and collect you later too.'

'Thanks, Daddy.'

'Though God knows what sort of reception I'll get when I tell your mother where you've gone.'

'I'm only going to meet a friend.'

'Yeah, I know, I know.'

As I step out of the car at Lesley's house, my father tells me that he'll collect me at five o'clock.

'OK.'

'And you'll behave yourself, won't you?'

'Of course I will,' I say, smiling in the door at him.

For the first time, age sixteen, I get to hang around the town with Lesley and two girls from her class. At last, a taste of independence.

We sit on a bench in the town square listening to *Ireland's Top 20* on Lesley's radio. Sharing her last two cigarettes between the four of us, Jackie, who lives in the same estate as Lesley, fills us in on the details of her first date with a boy called Pete.

'Did he take off his specs when he was kissing ya?' Lesley asks.

'Yeah.'

'Jaysus! Could he see where your mouth was?' Orla, the other girl, asks.

'Shut up.' Jackie makes a swipe at her.

'He didn't stick his tongue up your nostril, did he?' Lesley winks at me.

'Ah, fuck off, will youse? He was a fucking great kisser, if youse must know. He wore the face off me.'

'Oh, you randy wee bitch,' Orla says.

'You mean lucky,' Lesley says. 'I haven't had a decent snog in weeks. Did youse go far?'

Jackie opens the top two buttons of her shirt, revealing a big, dark red bruise just above the top of her bra.

'Oh my God!' I stare at the mark. 'Did he punch you?'

'No, he didn't, ya big innocent gobshite ya,' Jackie says. 'It's a love bite.'

Orla sniggers. 'She's in bad need of a fella,' she says to Lesley about me. 'You should fix her up with someone.'

'Would you be on?' Lesley says, nudging me.

I have no choice but to say yes. I want nothing more than to be like these girls – cool, wise, experienced and entitled to look down my seasoned nose at the likes of Kat Mulcahy or any other girl who hasn't the guts to live the way I intend to from this moment on.

'Don't tell me you've never kissed a fella.' Jackie stares at me with an incredulous frown.

Lesley throws her a disgusted glance. 'Of course she has. She met someone when she was on her summer holidays up in Mullaghmore, didn't you?' she says, turning to me, her big, brown eyes purging the lie.

'Yeah.'

'What was he like?' Orla wants to know.

'Oh, don't ask.' Lesley shakes her head. 'She's not ready to talk about him yet. It's a long story, isn't it, Frances?'

'Yeah.'

The girls are intrigued. 'Ah, go on, Frances,' Jackie says. 'We'll not breathe a word, will we, Orla?'

Lesley sneaks a look at me and makes a stupid face.

'On me mother's life,' Orla says, licking the tip of her index finger and crossing her heart.

I cover my face with my hands and laugh. My shoulders are shaking.

'Now look what youse have done, nosy bitches!' Lesley says, putting her arm around me. 'Can't you see she's still in bits over him? Just the mention of his name and she breaks down.'

'But we didn't mention his name,' Orla says. 'We don't know it.'

'Rock,' Lesley says.

'Rock!' the girls shout together.

'Yes,' Lesley says, and I moan hard with the pain in my ribs, 'as in Hudson, only twice the ride.'

'God! We didn't mean to upset you, Frances, honest,' one of the girls says.

'It's OK.' I wipe the tears from the corner of my eyes.

'If youse want to make it up to her, go 'way and buy some fags. There's nothing like a smoke in a crisis, isn't that right, Frances?'

'Mmm,' I nod, lifting my head for a puff of air.

'Jaysus, I'm really sorry,' Orla says, hugging me.

'Never mind sorry,' Lesley says, 'just get her a fag.'

Both girls root in their pockets but manage only 12p.

'Don't look at me,' Lesley says. 'I'm broke.'

I give them the 30p I have left after buying two bottles of Coke for Lesley and myself on the way down the hill from her house. It's still not enough for a packet of ten.

'Fuck it,' Lesley says, 'if I don't get some nicotine into my bloodstream quick, I'll smoke that bloody telegraph pole. Come on.' She takes my hand and pulls me to my feet. 'We'll be back in a few minutes,' she tells the others.

'Rock!' I say when we're out of their earshot.

'Well, it's better than Aloysius, isn't it? Or Francis. Oh, imagine that – Frances and Francis – poxy or what?'

'Definitely poxy.'

'Whereas Rock . . .'

'Oh God, what am I going to tell the girls the next time they ask me about him?'

'Don't get your knickers in a knot. We'll think of something.'

The shop door squeaks as she pushes it open.

'Shop,' a woman shouts from a room behind the counter.

A man in his forties comes out in his Sunday best. 'Well, lassies.'

'Hello, Mister Jermyn,' Lesley says. 'Oh, look; you're wearing the same tie that I gave my daddy for Father's Day. You were with me when I bought it, Frances. Remember I couldn't make up my mind between it and the blue one?' She gives me a dig.

'Yeah.'

'It goes lovely with that suit. You've great taste.'

'Oh, th . . . th . . . th . . . th . . . thanks very much, love,' the man says, straightening the tie. 'Though I didn't pick it myself. I'd be no good at that crack.'

'It doesn't matter who picks the clothes, Mister Jermyn, so long as there's a decent peg to hang them on. And you're not a bad peg, is he, Frances?'

'No.'

'Oh, you'd give a fella an awful big head, so you would,' the man laughs. 'Anyway, what can I do you for?'

'Just a couple of bags of cheese and onion please.' Lesley holds out her hand to me for the 30p.

'Twenty-six pence please, girls.'

Lesley hands him the money, leaning across the counter when he turns to the till. 'They're good, sturdy boxes, them Tayto boxes, Mister Jermyn. Would you have any to spare?'

'God knows, I might, love. Why?'

'I've a whole load of stuff at home ready to take out to the sale of work, only I have nothing to put it into.'

'What sale of work is this?'

'They're having one out in Crosslea where Frances lives. It's for Trócaire, isn't it, Frances?'

'Yeah.'

'Well, if youse hang on there a minute, I'll have a wee gander out the back and see what I can come up with.'

'Are you sure you don't mind?'

'Not at all. Why would I?'

'Thanks.'

'How many do you need? One . . . two?'

'Two'd be great, cos she has a pile of stuff needs packing too, haven't you, Frances?'

'Mmm,' I nod.

As he disappears through the swinging doors, Mr Jermyn is whistling chirpily.

Before I have time to draw breath and ask Lesley what she's up to, she's in behind the counter swiping packets of fags from the cigarette dispenser.

'Lesley!'

'Shut up, will you?'

I'm hopping from one foot to the other. My heart's doing a sprint.

'Jesus, Lesley, hurry up, I think I hear –'

She slips back out from behind the counter and starts stuffing cigarettes into my jacket pockets. I try to protest but it's no use; there's a packet in each pocket and two more stuffed into her bra.

'Take the guilty-looking face off ya,' she says, zipping up her bomber jacket, 'unless you want to get caught.'

Get caught! What's she talking about? I haven't done anything.

Mr Jermyn backs his way through the doors carrying two boxes, walks out to the customer side of the counter and hands one to each of us.

When we thank him, he holds the front door open for us.

'I don't care what people say about you youngsters today

having no religion about you, as far as I'm concerned what you girls are doing now is far more important than any amount of praying.'

'And I don't care what some of the smart alecks of teenagers say about you adults,' Lesley says without a hint of mockery, 'I don't think you're a generation of morons.'

As soon as I hear the shop door close, I start to run. I'm convinced that Mr Jermyn will notice the missing cigarettes straight away and come tearing down the street after us.

'Relax, will ya?' Lesley says, catching up with me.

'I can't believe you did that. What if he cops the missing fags?'

'He won't,' she says, taking the box from me and throwing both down the mouth of an alleyway. 'He'll be back in front of the telly now, watching the afternoon film.'

'How do *you* know?'

'Did you not hear the cowboys and Indians fighting every time he came through the swinging doors?' she says, breaking into a tribal dance on the footpath, tapping her open mouth and imitating an Indian war cry.

I fold over laughing. I can't help it. She could have got us both arrested for shoplifting and it wouldn't have cost her a thought. But I don't care. I still love her – my crazy, beautiful friend.

Lesley changes her mind about going back to the town square. She wants to sell some of her cigarettes to her brother Keith, so that she'll have the money to go out dancing later on.

'What about the girls, Lesley? They'll be expecting us.'

'Yeah. And they'll be expecting free fags too. Fuck them. Come on,' she says, linking my arm.

Half-way up the hill to her house, we stop at the children's playground and sit on two swings. There's no one else around.

The chains screech as we throw back our heads and swing as high as we can.

'Yahoo,' Lesley roars, and I turn my bobbing head to look at her. Her neck is elongated. Her black tresses are flying through the air like an open fan, skimming the ground each time the swing drops downwards.

I haven't been on a swing since Aunty Lily died and I've forgotten how good it can feel. I love the soothing motion, the wind in my face, the way I can close my eyes and think about nothing.

When I hear Lesley's shoes scuff the gravel, I snap out of my trance and slow down the swing.

'Wouldn't it be great if we didn't have to go home at all?' she says, straddling her seat to face me.

'It's all right for you. Your parents are really liberal.'

'My parents don't give a shite. There's a bit of a difference.'

'I wish my mother didn't give a shite. I swear, she's worse than Hitler.'

She extends her right arm and roars at the top of her voice, '*Sieg Heil!*'

An old woman passing by on the footpath staggers and looks anxiously around to see where the outburst has come from.

'Was that you, young Kelly?' she says, looking through the wire at us.

'No, Missus Costello, it was this one here,' she points at me, 'she's my German pen pal.'

The woman ogles me suspiciously.

'Up Ireland,' she croaks, punching the air with her knobbly fist. 'Never mind your oul *Sieg Heil*.'

When we burst out laughing, she mumbles something and then hobbles on.

'Lesley, you get on well with your *mother*, don't you?'

'I did . . . until yesterday.'

'What happened?'

'I had a big row with her.' For a moment her eyes look glassy.

'Over what?'

'Not helping her out around the house,' she says, taking two cigarettes from the packet. 'Sandra was working yesterday, so I was supposed to do the shopping, the vacuuming and a whole load of other crap as well.' She strikes a match and we light up. 'I told Mammy I had to call down to Jackie first, but promised to be back in an hour. That was at ten in the morning. I didn't get home until ten last night.'

'You're codding me.'

'I'm not,' she says, smirking.

'Were you not shitting a brick going home to face her at that hour?'

'No. Why should I be? I'm not her bloody slave.'

'What did she say?'

'She went pure mental . . . attacked me with a wet fucking dishcloth, the demented bitch. I swear, I was just waiting for her head to start spinning, like that possessed kid's does in *The Exorcist*.'

'Did you not feel awful guilty, letting her down like that?'

'Says she who'd stick a knife in her own mother if she got half a chance.'

'That's different. My mother *is* a demented bitch. But your mother . . . she doesn't be well, does she?'

'Hey, whose side are you on? She said some really rotten stuff to me, so she did.'

'Like what?'

'That I was just like my stinking father.'

'What did she mean by that?'

'That I'm a liar and a cheat, I suppose, cos that's what he is.'

'Oh.' Her father had made me feel very uneasy the day I'd met him on his upstairs landing, but Lesley has never talked much about him one way or the other.

'She must really hate me, comparing me to that oul bastard.'

'Is he really that bad?'

'No, he's worse.'

'How?'

'Well, he's hardly ever home for starters, and when he is, he struts about the house like he's lord of the fucking manor. Mammy could collapse in front of him from an asthma attack and he'd barely lift his head up over his newspaper to check if she was still breathing.'

With reluctance, I remember my surprise at Lesley's own indifference towards her mother when we'd found her bent over the kitchen sink, gasping for breath.

'It'd probably suit him down to the ground if she croaked it. Then he could hammer away at the widow across the border and have nobody to nag him about it.'

'What?'

'He's having it off with some widow woman from Keady.'

'You mean he's having an affair?'

'Yeah.'

'Jesus, I can't believe that! I've never known anyone to have an affair before . . . except for President Kennedy that is . . . him and Marilyn Monroe.'

'Well, I suppose if my mother was living in the White House with a shitload of servants, she wouldn't give a bollocks, but seeing as he spends half his wages keeping yon tramp in gin –'

'You mean, your mother knows?'

'Yeah – they're always rowing about it. It's no secret: everyone knows.'

'Janey Mac, that's awful.'

'The whole reason we came home from England was because Mammy couldn't stick his cheating any longer. We lived in a huge estate, ten times bigger than where we're living now. According to Sandra – she remembers better than I do – there was always some husband or other banging on our front door claiming that Daddy was screwing his missus.'

'Oh, my God.'

'She was going to leave him, but then he promised her he'd change, and, like an eejit, she believed him.'

'The poor woman.'

'Huh.' Lesley looks offended. 'After what she said about me, she can shag off. I can't stand either of them now.'

'At least she's not as bad as my mother.'

'Well, we can't choose our parents, can we?' she says, stamping on the butt of her cigarette, 'but we can choose our friends.'

'You're the best friend I've ever had, Lesley. And no matter what your mother says, I think you're . . .'

'Go on,' she says when I hesitate. She has a big grin on her face.

'Smashing,' I say, hoping that she won't think I'm stupid for being so corny.

'I know you do,' she says, tossing back her hair. 'You're not so bad yourself.'

Just to hear her say those words is such a big deal to me. I'm as close as I've ever been to bursting with joy, and I don't want the feeling to pass.

'Fuck them all,' she says, winding the swing around tight,

'your parents and mine.' She lifts her feet off the ground, throwing back her head as the chains unravel at speed.

She's smiling at me from upside-down. I can't take my eyes off her. I have to stop my hands from reaching out and stopping her mid-spin.

Don't be daft, I think, you're not a lesbian; you don't fancy her.

'What are you thinking?' she says, sitting up straight as the swing squeaks to a halt.

'Same as you,' I say, blushing with guilt over my private thoughts. 'Fuck them all.'

3 November 1999 (afternoon)

I went to the shop to buy cigarettes this morning. There was a new woman behind the counter. Not very friendly. When she handed me my change, she shook her head and looked me up and down. I'm sure she was letting me know that she knows who I am and what I've done.

I gave him back, I wanted to tell her. But I didn't. Instead, I hurried back to my room and smoked three cigarettes in a row.

Her eighteenth birthday

I switch off the TV and sit on the end of the bed staring at the blank screen. My ears begin to buzz. I can't take in what I've just heard. I don't want to. Surely all that hysteria couldn't have been about me.

Don't be daft, I think. You only heard the tail end of the bulletin. You didn't get the whole story.

Baby boy . . . Henry Street . . . kidnapped. Jesus!

My heart is pounding. I feel like I'm having one of those dreams where I've just fallen off a cliff. Oh God, please, wake me up before I hit the ground. The seconds tick away. The baby is getting restless. His head feels as if it's crushing the bones of my upper arm and I know it's no illusion.

'Nathan,' I whisper, looking down at him, 'what have I done?'

He doesn't care. All he wants is his soother. I find it in the baby-bag, put it into his mouth and lay him down between the two pillows. Without him in my arms, my chest feels cold and I shiver. The crying woman I've seen on the TV is knocking on my brain but I can't let her in; she'll have to wait.

I pace from one side of the bed to the other, trying to breathe properly: in through my nose . . . hold, out through my mouth . . . slowly. But my heart isn't fooled by my artificial composure; it's jumping about with my thoughts. The Gardaí are scouring the country for me. What if the receptionist suspected me? They could be on their way to the hotel right now.

I hear footsteps out on the corridor. Is that them already! No. No, it's OK. Whoever it is has just walked by my room. Thank Christ for that.

But what about the two old women in the coffee shop? They'd have no problem giving the Guards a detailed description of me and Nathan. They never took their prying eyes off us. Or the lad who helped me with the car seat – he might even remember my car registration. If he does, it'll not be long until they track me down. The thought makes my legs go rubbery and I have to sit down again. What if they find me? And arrest me? I just couldn't handle it. I'd crack up. All

I want now is to drive home, tiptoe up the stairs, climb into my bed and pull the blankets tight around me.

A rap on the door makes me yelp and Nathan opens his mouth and bawls.

'Who is it?' I whimper, but no one answers.

I creep across the room and open the door, just a crack, to check who's there. When I see a waiter standing outside the next room with a tray in his hand, I shut the door and hurry back to comfort Nathan.

'Please be quiet. Oh please, I'm begging you, be a good baby.'

He won't hold the soother in his mouth and he won't stop wailing. He's driving me mad because I can't think what to do. When I pick him up to rock him, it hits me that my feelings for him have changed. The bond is gone. I know now that he isn't mine and that he was never meant to be. I'm not even sure I like him any more. Part of me resents him for being there, in the wrong place at the wrong time.

'Stop crying, for Jesus' sake.'

He's getting worse.

'Please, shut up,' I cry, laying him back down on the bed. Maybe a bottle would help. I open one of the new ones I've bought and rinse it under the tap. As soon as I have him settled, I think, while pouring in the formula, I'll pack my stuff and go.

My shoulders are burning with pain as I sit hunched on the bed feeding him for the last time. Careful not to upset him again, I don't bother taking the bottle away to wind him, and he guzzles it down to the last ounce without a break. His body feels relaxed now and he's beginning to fall asleep. I hum a lullaby and rock him gently, all the while thinking about my next move. I'll leave the room key on the bedside locker and the door unlocked. Then I'll ring the Guards. But not from the hotel – that would be risky; I'll phone them from the nearest kiosk and let them know where Nathan is. By the time the child is fully asleep, I can see myself back on the motorway to Dublin. I sit him into his seat and fasten the buckle. Then I gather my stuff and throw a bag over each shoulder. A surge of relief washes over me as I walk towards the door.

'Goodbye, Nathan,' I say, turning round to take a final look at the child. His head is leaning to one side. His lips and cheeks are twitching as if he's still sucking on the teat of the bottle. His two closed fists look as soft as teddy paws. He seems completely content.

'Don't wake up,' I whisper, blowing him a kiss.

But what if he does? What if he wakes up before I even get as far as the car? He could be all on his own for ages. The thought of his big, blue, trusting eyes scanning the room for a motherly face, waiting to be touched, fed, comforted, breaks my heart.

'You'll be home with your mammy soon, I promise,' I say, turning the doorknob.

He lets out a long, quivery sigh. Anyone would think it was his last breath. My shoulders slacken and I don't stop the two bags from sliding down my arms and plopping on to the floor. My body folds and I fall to my knees in tears.

By the time I stop crying, it's getting dark and I feel exhausted. All I want is to put an end to this nightmare. Nathan is still sleeping. I crawl across the room to the telephone, pick up the receiver and phone reception.

'Reception.'

'I need the number of the local Garda Station.'

She gives me the number and asks if I'm OK.

'Fine,' I say and hang up.

After a few deep breaths, I pick up the receiver again and dial the number.

4 November 1999 (10 p.m.)

The rebellion against my mother was like dance. Once I started it, there was no turning back. I had to dance it out until the bitter end.

No turning back

Over the following year, I'm not sure which galls my mother more: the humiliation of having a daughter who has, as far as our neighbours are concerned, gone wild, or the realization that she has, despite her best efforts, lost control of me.

Within three months, my grades have dropped considerably, and I'm moved from the honours to the pass classes for French, Maths, History and Irish, where Lesley is causing havoc. She has Mr Sweeney, our middle-aged, thick-spectacled, badly dressed Irish teacher, driven round the bend with her endless disruption. She arrives late for class most days, with the waistband of her skirt turned down so many times that there's only a few inches between the bottom of her jumper and the hem of her skirt. As she passes his desk, she drops a book and bends down to pick it up, groaning with the exertion. The rest of the class snigger behind the pages of *Peig*.

'Why are you late for class again, Miss Kelly?'

'Oh, I'm really sorry, sir, but I was feeling very dizzy. I think I must be due my –'

'OK.' Mr Sweeney shifts about in his chair. 'Just sit down quietly and get your book out.'

'Right, sir. Sorry, sir. And pass no remarks on me if I'm a bit crabby today, sir, but you know how it is.'

'That's enough, thank you very much, Miss Kelly.'

'You're welcome, sir . . . any time.'

After that, *Peig* hasn't a hope in hell.

Sometimes Lesley drifts off on her own, without telling anyone, even me, where she's going or what she's up to.

'I just wanted to be on my own,' she says huffily, when I question her about where she's been and, although I feel a little hurt that she's holding back on me, it makes me crave her company all the more. So, when she invites me to skive off with her, I jump at the opportunity. We spend ages creeping around the corridors, 'dodging penguins' as she calls it. We go to the convent chapel and smoke in the confessional box. If we're peckish, we head down to Sister Bernadine, the old, wrinkly nun in the refectory who's half-deaf, and con her into giving us something to eat. She never remembers us from one time to the next.

'What's your name?' She has her hand on Lesley's elbow and is looking up into her face.

'Kimberley,' Lesley says. 'Kimberley Wilde. But you can call me Kim.'

'What's that?'

'Kimberley, Sister,' Lesley shouts. 'Like the biscuits.'

'Oh.' She looks confused. 'Why did your mother call you after a biscuit?'

'Because it's her favourite biscuit, Sister. She eats them morning, noon and night.'

'Does she not have a favourite saint?'

'No, Sister, more's the pity,' Lesley shakes her head, 'but I suppose I'm lucky that she's not too fond of Fig Rolls.'

Sister Bernadine is won over. Again. She strokes Lesley's arm, turns to me and says, 'You're not called after a biscuit, are you, like this poor child?'

'No, Sister. I'm –'

'Kate,' Lesley says into her ear. 'Kate Bush. Isn't she lucky to have such a lovely name, Sister?'

'It's a grand name all right. But never mind, Kimberley, you got the looks.'

'Oh, thank you, Sister.' Lesley hugs the nun gently, sticking out her tongue at me as she leans over the little woman's shoulder.

'I know I shouldn't ask, Sister,' she pulls back, looks at the ground and twiddles her thumbs, 'and I wouldn't only you're so kind, but have you any leftovers that I could have for my lunch? My stomach's rumbling. Can you hear it, Sister? Listen.' She lifts up her jumper and exposes her midriff.

Sister Bernadine looks at it with a squint, as if somehow her eyes might do the job of her ears.

'Ah, I'm a bit hard of hearing,' she says after a few seconds' silence.

'Can *you* hear it, Kate?'

I walk over and put my ear to Lesley's stomach. 'God, it's like an orchestra in there.'

'Come on, come on.' Sister Bernadine ushers us over to the long dining table.

'Anything but bread and jam, Sister,' Lesley shouts when

she sees the nun with her hand on the lid of the bread bin. 'I can't look at the likes of that at this time of the month.'

'What was that?'

'I said, that's all we've had to eat at home for the last month.'

'Poor wee mite,' Sister Bernadine says, shuffling across the refectory towards the refrigerator.

I learn how to take a good dressing-down from both my parents and my teachers, without being in any way affected by their anger. As Lesley says, 'What can they do, only eat the arse off ya?'

Absolutely nothing. I'm beyond their control.

Lesley fixes me up with boys and I kiss them up against the wall at the back of the youth club hall. I don't hate it, but it doesn't do a whole pile for me either. Maybe that's because she always keeps the best-looking boys for herself.

She's delighted when one of Keith's friends tells her that, from what he's heard, I'm a mighty good shift. 'Isn't it great?' she says. 'At last you're getting a reputation.'

I stop bothering to get permission off my parents to go into town to meet Lesley; I just walk out the front door and hitch a lift from the outskirts of the village. When he cops me leaving the house, my father follows me in the car and offers me a lift.

'You don't have to.'

'I don't like you taking lifts from strangers,' he says. 'Now, hop in.'

He offers to collect me when I'm ready to go home. I tell him that I'll give him a ring if I'm stuck for a lift.

'Promise,' he says, as I get out of the car.

'OK, OK.' I wish he'd stop caring so much. It makes me feel guilty.

'You know, it's not right what you're putting your mother and me through. All we have ever – '

'Goodbye, Daddy,' I say, slamming the car door.

I watch him drive away. My heart aches. I wish I could make him understand that I'm not trying to hurt him, but that I can't avoid it either. He's always there between myself and my mother; he's in my line of fire.

When I'm at home, I spend endless hours alone in my bedroom. I don't do much besides listen to music, daydream and wait for Lesley to ring. Sometimes I pick up one of my schoolbooks and flick through the pages, but I've no inclination to study; I find it hard to see the point. I've lost all interest in getting good grades. What difference would it make? The only thing that matters to me now is being popular, or being with Lesley; they're much of a muchness.

One night, I'm sitting on the edge of my bed trying to give myself a love bite on my shoulder – Lesley has shown me how – to Roxy Music's 'Dance Away the Heartache'. I'm going to try it out for real on Friday night if I get off with someone at the youth club.

Downstairs, there's an argument brewing. I think it might be about me. These days it usually is. When the song is over, I turn down the volume.

'She has you down for a right mug,' my mother says, 'chauffeuring her around like Lady Muck, instead of having the backbone to stand up to her.'

'There are all sorts of funny boys driving the roads nowadays. I don't want anything bad to happen to her.'

'If it does, it'll be her own fault.'

'If it does, I won't be able to live with myself.'

'A lot worse could happen to her if she carries on keeping company with Lesley Kelly. She's a cute hawk, that one, and she's leading Frances a merry dance.'

'A girl of her age needs a pal.'

'A girl of her age needs a firm hand.'

'We've done our best.'

'So we throw in the towel, do we? Let her win?'

'It's not about winning and losing.'

'Hah! It is, as far as she's concerned. The girl is laughing at us, Joe.'

I want to shout down the stairs that it's only *her* I'm laughing at.

'Look, I'll talk to her again, if you like.'

'Talk! Ah, for God's sake, have an ounce of wit. She hasn't a notion of listening to anything you or I have to say; she's already made that perfectly clear.'

'What do you want me to do then, lock her in her room?'

'You could do worse.'

'It wouldn't work.'

After a lull, one of them opens the door into the hall and I reach out to turn up the volume on my radio.

'I know what my father would have done,' my mother says, before I twist the knob.

'What?' It's my father at the door. 'You think I should *beat* her?'

'It might put manners on her.'

'She's sixteen.'

'She's out of control.'

'What's wrong with you, Rita? Have you forgotten what that man did to Lily?'

'Lily!' my mother shouts. 'Lily! Will you have a tither of wit, you stupid man? Lily was no victim. You said as much yourself. She went out of her way to look for trouble. Never mind who she hurt in the process. Are you trying to tell me now it wasn't all her doing?'

'Rita, let's not go down that road again. We've been over –'

'DON'T YOU DARE TELL ME WHAT I CAN OR CANNOT TALK ABOUT.'

'OK, OK. I'm sorry.'

'Sorry,' she sneers. 'Is that all you can say? God, but you're the weak man, Joe Fall. You have no moral fibre, no courage of your convictions. And I should know better than to expect someone like you to have any control over a devious little tramp who's determined to get her own way.'

Sometimes I visit Aunty Lily's grave. I still miss her. My mother has had the grass dug out and now the grave is covered with shiny grey pebbles. It looks so cold. I feel sorry for Aunty Lily because she's all on her own in a double plot. Xavier is living back in London with his daughter Madeleine now and, despite his original intention of being buried with my aunty, has since decided to be laid to rest with his first wife, whenever the time comes.

'I wouldn't blame the man for changing his mind,' was my mother's comment when she received a letter from Madeleine not long after his return to London, informing her of the new arrangement.

My mother's change of heart towards the sister she nursed with such unfaltering devotion makes no sense to me.

One day, as I'm sitting on a bench in the town square waiting for Lesley, I notice the daffodils in the flowerbed and think of

Aunty Lily. There was a vase full of them on her bedside locker a couple of weeks before she died.

'First daffodils of the year,' she'd said. 'Aren't they very cheerful?'

'A penny for them,' Lesley says, touching my shoulder.

'I was just thinking about Aunty Lily. She was mad about daffodils.'

'Well, seeing as she's in no fit state to pick them herself,' she says, walking over to the flowerbed and plucking a daffodil, 'we'll pick a bunch for her. Come on.'

While we walk to the graveyard, I tell Lesley about Aunty Lily and about how my mother has stopped visiting her grave.

'I don't know why she's turned against her,' I say. 'She couldn't do enough for her when she was ill.'

'Maybe it's something to do with her will. Families always fall out over money.'

'I doubt it.'

'Don't be so sure.'

'No. I know my mother, and getting upset over a few pounds wouldn't fit in with her holier-than-thou image. She wouldn't give in to it.'

As we walk through the graveyard gates, Lesley cups her hands around her mouth and shouts, 'Aunty Lily, where are you?'

'Would you ever shut up?' I say, pulling her along the path between the graves.

Some of the plots are smothered with flowers.

'Don't be so fucking greedy,' Lesley says, lifting a wreath off one and putting it down on a grave that is overgrown with weeds. 'There you are, you poor forgotten bastard.'

'Here she is,' I say, laying down the daffodils on Aunty Lily's grave.

'How's she cutting, Aunty Lily? I'm Lesley.'

'The girl who used to dance like a French tart doing the cancan.'

'What?'

'Ah, nothing.'

I have to pile pebbles on top of the stems of the daffodils to keep them from scattering in the breeze. Lesley is leaning on the headstone watching me.

'Do you think she knows we're here?'

There's a robin perched on a nearby headstone.

Fly away, I think. Fly away and I'll know it's a sign. I stare at it, willing it to spread its wings, but it doesn't.

'Nah,' I say, looking at Lesley and shrugging. 'Probably not.'

When I look back, the bird has gone.

4 November 1999 (middle of the night)

Sometimes the happy memories are as disturbing as the sad ones. They remind me of what I had, and lost. I don't believe I will ever reach the same level of happiness again because now I know that love is never as real as it feels. Love is one-sided, dependent. It makes fools out of us. Love makes us lonely. Look at Aunty Lily alone in her grave, after all the devotion and all the tears. What happened to the love there? Did it ever really exist? And if so, where did it go?

5 November 1999 (after lunch)

Every time I hear the phone ring in the distance, I pray that someone will come and knock on my door to say, 'It's for you.'

I badly need to hear from my father. The last time I spoke to him was on the phone from Kilkenny Garda Station.

Goodbye, baby

'Kilkenny Garda Station.'

In trying to blurt it all out as quickly as possible, I'm stuttering and snivelling and the Guard on the other end of the line tells me to slow down and take my time, because he can't make out a word I'm saying. I tell him again who I am, what I've done, where I am and how sorry I'm feeling. He says it's OK, to take it easy and to make sure to stay exactly where I am.

'Tell whoever's coming over that the baby's asleep and not to bang on the door or they'll frighten him.'

'I'll tell them.'

I hear crackly sounds in the background followed by urgent voices.

'And tell them to turn off their walkie-talkies. The noise of them would waken him and I'm just after getting him off to sleep.'

'Sure, Frances. Is he OK?'

'Yes, of course he is.'

'That's good. That's the main thing.'

'Are they on their way now?'

'They are.'

'Thank you.' I hang up.

Suddenly everything seems deadly quiet and for a split second it occurs to me to make a run for it, but I haven't got the strength, and, anyway, how far would I get?

Anxious to be ready to leave when the Guards arrive, I crawl back across the room, pull a cardigan from my bag and slip it on. Then I curl up on the floor, resting my head on my travel bag and holding my knees in my arms. My eyes are sore and heavy. I'd give anything to be able to sleep.

Nathan lets out a sudden, sharp cry and then spews most of the contents of his bottle down the front of his baby-gro.

'Oh no! Not now.'

My hands start shaking. Having to change him seems like such an ordeal; I'm all worn out. But I can't ignore his screaming and I don't want the Guards to think that I couldn't or wouldn't bother to look after him properly. I clamber to my feet and over to the dressing-table, where I've left my shopping. My face is tingling with perspiration as I rummage through the bags, like a madwoman, until I find a baby-gro.

'Hurry up, hurry up,' I tell myself as I lift him from his seat. I'm humming as I'm changing him, trying to keep myself calm, but it's hard because he's roaring his head off and squirming as if he's in terrible pain.

'I'm sorry,' I sob, 'but I'm doing my best.'

My clumsy fingers have to open and close the fasteners on his baby-gro several times before I get it right. It must be at least ten minutes since I've rung the Guards. Surely they should have come by now. I don't know how much longer I can stick this pressure. My head feels like a time bomb on its final ten-second countdown. I need them to take Nathan away. Now.

I start walking around the room with him on my shoulder and singing:

> Hush little baby, don't say a word
> Mama's gonna buy you a mockingbird . . .

He keeps jerking back his head and my arms feel weak from trying to keep a tight grip on him.

> And if that mockingbird won't sing . . .

'Frances,' a man calls from the far side of the door. 'This is Sergeant Hennessy.' He has a gentle, fatherly voice.
'It's over, Nathan.'
I hurry across the room and open the door.
'Mind how you hold his head,' I say, laying the baby in the sergeant's arms.

The next couple of hours are all mixed up in my head, I don't remember half of it. Some bits are clearer than others, like the bangharda nudging me in the back of the squad car and telling me not to fall asleep, that we're pulling into the station. But I'm not actually falling asleep; I just have my eyes closed. I'd been thinking about the last time I'd spoken to my mother. Back in the hotel room, they had asked me about my family: had I a husband, children?
'No,' I'd said. 'I live with my parents . . . sorry, not my parents, my father.'
'Where's your mother?'
'She died a year ago.'
It doesn't seem like a year ago since I'd last spoken to her. I can still remember it as if it was yesterday . . .

It's a beautiful summer's evening. My father is painting the fence in the back garden. My mother is sweeping the front doorstep and brushing away the cobwebs from around the porch. I'm in the kitchen washing the head of lettuce I've just taken in from the greenhouse. On the surface, we seem like a normal, even harmonious, family. But I'm distracted. It's the day after my baby's seventeenth birthday. It's hard to figure out where the years have gone. My parents have continued to attend Mass on her anniversary every year, while I've never missed a trip to Dublin to buy her a present. And although we never mention her, she still manages to inhabit every molecule of the air we breathe. She's in every corner of every room, waiting for one of us to break the silence. But I can't. I still haven't accepted her death. Secretly I'm convinced that I'm destined to have another baby and that, in doing so, I'll bring her back from the shadows of death – new body, same soul. Only it hasn't happened yet, after seventeen years. That's what I'm thinking as I dab the wet lettuce leaves with a wad of kitchen roll.

Why hasn't it happened? What's wrong with me? My periods are like clockwork. I've had a smear test recently and everything is OK there. I've had sex with several people over the years, but haven't had as much as a late period to built up my hopes. Time is pushing on. I'm almost thirty-five years old, getting less fertile by the year. I pat my eyes with the kitchen roll.

I'm tired of having casual sex. I don't want to do it any more. The night before has left me feeling empty inside; and used. Usually when I go shopping in Dublin, I book into one of the city centre hotels for the night. It's no problem for a girl on her own to pick up a man in a bar: no problem at all. But I'm sick of it. If it doesn't work this time . . .

'Will I put on a few eggs for the salad?' my mother asks, coming into the kitchen.

'If you like.'

'Do you know who'll be visiting the village next week?'

'Who?'

'Father Vincent. He'll be staying with Nancy for a few days.'

Father Vincent has since been transferred to a small parish in County Donegal.

'Really.'

'Yeah. I was thinking of inviting the pair of them over for tea some evening. You'll be around, I presume.'

'I don't think I will, actually.'

'Why not? I'm sure Father Vincent will be expecting to see you.'

'Too bad.'

'Too bad! What's that supposed to mean?'

'It means that I'm not that pushed on the man and I don't fancy having tea with him.'

'Not that pushed! After all he did for you.'

'It was *you* he did favours for, not me,' I say, moving out of her way while she fills the saucepan with water.

'Excuse me, but it wasn't me he got the school secretary's job for, was it?'

'You were the one who asked him to pull a few strings, though, weren't you? I didn't give a flute whether I got the job or not.'

'Well, if you weren't that bothered, why are you still working there after all this time?' She lights the gas ring and puts the saucepan on the flame.

'Because . . .' I root in the drawer for tinfoil.

'Hah!' she sneers. 'You can't answer me that, can you?'

'Yes I can,' I tell her, tearing off a piece of foil. 'It gets me out of the house and away to hell from you for a few hours every day. And yeah, I suppose you're right, I should be very grateful to the wonderful Father Vincent for sparing me the agony of listening to you all day long. In fact, I think I might just kiss his holy arse as soon as he walks through the front door.'

'Oh, that's typical of you,' she says, nodding, 'dragging the conversation into the gutter. You always love to use shock tactics, don't you, with your tarty clothes and your foul mouth and your bad attitude. But where has it got you, eh?'

'Go up to my wardrobe,' I say, pointing to the door, 'and get me one item of my clothing that you consider tarty. Go on.'

'I'm not talking about what you wear nowadays.'

'Oh, I see. So you just want to drag up the past again, is that it?'

'Don't be stupid.'

'Calling me stupid now, are you? And you think that *I* have a bad attitude.'

'As usual you're twisting my words, Frances, and well you know it.'

'How can anyone twist the meaning of "Don't be stupid"? If I can do that, I'm not so stupid after all.'

'Oh no, you're a real clever clogs all right,' she says. 'Look at you – nearly thirty-five years of age, no husband, no children and still dependent on your parents. That's some success story, I must say.'

'Fuck you, Mother,' I say, looking her right in the eye. 'You know what? I hate your guts. How does that feel, your only child hating you? That's an equally outstanding success story, don't you think?'

'If that's how you feel, you know where the door is, don't you?'

'She really knew how to hit where it hurt.'

'Pardon?' the bangharda says.

'My mother knew I couldn't leave.'

'Leave where?'

'Home. I tried. I shared a house in Castleowen with a couple of girls for three or four months, but I didn't work out. It's hard to get close to people when you can't tell them what's really going on in your head.'

'Take it easy,' she says, patting my shoulder.

'I think the girls got fed up trying to figure me out. When they started ignoring me, I took the hint and packed my bags. I was better off at home, where I didn't have to pretend to be someone I wasn't.'

Most of the Guards are nice to me, especially Sergeant Hennessy. He's not angry with me at all; he says he understands.

'The baby has been taken to the hospital for a check-up,' he says.

'But I didn't harm him.'

'I don't doubt you, Frances, but we have to follow procedures.'

Most of the legal stuff he talks about goes right over my head. I don't care about my rights. I just want to go home.

I answer all their questions – my solicitor's, Sergeant Hennessy's, the bangharda's – and they take endless notes. I tell them everything they want to know. When the interview is over, the bangharda switches off the tape-recorder and my solicitor tells me he'll see me in the morning. As soon as he leaves, Sergeant Hennessy suggests that I ring my father.

'You might be glad of a friendly face in the courtroom tomorrow, and I'm sure he'd like to be there for you.'

'No.'

'Your name will probably be released to the press tomorrow, Frances. You don't want him hearing about your arrest on the one o'clock news, do you?'

'Oh, God no!' I bite my lip. '*You* ring him and tell him what I've done. And if he wants to talk to me after that, then fine, I'll talk to him.'

I become teary as Sergeant Hennessy explains the situation to my father.

'The poor girl is very distressed, Mister Fall,' he says. 'What she needs right now is the support of her family. And you, I believe, are the only family she's got.'

He pushes the bridge of his glasses up on his nose. 'Yes, yes, of course I understand that this must be terribly upsetting for you, but the lassie is in a state of shock herself.'

'It's OK,' I say, raising my hand, 'I don't want to talk to him.'

'Well, you could always ask her that question yourself; she's here beside me,' he says, nodding at me.

I shake my head.

'He wants to talk to you. It'll be OK,' he says, handing me the phone.

'Hello, Daddy,' I utter, barely above a whisper. 'Daddy, are you still there?'

'Frances, what have you gone and done?' He sounds so old, so feeble.

'I'm sorry, Daddy.'

'What in God's name were you thinking of?'

'I don't know,' I sob. 'I really don't know. I just wanted a baby.'

'So you went out and stole one!'

'No . . . yes, I know that's what I did but –'

'When you spoke to me earlier on, did you have the baby with you?'

'Yes. He was asleep.'

'Dear God!' he sighs. 'Dear, dear God!'

'It's all right; the baby's fine.'

'And what about the poor mother – is she fine? Will she ever be fine again?'

'I'm sorry. I didn't plan it, honest. It just happened.'

'How could you do that to any mother?'

'I don't know. I can't explain it. It felt like the right thing to do at the time. But I know now that it wasn't. I never meant to hurt anyone, I swear.'

'You never do, do you?'

'Oh, Daddy, if I could turn the clock back . . .'

'All I can say to you, Frances, is thank God your poor mother's not around to suffer the shame of this.'

I drop the receiver on the desk and turn away, burying my face in my hands.

My father has already hung up.

'It'll be the shock,' Sergeant Hennessy says, replacing the receiver. 'Give him time; he'll come round.'

5 November 1999 (bedtime)

I have this dream sometimes.

I'm doing a jigsaw puzzle, a thousand pieces. Though it's difficult, I'm making progress. I have all the edges done, lots of background, but in the centre there are holes, people without faces – I don't know what they're thinking – fingers pointing at blank pieces, hands holding empty spaces. It's almost complete, but I still don't know what the picture is trying to tell me. Frantically, I search every corner of the room for the missing pieces – under the table, behind cushions, in drawers. And then I find the empty box in a cupboard; it's upside-down, so I pull it out and turn it over to look at the lid. I have to see what the picture is supposed to look like. But when I do, the gaps are still there, staring out at me like ghoulish eyes. I shake the empty box and that's when I wake up, every time, still shaking.

7 November 1999 (evening)

It's been lashing rain all day. I haven't been able to get out for my walk and I'm feeling all cooped up. From my window I can see a man dashing from his car towards the front of the building holding a newspaper over his head.

Run run as fast as you can . . .

The gingerbread man

It's a dull, drizzly September afternoon. I've just turned seventeen, and I'm in my fifth and final year at secondary school. Lesley and I are propped up on the classroom windowsill during lunch break and, as usual, she has no lunch with her. I offer her a cheese sandwich.

'They're not slices of bread,' she says, curling her lip, 'they're slabs. Has your mother never heard of the sliced pan?'

'You don't want it then?'

'No, thanks. I'd rather starve.'

I take a bite, more to fill the hole in my stomach than for pleasure.

'Would you look at that shower of eejits?' Lesley says, looking out of the window at the girls from the cross-country team who are jogging by in their shorts and T-shirts like a posse of drowned rats.

'Talk about gluttons for punishment,' I say.

'Jesus! The big rosy cheeks on that Hickey one.'

'God, yeah, you could fry an egg on them.'

'Hickey by name, hickey by nature. Look at the legs on her, would ya? All joking aside, I've seen thinner tree trunks.'

'And that boulder of a backside must weigh a ton,' I say smugly. 'Any wonder she's paddy last?'

'No she's not,' Lesley sniggers. 'Here's Mulcahy coming round the corner.'

'Gawd, to think that this time last year, *that* was my best friend,' I say, cringing.

'Move your sweaty arse, ya gom ya,' Lesley shouts, tapping the window.

Kat looks up and gives us a wave. I turn away to laugh. Lesley waves back. When Kat turns the corner and there's nobody left to make fun of, Lesley sighs and says she's bored.

'Do you want to go down to the bicycle shed for a fag?' I ask her.

'May as well, I suppose, but let's head over to the refectory first and see if we can scrounge some grub. I'd eat the face off a scabby pig.'

'But not my cheese sandwich.'

'Definitely not your cheese sandwich.'

The shortest route to the refectory is across the courtyard from the main doors of the school.

'Hang on a sec,' Lesley says, sitting down on the steps outside. 'Here's the bread man. Perfect timing.'

The bread man is a fast-talking, middle-aged, bald man who, for as long as I can remember, has been delivering supplies to the convent every Wednesday between noon and two o'clock. If he happens to arrive during the lunch break, Lesley nicks a handful of goodies from the back of the van while he is carrying in trays of loaves, cakes and buns to the refectory. Luckily for us, he allows Sister Bernadine, the old doting nun, to talk him into having a quick cup of tea before he gets back on the road.

'One of these days he'll skip the tea and you'll get caught,' I tell Lesley.

'I don't care. The way I see it is, if the poxy boarders can eat cake, then so can we.'

A few yards away from us, the van pulls up.

'You do the usual, right?' she says.

'Right.'

The usual is me keeping an eye on the refectory door and coughing when I hear the bread man saying, 'That was lovely. Thanks, Sister. It's hard to beat the cuppa tea.'

The van door opens, and a lad of about twenty jumps out.

'It's a new fella,' I say, digging Lesley in the ribs.

He walks round to the back of the van and opens the door.

'Would you look at the strut of him?' Lesley says. 'He thinks he's hot shit.'

Inside the back of the van, he stacks loaves on to a tray.

'And what's more,' Lesley says, ogling him, '*I* think he's hot shit.'

'What about Buster?' Buster is Lesley's latest boyfriend. He's lasted all of three weeks – a record.

'Fuck him. You can have him if you like.'

'But he doesn't fancy me.'

'He thinks you're good-looking.'

'Did he say that?'

'Yeah.'

'When?'

'I forget. Now, will you shut up! I'm trying to keep my eye on this fella so's I'll know when to make my move.'

'You're not going to chance robbing off *him*, are you?' I say, as he steps down from the back of the van.

He notices us watching him and winks.

'I certainly am,' Lesley says, grinning. 'And what's more, I'm gonna make sure I get caught.'

'Are you mad? Why?'

'Stay there,' she says, running across the courtyard and climbing into the back of the van.

'If you get caught,' I say, walking towards her, 'you'll be expelled.' She's leaning against a rack of bread with a jam roll in her hand. 'Oh shite!' I giggle nervously, 'here he's coming now.'

'Hiya,' he says, strolling towards me with a spring in his step.

'Hello.'

He looks into the back of the van and sees Lesley.

'What are you doing in there?' He has a strong Northern accent.

'Having a snack,' Lesley says, tearing the wrapping off the jam roll.

'Hey,' he says, looking at her in amazement. 'I hope you're gonna pay for that.'

'I don't have any cash on me. Is there any other way I can pay you?'

'You're a cheeky wee mare, aren't you?' he says, jumping into the back of the van beside her.

'Yeah,' she says, running her finger round the swirl of jam and rubbing it on to the tip of his nose.

'Ya wee rip ya,' he laughs, wiping his nose on the sleeve of his white coat.

'Ya wee rip ya,' Lesley imitates his accent.

'Will you tell her to get out?' he says, looking at me. 'If them nuns catch her in here, I'll end up getting the sack.'

'Come on, will you, Lesley?'

'OK, OK,' she says, lifting another jam roll and jumping out.

'Gimme that back,' the fella says, holding out his hand. 'One's enough for youse.'

Lesley stuffs it up her jumper. 'If you want it, come and get it.'

He shakes his head and starts restacking the tray. 'Youse convent girls are stone mad, so youse are,' he says. 'Fucking mental.'

I like him. He's good crack.

'Where are you from?' Lesley asks.

'Enniskillen.'

'Are you orange or green?'

'Guess.'

'What's your name?'

'Johnny.'

'Mmm. Surname?'

'Connolly.'

'Definitely green.'

'Aye,' he says, stepping down with a trayful of goodies. 'Now let me past, will ya, before that wee nun in there sends out a search party for me?'

'I want him, Frances,' Lesley says as soon as he's out of sight.

I know she'll have no problem bagging him. Lesley always

gets what she wants. For once, though, I feel a twinge of jealousy; I'm not sure why.

'So where's baldy today?' Lesley asks, when he comes back out.

'Who?'

'The man who usually comes.'

'He's retired.'

'So you'll be here again next week?'

'Aye,' he says, closing the door. He gives me a questioning look. 'Are you always this quiet?'

'No,' I say, blushing.

'I'd say not. You, cheeky,' he says, tickling Lesley's side, 'owe me seventy pence.'

'I might pay you next week,' she says, 'if you're lucky.'

'I'm always lucky, me. Lucky's my middle name.'

He flicks his hair and gets into the driver's seat.

'Roll on Wednesday,' Lesley sighs, as Johnny drives away with his elbow jutting out the window, bobbing his head to the rhythm of some rock song on the van's radio.

We spend every spare minute of the following week pining for Johnny and trying to recall every last detail of our encounter for Jackie and Orla.

'He has a reddish mullet,' I say.

'A carrot head! Ugh!' Jackie screws up her face.

'It's not orange,' Lesley says. 'It's brownish red.'

'It's more sandy red,' I say.

'It's still red though,' Jackie moans as she takes another bite of her gingernut.

'That's the exact fucking colour there,' Lesley says, snapping the rest of the biscuit out of her hand and holding it up for inspection.

'The gingerbread man, bejaysus,' Orla says, and we all burst out laughing.

'If he's the gingerbread man,' Lesley says, 'then I'm the fox and I intend to savour every morsel.' She pops the piece of Jackie's biscuit into her mouth, moaning with pleasure as she chews.

'Ah, but you're forgetting one thing, Lesley. This one fancies him too,' Jackie says, poking me. 'Don't you, Fall?'

'No way.' I shake my head for emphasis.

'Hands off,' Lesley says, half joking, half threatening.

'Don't worry,' I say. 'It was you he was flirting with, not me.'

The following week, the bread van arrives just after twelve and we're still in class. Jackie and Orla, who are sitting near the window, are swinging back on their chairs and straining their necks to get a proper look at Johnny Connolly. Lesley keeps sighing, rolling her eyes and looking at her watch in despair. By the time the bell rings for lunch break, the gingerbread man is getting back in his van. From the window, the four of us watch him drive away in the rain.

'Oh no,' Lesley says, pressing her forehead against the weeping windowpane. 'Now I have to wait another whole week.'

Orla puts her arm around her. 'I see what you mean about him. He's a bit of all right, isn't he? Even with his red hair.'

'Ginger,' Lesley and I say in unison.

Nobody seems to notice that I'm as disappointed as Lesley is.

By the time Wednesday arrives again, all four of us are keyed up at the thought of seeing Johnny. We spend the eleven o'clock break in the toilets trying to make ourselves look cool.

'I'm gonna snog him in the back of the van,' Lesley says, rubbing strawberry-flavoured gloss on her lips. 'Youse can keep an eye out for the penguins.'

I'm standing next to her, finger-combing my hair and spraying it to make it stand up in the right places. I can't help looking at Lesley's reflection and feeling that I don't stand a chance. Although I'm tucks more confident about my appearance than I was a year earlier, I know I'll never be what Lesley is – irresistible. Even *I* want to touch her silky skin and kiss her yummy mouth. She catches me eyeing her and gives me a grin as if to say: you're right, you can't compete; look at me, I'm gorgeous.

'Right, girls,' she says, turning to face Jackie and Orla, 'which way should I wear my hair?' She throws her head forward, tussles and sprays it and then throws it back. Her jet-black hair is full and curly, and begs to be touched.

'It's fab like that,' Orla says.

'What about this?' Lesley bunches it into two ponytails, making herself look almost innocent.

'Definitely like that,' Jackie says.

'No, leave it loose.' Orla is adamant. 'It's far nicer.'

They argue until Orla eventually says, 'What do you think, Frances?'

Although I'd prefer it loose, I look at Lesley and say, 'The way you have it now.' I'm hurt that she hasn't asked me for my opinion herself.

'Nah,' she says, pulling out the bobbins, 'I think I'll leave it loose.'

At a quarter past twelve, we hear the van coming up the avenue and look at each other across the classroom. Miss O'Dowd, our history teacher, is rabbiting on about dictatorship.

'Hands up,' she says, 'those of you who can give me an example of a dictator.'

Lesley puts up her hand. I'm surprised she's been listening, considering that we've just heard the bread-van door swing open.

'Yes, Lesley?'

'I think I'm gonna puke, Miss. Can I go out to the toilet?'

'Yes, of course you can. Frances, you go with her.'

'It's all right, Miss,' Lesley says, as I'm about to get off my chair. 'I'll be grand on my own.'

I feel as if I've been kicked in the teeth. I can't believe she's freezing me out. Jackie and Orla are nudging each other and tittering. About five minutes later, Jackie asks the teacher if she should check on Lesley.

'Yes, go ahead. It's almost lunchtime anyway.'

When the bell rings, Orla grabs me by the elbow and hurries me along the corridor towards the main doors.

'Who took the butter off your bread?' she says.

'I'm pissed off with Lesley.' I feel guilty as soon as I say it. I've never talked about her behind her back before.

'Why? What did she do?'

'It doesn't matter.'

'With a face like that, it must matter.'

'It's nothing. It's just when she said she didn't want me to go outside with her . . .'

'Ah, you can't blame her for that. All she wanted was a chance to nab Johnny on his own.'

'Yeah, I suppose.' Deep down, I know Orla has a point and that I shouldn't be behaving so childishly, but I can't help how I feel.

'God,' she says, looking at me suspiciously, 'you really do fancy him too, don't you?'

'No. I swear I don't.'

By the time we get outside, the gingerbread man is driving away. Lesley and Jackie are sauntering towards us, linking each other and wearing triumphant smiles.

'She did it,' Jackie squeals. 'She shifted him.'

Though I try, I find it hard to join in Jackie and Orla's screaming-fan antics.

'He's the best kisser *ever*,' Lesley says, pulling me over to the wall to sit down.

I wonder if she's trying to make me jealous or if it's simply me being over-sensitive.

'A ten out of ten?' I ask, not wanting her to cop my bad mood.

'No, an eleven.'

I can see she expects me to be thrilled for her. And why wouldn't she? Along with Jackie and Orla, I've always been happy for Lesley to have her own way, to get off with all the best-looking lads and leave the not-so-hunky specimens to her not-so-beautiful friends. That's the way it has always been.

'I swear, Frances,' she says, laying her head on my shoulder, 'I'm gonna marry him.'

I toss and turn in bed that night. My blood is boiling. I'm not sure who I'm mad with or jealous of. I've never seen Lesley so smitten. Since she's met Johnny, she seems distracted to the point where nothing else matters, even me. Maybe that's what's getting to me. Or is it that I have feelings for the gingerbread man myself? There's just something about him. I cannot sleep. I'm all mixed up.

Every time Lesley rings, it's Johnny this and Johnny that, and I listen because I always listen to her and tell her how lucky she is. Part of me still suspects that she's purposely rubbing my nose in it, but why should she be? She doesn't know I fancy him too.

My feelings for Johnny are confirmed when I see him again the following week and he says, 'How's about ya?' in his sing-song accent, his dark green eyes glinting at me.

'Oh, I'm fine,' I say, unable to stop myself from smiling.

'Indeed ya're,' he says, grinning at me.

Over the following few weeks, Lesley tries to make a date with him away from school, but he keeps giving her vague excuses – he's promised to do a favour for a man on Sunday; he has to take his car to the garage; it's his granny's eightieth birthday. When she tells him that there's more to a relationship than a quick snog in the back of his van, he laughs and says, 'I'm not complaining, love.' She's not happy, but the air of mystery about him makes her want him all the more. When she offers to take the bus to Enniskillen to meet up with him over the weekend, he fobs her off again.

At Lesley's request, the four of us meet up in the Coffee Pot one Saturday afternoon to have a chat about what she should do about the gingerbread man.

'Bastard,' she says, almost in tears. 'What's he hiding?'

'Ignore him the next time he comes to the school,' Jackie says. 'Play him at his own game and see how *he* likes it.'

'You're right,' she says, as a tear rolls down her cheek. I can't stop my hand from reaching over and wiping it away. She looks just as beautiful when she's sad as she does when she's happy. 'But the thought of not seeing him on Wednesday . . .'

'You know fellas,' Orla says. 'You have to play hard to get.'

'I do . . . did, till I met Johnny. Maybe we should head down to Enniskillen tonight. He might be at the Tropicana – that's where all the Catholics go. I was there a few times with our Sandra.'

'You'll have to count me out,' Orla says. 'I'm on curfew after being out so late last night.'

'I'm going to the cinema with Pete,' Jackie sighs. 'Sorry.'

Lesley looks at me with big doe-like eyes.

'Yeah, OK.'

I've never been across the border before and I'm dead nervous. Lesley and I are sitting in the lounge of the Imperial Hotel in Castleowen having a cigarette and sharing a vodka with a dash of lime. Raging with me over having my hair dyed peroxide blonde, my father hasn't given me any pocket money.

'If that's how you choose to spend my hard-earned cash,' he told me, 'you can do without it.'

'All it cost me was two pounds. Sandra only charged me for the dye.'

'And cheap-looking it is too.'

I've had to withdraw the last fiver from my post office savings account to fund my night out. Between Lesley and myself, we've barely enough to pay into the nightclub.

'Never mind,' Lesley says. 'We'll chat up some fellas and get them to buy us drinks.'

I've been drinking since the summer, when I discovered that alcohol was the answer to my biggest problem – lack of confidence. So far I've stuck to vodka because Lesley says my parents will never smell it on my breath. I don't want them knowing I've started boozing. Somehow my mother would find a way of making it my father's fault and then he would look at me with his how-could-you-do-this-to-me? expression. It's best to spare him the persecution and myself the guilt. At least now I can have a conversation with a boy without turning puce and getting tongue-tied.

'What if we get shot?'

'I don't fucking care. I can't live without Johnny anyway.'

Shortly after nine o'clock, we walk to the outskirts of the town and stand at the edge of the footpath with our thumbs out. Cars whizz by. One man slows down just as he passes us and drives off as soon as we start running towards the car.

'Fucking wanker,' Lesley roars, giving him the fingers.

When we hear another car approaching, Lesley sticks out her leg and the car screeches to a halt.

A rough-looking man of about fifty rolls down his window. 'Where are youse heading to, lassies?'

'Enniskillen,' Lesley says.

'Hop in so. Youse are in luck.'

'I don't like the look of him,' I say, tugging Lesley's sleeve.

'It's all right; he's just an old farmer,' she says before opening the door.

She sits in the front, leaving me in the back with a sleeping, drooling dog. I'm terrified of him waking up, so I lean against the door, keeping as much distance as possible between us.

'What's the big attraction in Enniskillen?' the man asks.

'I'm meeting my boyfriend at the Tropicana.'

'He must be a bit of a Casanova if you're willing to travel thirty-odd mile to get to him.'

'Yeah, he's a lovely guy.'

'From Enniskillen, is he?'

'Yip. Are you?'

'Aye, just a couple of mile outside it.'

'Maybe you know him – Johnny Connolly?'

'Johnny Connolly. Mmm. What's the father's name?'

'Dunno.'

'What part of Enniskillen is he from?'

'Dunno that either.'

'You don't know too much about him, do you?'

'We only met a while back.'

'Oh, I see. A new romance, is it?'

'Yeah.'

I can't take my eyes off the dog. Every time his ears twitch, I'm sure he's going to wake up and go for me.

The man scratches his flaky bald patch with his grimy fingernails. 'Well, there's the Connollys of Pearse Hill,' he says, flicking a bit of dandruff over his shoulder, 'and the Connollys of Fernduff. Then there's a couple of families of them down beyond Erne View . . . a right scabby bunch they are. And there's a Danny Connolly out my road – he has a slap of sons; it could be one of them. What did you say your buck's name was?'

'Johnny.'

'Johnny, Johnny . . . no, it doesn't ring a bell. I'd want more to go on than that.'

'He's a bread man and he has ginger hair.'

'Nah,' he coughs, clearing his phlegmy throat and sending a lumpy spit flying out into the night 'Still can't place him,' he says, winding up the window. 'Though he'll not be one of Danny Connolly's. Them lads are all very dark; they're like a bunch of Spaniards. Anyway, whoever he is, he's a fierce lucky fella having a looker like you.' He pats Lesley's bare knee.

A couple of miles later, he turns down a narrow lane off the main road. With held breath, I look around me as branches reach out from the overgrown hedges and tap on the windscreen with skeletal fingers. I dig my knee into the back of Lesley's seat, but she just keeps nattering away to the man as though nothing untoward has happened. I can't see anything ahead of us, only one gloomy bend after the next. I'm convinced that we're going to be attacked.

'Excuse me,' I say, sitting up, 'where are you going?'

'I'm just taking a bit of a detour to avoid the checkpoint,' he says. 'I don't want them Limey fuckers rooting in the boot of the car. Besides, if they startle Blackie, he'll go for them bald-headed and they'd not think twice about burying a bullet in the back of his skull.'

Although I'd been dreading the prospect of having to go through a checkpoint, I'd give anything to be out on the main road again heading in that direction. This is it, I think: my comeuppance. And bloody good enough for me it is too. Oh God, the thought of losing my virginity like this . . . to that. Where is he taking us? Will there be anyone else there? A gang maybe. Jesus!

'I feel sick.'

'Roll down the window and stick your head out,' the man says.

'I'm gonna throw up.'

He puts his foot on the brake. I pull the lever, but the door won't open. I try again, this time banging against the door with my shoulder. It still won't budge. I'm trapped!

'Hop out and open the door for her,' he tells Lesley. 'The cursed thing will only open from the outside.'

'Are you all right?' Lesley asks, as I step out. 'You're as white as a sheet.'

I slam the door shut and grab her arm.

'I think he's gonna rape us,' I whisper, turning towards the ditch and pretending to vomit. 'Let's make a run for it.'

'Don't be daft. He's a harmless oul eejit.'

'How the fuck do you know?'

'Cos if he was gonna try anything, he'd have done it by now.'

'He touched your knee.'

'So what? You could hardly call that sexual assault, could you?'

'I don't care what you think, Lesley – I'm not getting back into that car.'

'Are youse all right, lassies?' he shouts out the window.

'Think about it, Frances,' Lesley says. 'If he really wanted to attack us, how far do you think we'd get if we started running now?'

'Oh, we've had it. We're dead meat. My mother was right all along.'

'Will you get into the car and don't be such a wimp. If he tries anything, you punch him in the face and I'll knee him in the balls, right?'

'Do I have any choice?'

'No.'

'OK, then.'

When I turn round, I see the dog sitting upright and staring out the window at us with a slobbery gob.

'Shite, the dog's awake!'

'You can sit in the front with me.'

As soon as we open the car door, the dog growls.

'Shut up, Blackie,' the farmer shouts, giving him a clout across the mouth. The dog whimpers and crouches down.

Several bumpy miles farther on, the lane widens and we see the lights of Enniskillen. I feel like crying with relief.

'I'll leave youse right to the door of the discotheque,' the man says, turning on his wipers, 'seeing as youse aren't exactly clad for that weather.'

'See,' Lesley mutters into my ear, 'told you he was a harmless oul eejit.'

*

The nightclub is packed and particularly rough. We can't see past the throng of people in front of us.

'How the hell are we gonna get home, Lesley?'

'Johnny of course.'

'But what if he's not here?'

'He will be. Now, shut up panicking and let's just concentrate on finding him. We'll split up. You go right and I'll go left.'

'No way. We'll stick together. If we split up, we'll never find each other. It's like a cattle mart in here.'

Already lads are nudging each other and eyeing Lesley. For once, she doesn't notice.

'I'm bursting for a pee,' I tell her as we pass the Ladies.

'OK, I'll wait for you here,' she says, leaning against a pillar.

I have to queue for ages behind two well-plastered women in their late twenties. One of them keeps staggering and stepping on my toes with her stilettos. With the dirty looks I'm getting from her slightly less drunk friend, I'm afraid to flinch, let alone complain. I'd rather keep my mouth shut and have my feet stabbed than grumble and risk getting my head blown off. Who knows what kind of weapons the Northern girls carry in their handbags?

It's the guts of twenty minutes before I finally make it back to the pillar to meet up with Lesley, but there's no sign of her anywhere. Where could she have gone? I hang around for ages waiting for her, feeling more vulnerable and panicky by the minute. A man, nearly as old as my father, starts chatting me up.

'Where are you from?'

I don't answer.

'I said where are you from?'

I look away, pretending not to hear him.

'Wanna dance?' he asks, tapping my shoulder.

'No, thanks.'

'Arragh, go on.'

'No,' I say, moving away.

As I scour the hall for Lesley, I vow to myself never to cross the border again. It's been a disaster from the word go. I can't find her on the dance floor, or at the bar, or upstairs on the balcony, so I go back to the pillar, but she's still not there. Not knowing where else to look at this stage, I'm on the verge of tears. As a last resort, I go over to a bouncer and ask him if he's seen a seventeen-year-old girl with long black hair wearing a denim mini-skirt and black T-shirt.

'I did surely,' he says.

'Which way did she go?'

'They went that way,' he laughs, pointing to his right and left, 'all two hundred of them.'

Bollocks, I think, walking away. When I hear the introduction to the Nolan Sisters' 'I'm in the Mood for Dancing', I perk up and circle the dance floor hopefully. I'm convinced I'll find Lesley somewhere in the middle, strutting her stuff and singing at the top of her lovely voice. Whenever we go discoing, she begs the deejay to play the record at least twice and then drags me out to the centre of the floor to boogie with her. She says it reminds her of when we were little girls. But by the end of the song, I haven't found her and I'm really starting to sweat, because I know that if she were still in the hall, she'd have made her way on to the floor no matter whom she had to knock down to get there.

At the end of the night, the Irish national anthem blares from the speakers, and the mob, who have just finished buck-leaping around the dance floor to Horslips' 'Trouble', are now standing to attention like an army of well-trained soldiers. I'm leaning against the wall by the main doors praying that wherever Lesley has spent the previous three hours, she'll come back to meet up with me there. But fifteen anxious minutes later, I'm still watching and waiting, and the hall is almost empty.

'Looking for me, sexy?' some fella slobbers. His breath is reeking of whiskey.

'No. For my boyfriend,' I say, turning my back on him.

My stomach is in bits. I don't know what to do next. The bouncer I'd spoken to earlier is dragging a bloodied skinhead by the scruff of his neck across the hall towards the exit. As soon as he's rid of the fella, I approach him again.

'Excuse me, can you help me? I've lost my friend and I've no way of getting home to Castleowen.'

'Castleowen!'

'Yeah,' I say, feeling stupid.

'Fuck me, it's hardly a quick spin out the road, is it?'

'No.' I burst into tears.

'Come on,' he says, walking me back inside the hall and sitting me down near the bar. 'Is there anyone you could ring for a lift?'

'No.'

'What about your parents?'

'They won't come,' I sob. 'They never cross the border.'

'If they want you home tonight, they'll have to cross it, won't they?'

'They'll kill me. I'm not supposed to be here.'

'Aye, they might. But they'll hardly leave you stranded all the same,' he says, tapping a cigarette from his packet. 'Want one?'

'Thanks,' I snivel.

After lighting my cigarette, he asks for my home phone number and goes behind the bar to make the call. With the shutters down, I can't see whether he's managed to get through to my parents or not. There are a few stragglers still staggering their way towards the exit. Another bouncer is walking behind them, urging them on like a farmer does with straying cattle. I could kill Lesley for landing me in this mess. That's if it is her fault. Maybe I should be worried, not angry. What if something bad has happened to her? It is the North after all. Someone might have copped her English accent (she still has a touch of it) and thought she was a Protestant, or a Unionist, or even worse – a terrorist. She could have got beaten up, knee-capped or, God forbid, killed. Jesus, such a night! I can't wait to be back on familiar territory. Without Lesley by my side, I feel out of my depth.

A couple of young lads are clearing glasses from the tables. Some of the drinks look as if they haven't been touched. There are several on the table in front of me. It's a shame to see them going to waste, especially when I'm in dire need of an injection of courage. I don't want my mother seeing me upset. She'd make mincemeat of me if she caught me with my defences down. Besides, the booze is only going to end up being emptied down the drain, so it could hardly be considered stealing. I pick up a half bottle of Coke and pour it into what looks like a shot of vodka. Afraid of being caught by the bouncer, I gulp it down quickly. One of the lads approaches the table.

'I saw that,' he says, grinning at me. He lifts a drink from his tray and sniffs it. 'Gin,' he says, handing it to me.

'Thanks. Is there anything to mix it with?'

'Just this,' he says, pouring in the end of a small bottle of tonic water. 'Are you Mac's girlfriend?'

'Whose?' I ask, taking a bitter mouthful and almost choking on it.

'Mac's. The bouncer.'

'Are you mad?' I splutter. 'That man must be fifty.'

'Don't let him hear you saying that. He's only in his thirties. And what's more, he's got off with younger girls than you.'

'Well, he's not getting off with me. He's just arranging a lift home for me.'

'I'll give you a lift if you like.'

'Too late, Ownie boy,' the bouncer says, coming up behind him and clipping his ear. 'Her very irate parents are on their way as we speak.'

'Sneaked out your bedroom window, did you?' the young lad asks, handing me another glass of spirits.

'No, I –'

'Oi,' the bouncer says, swiping it out off my hand. 'I think you're in enough trouble as it is, don't you?'

'Ah, come on, Mac, the poor girl may as well be hung for a sheep as a lamb.'

'Shut up, for fuck sake,' he says, plonking the drink down on Ownie's tray, 'and just get on with the job you're being paid to do.'

As soon as the bouncer turns his back, Ownie picks up the glass and sets it down by my feet.

'Thanks.'

'Just make sure Mac Bollocks doesn't see it.'

Shortly after three o'clock, the staff have finished clearing up and I'm three shots of liquor less concerned about having to face my parents than I'd been an hour earlier. In fact now it seems quite funny. As we leave the premises, Ownie offers to wait with me until my parents arrive.

'No need,' I say, spotting them driving into the car park.

'How about a quick kiss then?'

The bouncer clips his ear again.

'I'd better go,' I say, walking away feeling light-headed.

'Good luck,' Ownie shouts. 'Might see you here again some night.'

My father gets out of the car and, without looking up, opens the back door for me as I walk towards him. When I catch sight of my mother, I start tittering. I can't stop myself. She's sitting in the front passenger seat staring straight in front of her. Over her hair rollers, she's wearing a cream-coloured beret. She looks just like a head of cauliflower.

'Hiya, Daddy.'

'Hiya!' He peers at me with small glassy eyes and shakes his head. 'Is that all you have to say?'

'Sorry.' I glance at him briefly before climbing in.

My mother straightens herself up and, half turning her head, addresses my bare knees. 'This is a lovely carry-on on the Sabbath, I must say.'

'I was at a disco and missed my lift home. It's hardly the crime of the century, is it?' Whatever about my father, I've no intention of allowing *her* to make me feel guilty. 'Anyway, it's not the Sabbath, it's Saturday night.'

'It's long past midnight, in case you haven't noticed, madam. So that makes it Sunday. The Sabbath.'

My father gets back into the car.

'Normal people would call this Saturday night,' I mutter, 'but then again, you're not exactly what I'd call normal.'

'That's enough,' my father says, slamming the door. 'You have some explaining to do when you get home, young lady. A mouthful of bad manners is hardly going to appease things, is it?'

'And taking the door off its hinges won't help much either,' my mother snaps, glowering at my father as if he's as responsible for this situation as I am.

'This is neither the time nor the place to argue,' my father says shakily. 'Let's just get out of here.'

We drive in silence through the streets of Enniskillen and back out to the Castleowen road.

'I suppose this is all down to that Lesley Kelly,' my mother says.

'No it isn't.'

'Don't give me that. That's her excuse for a skirt you've on, isn't it?'

'No.'

'Well, you weren't wearing it when you left the house this evening.'

'You mean yesterday.'

'What?'

'Well, if this is the Sabbath, I left the house yesterday evening,' I say, sticking out my tongue behind her back.

She swivels her cauliflower head and considers me with narrowed eyes.

'What?' I say after a few seconds when she's still leering at me.

She raises her nose, takes a couple of suspicious sniffs and turns to my father. 'She's been drinking!'

'My God, you haven't, have you, Frances?'

'No way.'

'Hah!' my mother scoffs. 'You reek of alcohol.'

'Someone spilt a pint all over my clothes, Daddy. That's what the smell is of.'

'Absolute rubbish,' she yells. 'You're a lying little . . .' She shakes her head, racking her brain for a befitting insult.

'Am not am not am not am not,' I say, raising my voice above hers.

'. . . tart.'

'Oh, for crying out loud,' my father shouts, turning down his headbeams, 'will ye keep your voices down? We're approaching a checkpoint.'

As we drive slowly over two ramps into the glaring light, I feel a mixture of dread and giddy anticipation. A uniformed policeman approaches the car, followed by a soldier in his late teens carrying a rifle with as much ease as a girl of his age would carry a shoulder bag. When my father winds down his window, the soldier shines a torch into the back of the car, making me squint. The policeman examines my father's driving licence and talks into his walkie-talkie. As the torch scans every corner of the car's interior, my mother sits motionless, arms folded and eyes downcast, as if her survival depended on her stillness. Out of the side window I see two more soldiers lying in the ditch with rifles pointing in our direction. I slither down in my seat.

'Where are you going, sir?' the young soldier asks my father as he withdraws the torch. He sounds just like Keith, Lesley's brother.

'Castleowen.'

'And where are you coming from?'

'Enniskillen. We had to collect the young lassie from a dance.'

The policeman hands the licence back to my father.

'OK, Mister Fall,' he says. 'Have a safe journey.'

'Thank you,' my father says, 'and goodnight.'

No one utters another word until we've driven over several more ramps and across the bridge that takes us back into the Republic.

'Thanks be to the Lord God Almighty,' my mother says, blessing herself. She then turns to my father. 'I don't ever want to have to go through that again,' she whines. 'Them guns are very threatening.'

'Don't worry, Rita, you'll not have to.'

'I hope not.'

'You won't. I promise.'

Behind them, I'm rolling my eyes at her helpless little woman routine. I just don't buy it.

We travel on in silence until we're only a couple of miles outside Castleowen. By now, I'm getting it hard to keep my eyes open.

'The gall of you to tell me that you weren't drinking,' my mother says, when she sees me with my hand over my mouth. 'Look at her,' she says, nudging my father, 'she's going to throw up.'

'No I'm not,' I say through a yawn. 'I'm just tired, that's all. God, am I not allowed to yawn now?'

'I know by your eyes you've been drinking, Frances Fall. Do you think I came up the river on a banana skin?'

'No, on a spaceship.'

'How dare you!' she yelps, reaching back to take a swipe at me.

In an attempt to stop her, my father grabs her wrist and loses control of the steering wheel. The car swerves to the left.

'Jesus, Jesus, oh Jesus,' my father cries out, jamming his foot on the brake as we judder along the grassy bank, narrowly avoiding the drop into a ditch. Half crying and half laughing, I grab hold of my father's headrest and close my eyes. In the next few seconds, the only thing that crosses my mind is Lesley – will I ever see her again? Then, thump! The car comes to a halt and all three of us are jolted forward.

'Aaagh!' my mother shouts.

'Rita, Rita, are you all right, love?' My father's voice is trembling.

'No,' she cries, holding her hand to her forehead. 'I hit my head on the dashboard.'

'Let me see,' he says, trying to take her hand away.

'Leave me alone,' she screeches. 'Just leave me alone.'

'Please, Rita, let me have a look at it to see if you're cut.'

'Will you just get me home, you silly man!'

'I'm sorry, Rita. I shouldn't have interfered: I should've kept my eyes on the road.'

She takes a sudden, sharp intake of breath and winces as if she's in agony, though I have my doubts. 'Yes,' she whimpers, 'you should have.'

'There's gonna be changes,' my father says as he turns the key in the ignition. 'Do you hear me, Frances?

'Yeah.'

'I'll not have you putting Mammy through the likes of this again.'

Shite! She has him now. A wee bump on her head and she's a martyr to the bloody cause. Any excuse at all and he gives in to her.

'Lesley Lesley Lesley – where the hell are you?' I whisper, as I climb out of bed the following morning.

It's half past eleven. What if she's still in Enniskillen? What if she's hurt? Dead! I run across the landing to the bathroom. My head is throbbing. I'm sure my parents are waiting downstairs to confront me, but I haven't time to listen to them. I have to get out of the house and down to the kiosk to ring Lesley's. There's no way I could talk in peace from the phone in the hall. After scrubbing my mouldy mouth, I swallow several mouthfuls of tap water and put on the jeans and jumper that have been lying in a ball at the bottom of my bed for almost a week. Then I sneak downstairs and out the front door. It's only then I realize my parents aren't home. The car isn't parked in its usual spot, in front of the sitting-room window. I'd thought that the deadly silence in the house when I woke up earlier on was down to the atmosphere, not their absence. Where could they be? Ten o'clock Mass is long over. In fact, I'm surprised my mother didn't insist on dragging me along. Just as the front door clicks shut, I realize I haven't taken any money with me for the phone, and I've forgotten my key. Nancy has a spare. Although I don't feel comfortable about calling at her house – she's very frosty with me these days – I have to get back in the house, so I hurry down the street and knock on her door. I'm surprised when there's no answer; her car is in the driveway.

'She's away with your parents,' Susan Scully shouts from across the street. 'I saw her getting into their car about an hour ago.'

'Thanks.'

A few doors down, I see my primary school teacher, Master Fitzgibbon, coming out of his mother's house and getting into his car.

'Hello, Master,' I say, walking towards him. I still him call that. Everyone does.

'How're you doing, Frances?'

'Grand. You're not heading into town by any chance?'

'No. Why? Do you need a lift?'

'Ah no, it's OK.'

'Come on. I'll run you in.'

On the way, he tells me I've changed. That of all the children he's taught over the years, I've surprised him most. I like that.

'Any thoughts on what you're going to do after the Leaving Cert?'

'Move to Dublin,' I tell him, because that's what Lesley and I have planned. We're going to share a flat and have a great social life.

'To study what?'

'Nothing. I just want to get a job.'

'You haven't considered university?'

'No way. I've had my fill of school.'

'Your parents must be a bit disappointed.'

'It's *my* life, Master.'

'Indeed it is. But there aren't that many decent jobs on offer nowadays if you haven't a degree in your back pocket.'

'I don't really mind what I work at. I'm just looking forward to getting away.'

'Yeah, I can see that.'

'She's still in bed,' Lesley's mother says. 'Come on in, love.'

'So she's home?'

'Only a couple of hours,' Sandra says, coming out of the sitting-room with her hands on her waist. 'Where the hell were ye last night?'

'Don't jump down the lassie's throat,' her mother splutters through a cough. 'Anyway, Lesley's already told us what happened.'

'Lesley fed us a cock and bull story and well you know it.'

'Innocent till proven guilty, Sandra.'

'Ah, will you cop on to yourself, Mammy. When it comes to Lesley, you've blinkers on. Come on, you, Miss Butter-wouldn't-melt-in-my-mouth,' she says, taking my elbow and leading me into the sitting-room. 'Sit down and give us *your* version of the story.'

'Stop bullying her, will you?' her mother says, sitting down beside me and patting my knee. 'If youse missed your lift, youse missed your lift. Youse did the right thing waiting at the depot for the first bus.'

'Oh, Jesus wept,' Sandra shouts, shaking her head in frustration. 'I give up,' she says. 'I've fucking had it with Lesley. She's your responsibility, Mammy, not mine.'

'Don't worry, she'll calm down,' her mother says when Sandra leaves the room.

I'm flabbergasted. I'd have thought Sandra would be cool over something like this and that her mother would be the one to hit the roof, not the other way around, especially after some of the things Lesley's been telling me about her mother lately. I was beginning to dislike the woman. Something doesn't add up.

'You'd swear *that one* never put a foot wrong herself,' she says. 'Since she got engaged, she's turned fierce sensible.'

'It's true about us missing our lift, Missus Kelly.'

'Arragh, I know it's not. But if *I* don't stand up for Lesley, no one will. The boys are giving out stink about her; they don't like their little sister getting a bad name for herself. They were the same with Sandra a couple of years ago. Indeed, my own brothers were the same with me, for all the good it did. I still ended up with a wrong one.'

'Sorry.'

'What for?'

'Lying.'

'Show me a teenager who doesn't tell the odd porky. We all did it in our day. You're a heck of a nice kid. I'm glad our Lesley has you. You'll keep an eye out for her, won't you?'

'Of course,' I say, delighted with the responsibility.

'And youse'll be careful when youse are hanging around with lads?'

'Yeah.'

'Good,' she says, struggling to get up. I can hear her wheezing. 'Cos they're all the same – sex flipping mad. You can go on up to her, if you like.'

Lesley is still asleep. Careful not to disturb her, I tiptoe over to the double bed and ease myself down on Sandra's side, laying my head on the pillow. She looks gorgeous lying facing me, still in her black T-shirt, dark tresses splayed across her pillow, one silky leg out over the blankets, skimpy black knickers revealing the beautiful, sexy flesh of her hip. I can feel the warmth of her breath on my face. The thought of going to Dublin and waking up beside her like this every morning fills me with longing.

In her sleep, she scratches her nose, wiggles about and turns her back to me. Without thinking, I put my arm around her waist and nestle into her. It feels natural being so close to her. When I start caressing her tummy, she sighs peacefully. I don't stop until she takes my hand and puts it on her breast.

'Lesley,' I whisper, checking that she's awake and aware of what she's doing.

'It's OK,' she says softly. 'It's lovely.'

We lie like that for ages, just breathing. I'm not afraid or embarrassed. I'm no longer bursting to hear what happened to her the night before. That can wait, now that she's safe in my arms.

'Wake up, Frances,' Lesley says, pulling back my eyelids.

'Did I fall asleep?'

'Yeah.'

'For how long?'

'I dunno,' she says impatiently. 'About an hour. But never mind that; I've something to tell you.' She sounds all keyed up.

'What?'

'You have to swear on your life not to breathe a word.'

'Is it about last night?'

'Yeah. Now swear.'

'I do.'

'Say it, Frances.'

'I swear.'

She sits up on her knees. 'I nearly got raped last night,' she whispers.

'What?'

'Shut up, will you? Someone might hear you.'

'Oh Jesus, are you all right? What the fuck happened?' I feel sick at the thought of anyone hurting her.

'When you were in the loo, this fella, at least in his mid-twenties, started chatting me up. I told him I had a boyfriend. He said, "Who, The Invisible Man?" "No," I said, "his name is Johnny Connolly if you must know." He told me he knew him.'

'And did he?'

'No, but I didn't know that, did I?'

'The bastard. So what happened then?'

'Oh God,' she says, putting her hands over her eyes, 'you'll kill me for this bit.'

'Why?' I ask, gently taking her hands away.

'He told me he'd been drinking in some pub or other with Johnny before he came to the disco and reckoned he was still there. I asked him if he'd go and tell him that we were at the disco – you and me, but he wouldn't, not unless I went with him.' She looks at me, her brown eyes begging forgiveness. 'I told him I had to wait for you, honest to God, Frances, I did. And I waited for ages. But he kept saying that if we didn't leave straight away, we'd miss him; he'd be gone. He told me we'd only be fifteen minutes or so and that I'd find you when I got back.'

She closes her eyes as if she's about to cry.

'It's OK,' I say, touching her shoulder. 'I'd probably have done the same thing.' That's a lie; I'm sure I wouldn't have.

'As soon as we drove off, I got this real creepy feeling . . .'

'Like *I* had when we got into that farmer's car.'

'Yeah, only in your case it was a false alarm. This fella was the real McCoy. I told him I'd changed my mind, that I was worried about you and I wanted to go back. But he wouldn't listen. He kept saying, "Relax, will you? We're nearly there."'

'You must have been scared stiff.'

'I was, especially when he rolled up his sleeves and I saw a big King Billy tattoo on his arm.'

'Oh Jesus!'

'I swear, I nearly fucking wet myself. I've heard about these boys – Proddies – who go hunting for Catholics to kill. I was sure I was dead.'

'What did you do?'

'There was fuck all I could do. The streets were deserted; he had muscles on him like the Incredible Hulk and a face on him like King Kong. There was only one thing for it.'

'What?'

'I had to talk my way out of it.'

'But how? What did you say?'

'I hadn't passed any remarks when I saw the tattoo, so I pretended to think he was a Catholic. I said "Ian," that was his name, "can I tell you a secret? Only you've got to promise not to tell anyone." "Go on," he said. "If my family find out," I said, "I'm dead." Next thing, he switches on the indicator and pulls over.'

'Oh, my God.'

'My heart was in my gob. "What is it?" he said. I wasn't sure if I was doing the right thing, cos you never really know what a Northerner is thinking. But it was too late to change my mind, so I just blurted it out.'

'What?'

'"Johnny and me shouldn't be going out together," I told him. He says, "Why the fuck not?" "Because I'm a Protestant," says I. "Please don't fucking shoot me."'

'That was a flipping brilliant idea. What did he say?'

'"You're fucking joking me. So am I."'

'God, how did you think of it? You're deadly at stuff like that.'

'But that wasn't the end of it. He was fucking ripping. He grabbed my hair and stared at me real threateningly. You should have seen the face of him. I was waiting for his bloody eyeballs to pop out on to my knee.'

'Jesus, I'd have died of a heart attack.'

'"Are you screwing a fucking Catholic?" he said. At this stage, his face was so close to mine, I thought he was going to head-butt me. "No," I said, "I've only met him a couple of times, but I'll break it off with him now, I promise." "You'd better," he roared, yanking my hair. It hurt like mad.'

'The bastard.'

'Then he told me to get out. When I opened the door, he practically kicked me out on to the footpath and said that if he ever saw me hanging around a Catholic area again, he'd . . .' She looks away and shivers.

'What? What, Lesley?'

'. . . rape me and then shoot me,' she blurts, flinging herself face down on to the pillow.

'Oh, thank God you're OK,' I say, stroking her hair.

'Thanks.' Her voice is muffled.

'You must still be in shock.'

'It hits me in waves.'

'You poor thing. How did you get home in the end? Did you really get the bus?'

'Yeah. It took me half the night to find the depot. And when I did, there wasn't a sinner there, only myself.'

'It wasn't open?'

'At that hour of the night? No. It was about seven o'clock before one of the bus drivers showed up.'

'So you weren't lying to your mother after all. You just didn't tell her the whole story.'

'It doesn't matter what I told her; she doesn't believe a word of it.'

'She's not mad with you, though. I was talking to her earlier on and she was standing up for you.'

'She's only doing that in front of you. She met me at the door this morning with a clout in the mouth. I bet she didn't tell you that, did she?'

'You're joking!'

'I am not,' she says, turning an offended face to me.

'No, I believe you; it's just that . . . she seemed so understanding. She even asked me to keep an eye on you.'

'The cow!' she says, rolling over on to her back. 'She wants you to spy on me.'

'I don't think she meant it that way. She –'

'You just can't see through people, Frances. You're far too gullible.' She turns on her side and starts tweaking my fringe. 'I told you what my mother's like. She hates me.'

'The *bitch*,' I say, sighing with anger. 'The rotten, two-faced bitch.'

'Don't let it bother you,' she says, running her fingers down my cheek. 'I don't.'

'The sooner we get to Dublin, the better.'

'Mmm. And listen, let's tell Jackie and Orla that we changed our minds about the Tropicana because you had a headache or something.'

'Yeah, OK.'

'Cos I can't bear to tell anyone else what happened.'

'Even Johnny?'

'Especially not Johnny.'

'Don't worry,' I say, feeling closer to her at that moment than I ever had or would, 'your secret is safe with me.'

By the time I get home, it's after eight o'clock, and the doubts I had the night before over the wisdom of my rebellious behaviour are now null and void. If anything, spending the day with Lesley has strengthened my resolve. When I told her about my parents having to come to collect me, she said, 'You don't owe them an apology. They did you a favour, that's all.'

Having forgotten my key, I have to ring the doorbell. The hall light goes on, and through the frosted glass I see my mother approaching the door. She delays a few seconds before letting me in, clearing her throat as if she's about to deliver a speech.

'Jesus!' I cringe at the rawness of the bruise over her left eyebrow. 'I didn't realize . . .'

'Well, how would you?' she says, her tone ridiculously formal. 'You were drunk.'

'It was dark,' I say, unzipping my jacket and wondering if her strange mood could be the result of delayed concussion.

'There's someone here to see you.'

'Where?'

'The sitting-room.'

'Who?'

She nods towards the door, intimating that I should see for myself. Warily, I pass her, stopping outside the sitting-room door to reconsider.

'Excuse me,' she says.

When I step back, she opens the door and walks in ahead of me, bowing like a housemaid delivering a guest.

'Ah, there she is,' Father Vincent says, sounding surprised, as if he hadn't heard the doorbell, or my voice in the hall. He folds his newspaper and tosses it on to the coffee table. 'Where have you been till this hour at all at all?'

His podgy cheeks look like two big lumps of cooked ham. He must have been sitting by the fire all day waiting for my return. The living-room door clicks shut. I look behind me to find that my mother has vanished. I hadn't heard her move.

'I was in town,' I say. 'Why?'

'With young Kelly, I suppose.'

'So?'

'Why don't you sit down?'

'I've things to do upstairs.'

'I'm sure you can spare five minutes.'

Rolling my eyes, I perch myself on the armrest of the sofa.

'Did you fall?'

'No. Why?'

'I thought maybe,' he points to the rip in my jeans, 'you tore your slacks on something.'

I have to turn away to laugh.

'Did I say something funny?' He's irritated.

I shake my head.

'Well then, what are you laughing at?'

'Nothing,' I giggle.

'Begod, I can see why your mother is worried about you so.'

It suddenly dawns on me that that's why my parents had called to Nancy's house earlier on. She could persuade her brother to intervene on their behalf. Surely I'd listen to him. Everyone listens to him, a man of the cloth, full of wisdom, understanding and, above all, clout. Apart from the Bishop himself, there isn't a man in the county could compete with Father Vincent in the 'clout' department. As a child, I felt privileged that such an important person was a regular visitor to our house. Now all I can see is a middle-aged, red-faced man with no neck, struggling to be taken seriously, and I can't help feeling sorry for him.

'Sorry, Father. What was it you wanted to talk to me about?'

'Alcohol.'

'Oh,' I say, trying to look serious.

He shifts awkwardly in the armchair and rests his inter-locking hands on his lap. 'And young fellas.'

Without interrupting him, I listen to his lecture, though I switch off half-way through it. From the outset, I know it's pointless, but I don't want to be nasty to him; he's never done me any harm.

'Do you see what I'm saying, Frances?' he says every so often.

'Mmm.'

I'm thinking about Lesley again, about the softness of her breast, about the way she looked at me and played with my hair. I close my eyes and breathe deeply.

'You're not falling asleep on me, are you?'

'No, Father.'

She and I have so much in common – we both love to dance, we've the same taste in clothes, music. Neither of us can wait to leave for Dublin. Both our mothers hate us, though I'd still rather have hers than mine. And then there's the gingerbread man.

'. . . because in my experience, and I've been around a while, as soon as a lassie gives a boy what he's looking for, he heads for the hills – him and his promises.'

8 November 1999 (evening)

Never mind him and his promises. What about her and her promises?

The end of a beautiful friendship

Sometimes Jackie or Orla tag along, but usually it's just me who hangs around the bread van keeping an eye out for the nuns and lay-teachers. Although I cannot see them, I can hear Lesley and Johnny kissing hurriedly inside the van like forbidden lovers. Afterwards her mouth looks red and swollen. Once he bites her lower lip so hard it bleeds.

'It stings like mad,' she says, licking away the spot of blood. 'He'll pay for that.'

'How do you mean? You're not dumping him, are you?'

'No way!' she says, looking at me wide-eyed. 'Never. I'm gonna bite him back.'

'You wouldn't!'

'Yes I would. He's tasted my blood, so why shouldn't I taste his?'

We meet up with Jackie and Orla and spend the rest of the lunch break sitting on a bench that faces out on to the sports field. A few yards away, girls are charging up and down the pitch shouting at one another and swinging their camogie sticks.

'Did you see that?' I say, when one of the players drops to her knees after getting belted in the stomach with the ball.

Lesley doesn't answer. She's staring straight through the action to the far side of the pitch, where a cluster of trees obscures the neighbouring field. It's as if she's looking through a telescope at something or someone none of the rest of us can see. I wish I knew what was going on inside her head.

In the middle of the night, I wake up to go to the toilet. While I'm at the sink washing my hands, I catch a glimpse of my reflection in the vanity mirror and suddenly feel irritated, I don't know why. After drying my hands, I go back and look again. Now I know. It's my eyes. They look so soft, so stupidly vulnerable. It's like looking into clear water – you can see right through me. In a fit of annoyance, I start pulling faces, trying to make myself look strong, provocative, unfathomable. Like Lesley. Her eyes are so dark, so deep, you cannot see where the dark brown begins and the black ends. It's well for her, being able to look in the mirror and see what she sees. Squeezing my eyes shut, I take a deep breath and imagine myself inside her body. Then, pursing my lips, I lean forward and kiss the cold glass.

'Idiot,' I murmur, opening my eyes and quickly wiping away the condensation. 'Stupid idiot.'

I pace the bathroom floor in a rage. I can't get Lesley out of my mind. The way she's been carrying on lately, it's ridiculous. The girl is obsessed. She hasn't the space in her head for anything or anyone else these days but the bloody gingerbread man. She hasn't the space for me. Feck him! Who does he think he is, coming between us like this? Teasing her, teasing me. I hold my bottom lip between my teeth, loosely at first, but gradually biting down harder. The pain makes my eyes water. Go on, I think, standing back in front of the mirror, bite harder. She says they're going to do it; they're going to go all the way. He's coming down to Castleowen on Monday evening. It'll be their first proper date.

'Ouch!' I put my hand over my mouth.

I don't know if I've drawn blood or not until I take my hand away and examine my bottom lip in the mirror.

Spineless coward, I think, creeping back across the landing to my bedroom. You just haven't got what it takes.

On Saturday night Lesley stays at home waiting for his call. He says he'll be ringing her to make sure she's not out with anyone else. She asks me to call to her house to keep her company.

'He's so possessive,' she says, beaming. 'If he thought I as much as looked at another man, he'd kill him, and then he'd kill me.'

'He said that?'

'Yeah,' she says, stretching out on the bed.

'Jesus!'

'I know,' she says, blowing smoke at the ceiling, 'what a cool way to die.'

'It was the best night of my life,' she says.

My skin begins to prickle.

Jackie, Orla and myself are huddled around Lesley in the cloakroom.

'So did youse do it?' Jackie asks.

'Twice.'

'Get out of here,' Orla says.

'Honest. Once in the front of the car and once in the back.'

Jackie looks over her shoulder to make sure no one is listening. 'What was his willy like?'

Lesley starts giggling. I can tell she's loving every minute of it – being the first of us to lose her virginity; having had the nerve to go through with it.

'Come on, quit laughing and tell us,' Orla says, nudging her.

'A fucking microphone . . . with hair.'

'Holy fuck!' Jackie screeches. 'What did you do – start singing into it?'

'Ah jaysus, that's disgusting,' Orla says, puckering her face. 'I think I'll join the fucking convent.'

A girl from third year with prominent teeth, who's sitting on the opposite bench, is smiling over at us. She reminds me of myself a couple of years earlier – the curious spectator, eager to join in the conversation, but much too shy to try.

'Oy, Bright Eyes,' Lesley says, giving her daggers, 'go nibble a lettuce leaf and keep your twitchy nose out of our business.'

The girl's face turns scarlet as she picks up her books and walks away.

'That's right, hop along. Just follow the signs for Watership Down.'

'Oh, you bitch!' Orla titters, when the girl is out of sight. 'That was lousy.'

'Too bad,' Lesley says, shrugging. 'She'll be all right if nothing falls on her.'

'How do you know?' I ask.

'What?'

'How do you know she'll be all right? She could be down the corridor crying her eyes out for all you know.'

'If she is, she's a fucking wimp.'

'If she is, it's your fault.'

'OK, OK, take it easy,' Jackie says. 'It's not the end –'

Lesley looks at me suspiciously. 'What's your problem, Frances?'

'I don't have a problem. I just feel sorry for the girl, that's all.'

'Why? What is *she* to *you*?'

'Nothing. I just don't like the way you –'

'The way I what?'

'Hurt people.'

'Oh, *people* now, is it?'

'You know what I mean.'

'No I don't. Tell me what you mean.'

'Ah, quit, girls, will youse?' Orla says. 'She's not worth falling out over.'

'Oh, but Frances thinks she is,' Lesley says, folding her arms and eyeballing me. 'Don't you?'

I've never challenged Lesley before and find it impossible to hold her stare. I have two choices. I can stick to my guns, insist that what she did was wrong and walk away. Or I can apologize for making a big deal over nothing. If I do the former, I know our friendship is over.

'Ah, don't mind me,' I say. 'I'm just in a bad mood.'

'It's all right,' she says, her face instantly softening. 'But next time, don't take it out on me, OK?'

'OK.'

'Thank God for that,' Jackie says. 'I thought we'd never get back to talking about sex. So, tell us more. Did it hurt?'

'A bit. But the sensation, I'm not joking youse, girls . . .' she says, closing her eyes, taking a deep dramatic breath and holding it for several seconds, 'I thought I'd died and gone to heaven.'

I'm fiddling with the loose change in my pocket, trying to disguise my jealousy with a smile. My lips feel strained with the falseness of it. If I wanted to, I could go straight to the phone, ring her mother and let her know what Lesley's up to. Even better still, I could tell her brothers. She'd be well and truly frigged then.

'Did you have one of them thing-a-me-jiggies?' Jackie says.

'You mean, did I come?'

'Yeah.'

'No, I exploded. It was bloody fantastic. Pure magic.'

'Did he?' Orla asks.

'God, yeah. It was so funny,' she giggles. 'You should've seen the face on him. It was like this.' She squeezes her eyes shut and starts screwing up her face and making grunting shouts. 'You'd think he was constipated.'

The girls are in stitches.

'I'll be back in a minute,' I say, hurrying away with tears in my eyes.

I cannot bear to listen to any more. Why is she being such a fool? Can she not see that he doesn't love her, that he's only using her? Maybe I should have told her how behind her back he winks at me and nudges me playfully, how he tells me I have wild sexy eyes, beautiful cheekbones, a cute bum. I know he's playing us both and I know I should have warned her. But if I had, she'd have turned against me. She's never seen me as a threat. I could tell him to get lost, but part of me is enjoying the attention, and, in a way I can't explain even to myself, I like being a threat to her, whether she knows it or not.

The week we go back to school after the Christmas holidays, Lesley is in bed with the flu. On the Tuesday night she rings me with a string of messages to pass on to the gingerbread man the following day.

'Are you writing them down?'

'Yes.'

'Good. And ask him if he has any messages for me.'

'OK.'

'And if he does, write them down as well, in case you forget like.'

'Don't worry. I'll record every word.'

'Oh thanks, you're the best. It's killing me not being able to see him this week,' she says, sighing.

'I know.'

He stands watching me with an impish grin as I sneak across the yard towards the van. Since the principal, PMT, told us she had received complaints from Sister Bernadine that some of the students were fraternizing with the bread man, Jackie and Orla have steered clear.

'How's about ya, chicken?'

'Hiya.'

'Where's the queen bee today?'

'She's sick. But I have a load of messages for you.' I start rooting in my pocket for the slip of paper.

'Who from?'

'Lesley, who d'ya think?'

He leans his face towards mine. 'But do *you* have any messages for me?' he whispers, his breath tickling my ear.

Before I have a chance to draw breath, he's in the back of the van stacking a tray as if he hasn't said a word. I never know how to react when he flirts with me.

'Fancy a spin?'

'What?'

'Fancy a spin in the van?'

'No.'

'You don't fancy it?'

'I can't. I have to be back in class in five minutes.'

'Who says?'

'PMT. She's warned us not to be hanging around you any more.'

'It hasn't stopped you though, has it? You're still here.'

'Just to give you this.' I hold out Lesley's note.

'Aye,' he says, ignoring the note as he climbs down from the van and passes me.

'The note, Johnny.'

'I think it's Lesley who scares you, not PMT,' he says, looking back at me over his shoulder. 'Would I be right?'

What does he mean? Scared of Lesley how? He must think I'm a lapdog. But I'm not. I've as much guts as anyone else. More than most. Why does he think that?

'That wee nun's for the birds,' he says, coming back out laughing. He has a lovely laugh. It makes his eyes sparkle. 'She's after asking me how Father Foley is. She must think I'm a priest or something.'

'Father Foley is the other bread man's brother – the fella who retired. He's a missionary. I heard them talking about him loads of times. He's out in Kenya, I think.'

'Fuck! I'm not that ancient-looking, am I?' he asks, climbing back into the van.

'No,' I say, smiling. 'You only look fifty.'

'Hey, you!'

'Here.' I hold out the note again.

'My hands are busy,' he says, arranging several apple tarts on to the tray. 'You read it for me.'

'Why do you want me to read it?'

'I told you. I'm busy.'

'Then put it in your pocket and read it later.'

'If you don't read it for me, I'm not taking it.'

He climbs back down and disappears through the refectory door with the tray. He's such a tease.

When he comes back out, he puts the empty tray into the back of the van.

'On second thoughts . . .' he says, jumping out and swiping the note from my hand.

'What are you doing?' I ask, when he starts tearing it up.

'There's no point in reading it. I have the hots for someone else.' He throws the pieces of paper over his shoulder and they scatter on to the damp ground.

'Have you a new girlfriend?'

'I didn't say that.'

'But –'

'I said I have the hots for someone else. Whether she'll be my girlfriend or not remains to be seen.'

I think it's me he's on about, but I don't want him to know what I'm thinking.

'Is she from Enniskillen?'

'No. She lives south of the border in a wee village called eh . . . oh damn, I can't think of the name of it. It begins with "C" I think.'

The bell starts ringing.

'I have to go,' I say.

'You don't have to do anything,' he says, taking my hand and bringing me over to the passenger door. 'Let me take you for a spin.'

'I can't. Anyway, Lesley's my friend . . . my best friend.'

'Young man . . .' Sister Bernadine says, coming out from the refectory looking confused.

'Hop in quickly before she sees you,' he says, opening the door. 'Just crouch down till we get away from the school.'

I'm in the van before I've time to think. My heart is going hell for leather. He walks round the front of the van and opens the driver's door.

'Just getting the delivery docket for you, Sister,' he says, winking at me and picking it up from the dashboard.

Five minutes later we're parked up a narrow lane that leads to a nearby wood. I suppose I could have told him to drop me off at the school gates and hurried back up the avenue to my classroom. And maybe I shouldn't have climbed into the van in the first place. But I did, because I'm not a coward and I'm not afraid of anyone, even Lesley.

'It's all right. You can sit up now,' he says, passing me a cigarette.

My legs are stiff from being on my hunkers.

'Why do you think I'm *afraid* of Lesley?' I ask, leaning towards him for a light.

'I don't think it.'

'But you said –'

'I *know* it.'

'Why should I be? What makes you say that?'

'The first day I met youse, you fancied me too . . .'

'I did n—'

'But you wouldn't flirt with me because you knew Lesley wanted to shift me. You were afraid to compete.'

'I'm not afraid of her.'

'No?'

'No.'

'Kiss me then.'

'I'm smoking.' Turning towards the window, I take a long, deep drag. 'It's freezing in here.'

'Don't change the subject,' he says, starting the engine.

'Where are you going?'

'Nowhere; I'm just warming up the van for you.'

'Oh.'

'Why won't you kiss me? Don't you fancy me?'

'No.'

'Liar.'

I take a few more drags of the cigarette, roll down the window an inch and peg it out. The sky has turned grey and the rain is pouring down. I know I shouldn't be here. By rights, it should be another lazy, humdrum school day, when the biggest decision I have to make is whether I should eat my sandwich before my apple, or my apple before my sandwich. Instead, I'm on the verge of a decision that could change who I am for ever. Part of me wants to give in and let everything that could happen, happen. I want to prove to myself that I too have the guts to do it. I want the thrill, the passion, the died-and-gone-to-heaven feeling. The one up on Lesley, God forgive me. But my conscience is struggling. How will I feel afterwards? And how will I ever look Lesley in the eye again?

'What do you think she'd do if she was in your position?'

'I don't know.'

'I think you do.'

As soon as I turn my face to his, our mouths find each other and we're kissing like long-lost lovers, like him and Lesley. He's holding my face in his strong hands. His thumbs are pressing into my cheekbones.

'You're mad for it, aren't you?' he says, breaking away and quickly climbing over on top of me.

He starts unbuttoning his white coat. If I don't say something now, it'll be too late.

'Wait,' I blurt, as he starts undoing the buttons of my cardigan.

'What?'

'I don't want to hurt Lesley.'

'Then don't tell her. I won't.'

'Do you not care about her at all?'

'I do. I think she's a great kid.'

'But you're going to break it off with her.'

'If it makes you feel any better, I won't,' he says, kissing my neck.

'Why are you messing us both about?' I ask, pushing him back.

'I'm not. I'd rather be with you.'

'Just to have sex with me?'

'Well, I wasn't going to ask you to marry me just yet.'

'You just want sex off us, don't you? You're just using us.'

'Will you relax, for God's sake. It's just a bit of fun.'

'But Lesley loves you. She wants to marry you.'

He rolls back over to his own seat and sighs. 'Lesley knows the score. I'm not into going steady. I explained all that to her the night she came up to the Tropicana.'

'What are you on about? When?'

'A couple of months ago. Not long after I met youse.'

'Oh. She never told me.' I'm thinking she must have gone back again with Sandra or something. But why didn't she tell me?

'She didn't want any of youse to know about it. She had a bad experience that night.'

'What happened?'

'The mad wee bitch hitched up on her own. She got a lift with some randy oul farmer and the dirty bastard tried to make a pass at her. She was in an awful state about it.'

Stop it, I tell myself. Stop thinking the worst.

'It took me the rest of the night to calm her down. She was dead lucky to get away.'

'How *did* she get away?'

'She told him she had two brothers in the IRA. Crazy bitch. She was chancing her arm there. If he'd been a loyalist, he'd have raped her and then he'd have killed her. And I told her that too.'

'So, he just let her go?' I ask, staring out into the mizzle.

'Aye. He opened the car door and kicked her out.'

'Where did *you* meet up with her?'

'Inside the disco. She was standing by a pillar looking out for me. I wouldn't mind, but I wouldn't have been there at all that night only it was my friend's twenty-first. The minute she saw me she burst into tears. She wanted to leave straight away, so we did. The poor girl was shaking.'

'What was she wearing?' I ask, taking off my cardigan.

'What do you mean, what was she wearing? What's that got to do with the price of butter?'

'Just tell me what she was wearing.'

'I can't remember.'

'Try.'

'But why?'

'Just do.'

'A denim mini, I think. Yeah, a wee slip of a thing. How could I forget? It barely covered her backside.'

'Like this,' I say, pulling my skirt up to my thighs.

'Aye,' he says, leaning over and whispering into my ear. 'Only not as sexy.'

'What did youse do all night?'

'I won't tell you,' he says, putting back the seat. 'I'll show you.'

11 *November 1999 (5.30 a.m.)*

It's pitch black outside, and eerily quiet. I've just smoked my first cigarette of the day, despite the promise I made to myself last night that I wouldn't smoke until after breakfast this morning. I've been bursting for one since I woke up nearly an hour ago. I'm more addicted now than I was eighteen years ago. In the last couple of days I've gone through sixty, and that was taking it easy. How desperate is that? I don't want to get cancer. When I die, I want to go out like a light, like my mother. According to my father, all she had time to say was, 'Tell Frances I forgive her.' I wish she hadn't bothered. I didn't want her forgiveness. The cheek of her to assume that I did. Why couldn't she have done the decent thing and told my father that she loved him, or that she was sorry for trampling his pride into the ground again and again, until the poor man gave up on his dignity? Something like that would have been more in her line.

My mother's death

It's a beautiful summer's morning. I'm up earlier than usual; I've a lot to do. The principal of the school has asked me to call at the office to help him sort out a few things before the school reopens in a few days. It's something we do every year. As I stand at the kitchen window sipping my tea, I watch my father out in the greenhouse checking his lettuces and tomatoes. Something about his demeanour makes me think that he has a lifetime of regret weighing him down. I can't help but pity him. Before I leave the house, I go out to ask him if he needs any errands done. I would be stopping off in town on my way home.

'No thanks,' he says, his back to me, 'but maybe you'd look in on your mother before you leave. She's not feeling the best.'

'After the way she spoke to me last night! Forget it.'

'All she asked of you was that you be here for your tea whenever Father Vincent comes over. Where's the harm in that?'

'Why did she ask, if she wasn't prepared to take no for an answer without insulting me left, right and centre? Why not just order me about like she used to do when I was a child?'

'More to the point,' he says, turning to me, 'why not say *yes* once in a while? Why do you make a song and dance about everything you're asked to do?'

'I don't.'

'You do.'

'Why do you always take her side? How come you never see my point of view?'

He picks up his can and starts watering the tomatoes. His eyes look weary. 'I do . . . at times, but it's hard. You make no effort whatsoever to get on with your mother. As a matter of fact, you seem to do everything you can to pull against her.'

'Because she's a bloody dictator and I've no intention of being her puppet any longer.'

'Arragh, you're living in the past, Frances. She's not trying to run your life for you. She asked you to tea, that's all. It was a simple request.'

'I'm always the one to blame,' I say, opening the greenhouse door. 'All this misery – it's down to me.'

'Frances,' he sighs. 'Frances, wait a minute. Frances . . .'

*

Nuddy Neary is standing just beyond the chapel gates. He doesn't even bother sticking out his thumb any more. Everyone knows that when he stands there with a gormless grin on his face, he's looking for a lift into town. I hate having him in the car – he gets on my wick – but if I don't stop, I'll be the talk of the village.

'Good lassie yourself,' he says, getting into the passenger seat. 'You're early on the go this morning.'

'Mmm.'

'A spot of shopping, I suppose.'

'No.'

'Or is it retail therapy they call it nowadays?'

Give me strength, I think, turning on the radio.

'You're looking well anyway.'

'Thanks.'

'So likely you're not on your way to the doctor's.'

'No, Nuddy. I'm a hundred per cent, thank God.'

'And it's a bit early in the day to be *doing* lunch.' He laughs with a snort. 'Have you heard that one?'

'What?'

'*Doing* lunch,' he chuckles. 'Doesn't it sound odious stupid?'

'It does. And no, I'm not doing lunch.'

'Are you visiting someone in the hospital?'

'No. Where do you want dropping off yourself?'

'Ah, don't worry about me. You can drop me off wherever you're parking.'

'I'm going to the school. That's the far side of town.'

'Are you not a few days early?'

'If you must know, I've a couple of jobs to get sorted before we reopen.'

'Oh,' he says, 'I never thought of that.'

'Well, there you are,' I say, hoping that now he's managed

to drag the information he wanted out of me, he'll shut his trap.

'Have you much to do?'

'Enough,' I say, turning up the volume.

'Like what?' he asks, raising his voice.

'Just bits and pieces,' I snap.

When he keeps his mouth shut for a mile or so, I'm pretty sure he's taken the hint.

'Will you be cleaning blackboards and battering the dusters off the walls?'

'I don't have a blackboard or a duster in my office.'

'Right enough, you wouldn't. I suppose you have a type-writer.'

'No. A computer.'

'A computer! Oh, I say. Very cutting-edge altogether.'

By the time he gets out of the car, I'm ready to scream.

'I'll see you so,' he says, closing the car door.

'If I ever see you again,' I say to myself as I watch him plod off, 'it'll be too bloody soon.'

As it turns out, it's the following night at my mother's wake. There must be a hundred people in the house at any given time. There's a constant queue on the stairs leading to her bedroom where she lies as stony-faced in death as she was in life. My father is sitting by the bed shaking hands with everyone who enters the room. Nancy has taken over the kitchen and is keeping the tea flowing all night. I can't sit down, so I mooch around from one room to another, picking up empty teacups and listening. Everyone is in shock.

'I was only talking to her the other morning.'

'She was the picture of health the last time I saw her.'

'Isn't the heart a fickle apparatus too, the way it can stop on you just like that.'

'And Joe says she didn't have any problems with blood pressure and that her last blood test showed that her cholesterol was low.'

'He's in an awful bad way, God bless him.'

'What exactly happened anyway?'

'She complained to Joe yesterday morning about feeling weak, so he told her to have a rest and stay in bed. Around one o'clock, she said she was feeling a bit better and asked him to bring her up a cup of tea. He was standing by the cooker waiting for the kettle to boil when, next thing, he heard an unmerciful thud. She'd collapsed on the bedroom floor.'

'Isn't that shockin'?'

'Ah now.'

I don't feel comfortable when they come up to me and shake my hand. I've no right to accept their sympathy, because I don't feel sad. I feel numb.

To escape the unwanted attention, I slip out to the back garden for a breath of air and a bit of peace. I sit down on the grass behind the shed where no one can see me. Nuddy and one of the postmen my father worked with before he retired come out for a cigarette. Nancy won't let anyone smoke inside the house. Unaware of my presence, the two men start chatting.

'Are you a relative?' Nuddy asks.

'No, indeed I'm not. I'm a friend of Joe's.'

'You're from about so, are you?'

'I am. Castleowen.'

'Oh aye.'

'I worked with Joe on the post for years.'

'Is that right? So you'd know him well then?'

'Oh I do, and a nicer fella you wouldn't meet.'

'You're right there. He is, he is,' Nuddy says with certitude. 'He's sound as a pound.'

'He's a broken man tonight.'

'Aye, the poor unfortunate,' Nuddy sighs. 'Did you know herself at all?'

'Not really, no. I might have met her once or twice, but I was never really talking to her.'

'Oh, indeed you weren't. She didn't talk to too many, the same one.'

'It was like that, was it?'

'I suppose I shouldn't speak ill of the dead, but I have to say: I was never that gone on the woman.'

'I heard she was a bit stand-offish all right.'

'A bit, me bollocks. Talk about tuppence-halfpenny looking down on tuppence.'

You're not as thick as you look, Nuddy, I think, as I twirl a blade of grass around my finger.

Gone on her or not, Nuddy attends her funeral along with half the parish. Father Vincent concelebrates the Mass with the parish priest, and Nancy reads the first and second readings, as well as the responsorial psalm, because I've refused to do either and my father isn't up to it. People remark that I'm a tower of strength and that it's a blessing for my father that I'm still living at home, because otherwise he'd be lost.

'Isn't she marvellous,' Mrs Scully says about me to Nancy, 'the way she's holding it all together for her father?'

'I don't think it has quite sunk in yet, has it, Frances?' Nancy says, rubbing the top of my arm.

*

Later that night, when my father and I are alone in the house, he starts talking about the funeral, how proud my mother would have been at the turnout.

'You were well represented too,' he says, stirring his tea.

'What?'

'All them teachers you work with – it was nice of them to show up.'

'They didn't go for *my* sake.'

'What do you mean? They hardly went for mine, did they? Sure, I don't know any of them.'

'They went for themselves.'

'What's wrong with you, Frances? Why do you talk like that? Can you not show a bit of gratitude to anyone for anything any more?'

'Why do I always have to be the grateful one? They were there out of duty, Daddy, not out of concern for me.'

'Lord God,' he says, looking up at the ceiling, 'you have some awful funny notions, wherever you get them.'

Not another word passes between us as we nurse our half-drunk cups of tea. I don't feel like finishing mine. All I want to do is lie down and sleep. I'm jaded. But I can't get up and walk away from my father. He looks so lonely.

Closing my eyes, I rest my head in my hands. She's gone, I think, remembering how as a child I used to dream about what my life would be like without her. Night after night, I'd lie in bed, imagining how that day at the *Feis* would have turned out if I hadn't had a mother. I pictured myself on the stage doing the reel in Lesley's red dance costume. Daddy is smiling up at me from the crowd. Afterwards, when I'm awarded the gold medal, Lesley skips across the stage and hugs me. She's wearing her silver medal on a green ribbon, like a necklace. She doesn't mind being second best. Daddy says I can invite her round for tea. Afterwards, we spend the evening playing – making a den in my bedroom, chasing each other up and down the stairs in a game of tag, sliding down the banister, jumping in puddles – all the things my mother forbade me to do.

My young head prayed that she'd die. My older head is glad that she has. The only catch is, I can't taste the freedom I've been longing for since I was eight years old. It's no longer there for the taking, because the wedge my mother so artfully lodged between my father and me still lingers – in the silence that surrounds us, in the lack of mutual understanding, in the resentment I feel towards him for grieving for her and in the resentment he feels towards me for not.

'I'm going to get it hard to climb the stairs tonight,' he says, pulling himself out of the chair as if his back was made of cement.

After he leaves the room, I break down in tears, because I know now that whatever my father and I had all those years ago is gone. And it's never coming back.

'You might forgive me,' I weep, picking up my mother's photo from the top of the dresser, 'but I will never forgive you. Never.'

11 November 1999 (midnight)

The only forgiveness I've ever wanted is Lesley's. That's why I turned up at the school reunion a few months ago, to see if she had forgiven, or could forgive me.

The reunion

'Lesley's in Australia,' Orla says, when I run into her in the lobby of the hotel. She's the only one who stops to chat with me. 'She married an Australian guy, Craig, two years ago.'

'Good for her.' I hope she doesn't notice the effort in my smile.

'She landed on her feet there: her hubby's loaded; owns a couple of restaurants.'

'Very nice.'

'Simon is working for him. Imagine; he's eighteen now.'

How could I forget?

'When did you last see them?'

'Four years ago in Manchester. It was myself and Dave's fifth wedding anniversary. We flew up from London and stayed with them for a weekend. You should've seen Simon; drop dead gorgeous – a dead ringer for his daddy.'

'And what about Lesley?'

'She looked a million, the bitch,' she says. 'I swear, only she had started going out with Craig, my Dave would have ended up dumping me and proposing to her. It was his first time to meet her. He thought she was a howl.'

'I'd say so. Does she ever come home?'

'Nah! Not since her mum died. Anyway, what's the crack with you?'

'Oh, I'm fine.'

'What are you at these days?'

'I'm working here in town.'

'Doing what?'

'School secretary.'

'And?'

'And what?'

'What's the story?'

'How do you mean?'

'Any man? Any kids? Where are you living?'

'No man, no kids. And I'm living at home.'

'I see,' she says, shifting from foot to foot and looking round her. 'Oh look, there's Jackie. I'd better go and say hello. Might see you later though, right?'

'Right.'

I don't bother going in for the meal. I'm too upset. It's not that I don't wish Lesley well – of course I do – but I had my heart set on seeing her again and rekindling our friendship. I hoped that perhaps she might have had similar feelings about meeting me again.

Why hadn't I listened to my father? – reunions were not for the likes of me.

'You'll find,' he said, 'that the only ones who'll show up will be them that's landed on their feet, careerwise . . . moneywise. People – they only parade success.'

'Don't worry,' I told him. 'Failure will stay at home where failure belongs.'

But as the days passed and the reunion date approached, the questions that had been prodding me from the day I'd received the invitation started doing hornpipes in my head. What if Lesley turned up? What if she was hoping to see me? What if she was willing to forgive? Looking for forgiveness? What if I found the courage to tell her the truth? What then? What had I left to lose?

15 November 1999 (evening)

Today I received my first letter since my arrival here – from Father Vincent no less. I couldn't stop laughing at first, but then I cried.

Dear Frances,

I hope this letter finds you in good health, physically, mentally, and, most importantly, spiritually. I am writing to you about a matter that will hopefully assist you in sorting out your future, as I am sure, at times, it may look bleak.

While I was visiting Nancy in Crosslea last week, I dropped in to see your poor father, who, I must tell you, is a much-troubled man. He and I spoke at length about your situation and of the possibility that you'll be discharged from the hospital either before Christmas or early in the New Year. Of course, we don't know what plans you have, if any, but I would imagine that returning to Crosslea would be not only unwise but also very difficult for you, in light of what's happened. Given the utmost respect I have, both for your father and your mother (RIP), I have gone to great lengths to find you a new home and job. A very dear friend of mine, Fr O'Malley, who is a parish priest in Bloody Foreland, happens to be looking for a live-in housekeeper, as Miss McDonnell, his current housekeeper, is retiring next month. I have told him about your background and he is willing, as a special favour to my good self, to hold the vacancy open for you until you are discharged. I don't know if you have ever been, but I have visited the area myself many times and I can assure you that Bloody Foreland is not only very picturesque but also home to the country's most welcoming people. It has the added advantage, of course, of being a long way

from Crosslea and therefore no one would know who you are. And
wouldn't that be a blessing?

   There would be no problem, whatsoever, if your father wanted
to visit you at the house, and even stay a night or two. Nancy
thinks that it's an ideal solution and has passed the details of this
offer on to your father, who, she tells me, is very anxious that you
accept it.

   I would ask you to let me know if you're interested as soon
as possible, as Father O'Malley has been good enough to post-
pone advertising the job until I get back to him with your
reply.

   Until I hear from you, take care of yourself and God Bless.
   Yours sincerely
   Fr Vincent

For thou, Lord, art good, and ready to forgive; and plenteous
in mercy unto all them that call upon thee. Psalms 86:5

19 November 1999 (afternoon)

I've written a letter. Sorry, letters. It's my fifth attempt. The
first one was to Father Vincent, telling him to stick his job
offer, to keep his nose out of my business and, while he was
at it, to tell my father to do his own dirty work in future. I
tore that one up. Why shoot the messenger? The second had
the same message, only I addressed it to my father. That's in
the bin too. The third was a short note to Father Vincent
formally declining the offer. Also binned. The fourth was an
angry letter to my father, asking him who the hell he thought
he was trying to run my life for me, and that he needn't worry
his cowardly head about me embarrassing him any more,

because I've no intention of ever living with him again. I haven't torn that one up yet. Here's the last one.

Dear Daddy,

I haven't yet thought about what I'm going to do when I leave here. I've been much too busy trying to figure out how I got here in the first place. Please let Father Vincent know that I won't be accepting the offer. Whatever I decide to do, I've no intention of hiding away for the rest of my life. I want to move forwards, not backwards, and I thought that, seeing as you're so concerned about my future, maybe you could help me to move on by answering a few questions for me.

All my life, I've been trying to figure out why we were such an unhappy family. Looking back on my childhood, which I've been doing quite a lot this past couple of months, I struggle to remember any happy times, and the few good memories I do have all occurred before Aunty Lily died. How come? What happened in the days and weeks after Aunty Lily's death that caused my mother to stop loving us? And Aunty Lily. Had it something to do with that row ye had with Xavier? Or that strange man who turned up at the funeral? I could never figure out why she was so unhappy and so angry. Somehow, I felt that it had something to do with me, but how could it have? I was just a kid. Why did you allow her to treat us the way she did? I don't blame you, Daddy. At this stage, I just what to know the truth. You might think it's none of my business, but it is, because it affected me as much, if not more, than it affected you. I have the right to know why my mother stopped loving me.

And then there's the issue of the marriage cert. I know I was born three months after your wedding. What I can't figure out is why you won't level with me after all these years. I understand that you don't want to let Mammy down by admitting she had sex

*before marriage, but the evidence is there that she did, either with
you or with someone else, even if it happened without her consent.
Did it?*

*These are the questions that have been haunting me for several
weeks, Daddy, so I hope you find the courage to be honest with
me. And I hope you're well.*

Frances

I won't post it for a couple of days.

21 November 1999 (evening)

I'm wondering if I should write to Lesley, now that I'm in a
letter-writing mood. Would it do any good? What would she
think, hearing from me after all these years? Would she really
want to know what has happened to me over the past few
months? Would she care? She would have, once upon a time.
She'd have loved the drama of it. She'd have been right there
in that courtroom. In the front row.

But people change, move on; well, most people that is.
Obviously she has. I wonder what her life is like – if she's
happy, if she ever thinks about me, and if she does, is she still
angry?

Falling out with Lesley

I'm in an awful state. I can't believe what I've done. The sex
was supposed to make me feel better, but it hasn't. It was
rushed, rough and vulgar. He never looked at me; he just
squeezed me, while I looked out over his shoulder at the rain

and cried. He didn't even notice. I don't ever want to see him again.

I've tons of homework, but I can't do a stroke, not until I've rung Lesley. She'll be waiting for my call. First, I need to calm down. I feel so emotional. I'm gutted over the way she dumped me in Enniskillen and then lied to me about it. Is that all she thinks of me – her best friend? I'm so angry with her, and Johnny, and myself, for that matter, because I've decided not to confront her about her deception. Instead, I'm going to forgive her: I love her too much not to. It's better to forget what I've heard and to carry on as usual than to risk falling out with her. Besides, I've already had my revenge, horrible as it was.

Several times I go down to the hall and pick up the receiver, but as soon as I start dialling, I panic and hang up. What if she's already been talking to Jackie or Orla? I'm not convinced they believed my story. They said they did, but their expressions didn't back up their words. They kept giving each other doubtful looks. On second thoughts, maybe I should tell Lesley the truth. I don't need to say that we went all the way, just that we had a kiss. If I explain how hurt I felt over her lying to me, she's bound to understand, isn't she? After all, we've both made mistakes. We both need to forgive and to be forgiven.

Just as I'm about to pick up the phone again, it rings.

'Hello.'

'Hiya.'

'Lesley!' Thank God she sounds cheerful. 'I was just about to ring you.'

'The gingerbread man beat you to it.'

'You've been talking to him?'

'Yeah, for a whole hour. He's coming down to see me on Friday night.'

Jesus! So much for him wanting me to be his girlfriend. Not that I want to be, but God, what's he up to now?

'I can't fucking wait,' she says. 'I feel like Rapunzel stuck inside this house for the past week. It's doing my head in. Bad as school is, this kip's way worse.'

'So you're still as mad about him as ever then?'

'Madder.'

'Oh.' I know now that if I tell her the truth, our friendship is over.

As she babbles on about what he said to her and what she said to him, it becomes apparent that he hasn't mentioned anything about me being in the van with him. He and I hadn't discussed what excuse I'd come up with for disappearing from the school for over an hour. As soon as the sex was over for him, he drove me back in silence as far as the end of the avenue, where he gave me a quick peck on the cheek and said he'd see me the following Wednesday. Luckily, my biology teacher was doing an experiment and had not noticed my absence.

'So, you weren't talking to Jackie or Orla this evening?'

'No,' she says. 'Not yet. But I'm expecting Jackie any minute. She met Keith down the town earlier on and told him she'd be calling over to see me.'

I have to tell her what I told the girls quickly before Jackie gets to her house to fill her in.

'Lesley, Johnny's really cracked about you.' I can hear the quiver in my voice.

'Do you really think so?'

'I know so. He told me.'

She screams down the phone. 'Yes! Tell me more.'

'I was nearly caught talking to him.'

'By who?'

'Sister Bernadine.'

'Ah, I wouldn't worry about *her*. She's seen me there with him loads of times. Sure, you know yourself, the daft oul bat hasn't a clue who's who.'

'She might be a bit doddery, but she's no fool. She must have known there was something going on when she complained to PMT about all the girls hanging around the bread van. Anyway, I had to get into the van to dodge her.'

'Why didn't you just run off like we usually do?'

'Cos I still had the note in my pocket, so I hopped into the passenger seat and ducked.'

She starts to laugh. 'Oh, you're a mad bitch, fair dues to you.'

'It wasn't fucking funny. I waited ages for her to go back into the ref so that I could get out, but she didn't. I'm telling you, she definitely suspected something, because she hung around outside waiting for Johnny to leave and I couldn't budge. I was trapped.'

'Ya poor eejit, ya.'

'In the end, Johnny had to drive off with me still in the van.'

'Go way.'

'Honest to God. I never felt as sick in my life. I thought, this is it, I'm going to be expelled and all because of Lesley Kelly and her mental love life.'

'Oh, sorry.' She's still giggling.

'It's all right.' I'm glad now I opted for the lie.

'So what happened then?'

'We parked out the road, had a couple of smokes and talked about you.'

'What did he say?'

'That he loved you.' Well, it is what she wants to hear. And with any luck, it might turn her off him. Any boyfriend who'd been foolish enough to mention the 'L' word to Lesley ended up getting the heave-ho within a week. 'I would've got out at the end of the avenue only he kept going on about you and asking me tons of questions. I'm telling you, he has it bad.'

'Do you really think so?'

'Definitely.'

'Then why does he act so bloody cool? I mean, even on the phone this evening, I practically had to beg the bollocks to meet me on Friday night. I just don't know what to make of him.'

'He's trying to keep you keen.'

'Are you serious?'

'Yeah. He reckons if he was all over you, you'd get bored.'

'That's the crafty oul fecker. He's playing games with me.'

'He's right though, isn't he? If he was smothering you with attention, you'd have dumped him long ago.'

'Johnny can give me as much attention as he likes. I'll never stop loving him.'

'You sound happy.'

'Happy! Cloud nine my arse, I'm on fucking Jupiter. I was beginning to think he was just using me.'

Shit! I've gone too far. I've built up her hopes, knowing that Johnny has every intention of letting her down. I didn't set out to hurt her, it's just . . .

'So youse didn't talk about anything else except me.'

'No, not a thing.'

'Lovely stuff! He really does have it bad so.'

'Don't tell him I told you what he said.'

'I won't.'

'In fact, as far as you're concerned, I just gave him the note and left.'

'OK. Oh, there's the doorbell now. It's probably Jackie. Hang on a second.'

I hear her telling Jackie that I'm on the phone.

'I'd better go. Jackie's in a tizzy about something. I'll talk to you tomorrow and thanks; you're the fucking best.'

'You're welcome.'

'Oh, hang on a second, Frances. What was that, Jackie?'

I hear mumbling in the background.

'Jackie wants to know if you've looked in the mirror lately.'

'Looked in the mirror? Why? What's she on about?'

'She wants to know what you're on about,' she says to Jackie.

'Tell her she'll know when she looks in the mirror.'

'She says –'

'Yeah, I know. I heard her.'

'Well, when you find what you're looking for, let me know, won't you?'

'Yeah, OK. I'll talk to you later,' I say, a horrible sense of uneasiness sweeping over on mc.

Standing in front of the hall mirror, I take several deep breaths before slowly raising my eyes in dread. What? I can't see anything unusual. Fair enough, my hair is a bit of a mess, but then my hair is always like that – wild-looking. It's all the gel I use. What am I supposed to be looking for? Do I look like I've just lost my virginity? Do I look like a slut? A liar? What's she on about?

Back in my bedroom, I start imagining the conversation that is taking place between Lesley and Jackie. It switches from talking about the good friend I am one minute, to calling me a scheming bitch the next. In fact, under the circumstances, it wouldn't surprise me if they were planning on battering the crap out of me.

Stop panicking, I think, flicking through my Maths book. Why would they? They don't know what I've done. They couldn't possibly.

I muddle through my homework as best I can, but at the back of my mind the question is still niggling me – What am I supposed to see in the mirror?

Before I go to bed, I go into the bathroom to wash my hair. Filling the wash-hand basin with warm water, I take off my cardigan and turn down the collar of my uniform blouse. As I lower my head into the water, I catch a glimpse of myself in the mirror, and there it is – a dirty big love bite on the side of my neck. SHITE! How the hell had I missed it? I turn the collar back the way it had been just to see if it covers the bruise. It does, except when I turn my head to the right.

When my mother calls me for school the following morning, I'm already awake.

'I suppose you are a bit on the pale side,' she says when I tell her I have a woeful headache and cannot go to school.

I spend the next three days moping around the house in my dressing-gown and slippers. With all the hours I have to rack my brains, I cannot think of a way out of the mess I'm in. By Sunday afternoon, I haven't made or received any phone calls. My mother says that if I'm not fit for school the following morning, I'll have to see the doctor, because three days is too long for anyone to have a headache. What am I going to do? I cannot face losing Lesley. Without her, my life is a joke. I should have rung her as soon as I saw the love bite and told her I'd had a snog with one of the boys from the village. Out of desperation, she might have believed me. But I was in that much of a heap at the time, I couldn't think clearly. She's bound to have come to the conclusion by now that I'm as guilty as sin.

'You didn't have any breakfast,' my mother says, nabbing me on my way out the door on Monday morning.

'I didn't feel like it.'

She's been watching me closely over the past few days. She knows there's something up.

As the bus pulls in at the school gates, I spot Lesley by the wall chatting with Jackie and Orla, and hiding a cigarette behind her back. As usual, they're waiting for me. I suppose that's a good sign. Still, it doesn't stop me from blushing profusely as I step off the bus and walk over to join them.

'Well, any crack?' Orla says.

'She's been sick in bed,' Lesley says. 'How the hell would she have any crack?' She rolls her beautiful eyes.

'Want a fag?' Jackie asks, holding out her packet of Major.

'Thanks.'

'How did your date go Friday night, Lesley?' It's the most natural question I can think of asking.

'It was all right,' she says, shrugging.

'Just all right?'

'Yeah. I'm getting a bit bored with him. I fancy someone else more.'

'You're joking. Who?' I can't believe it.

She smiles at me. 'That would be telling.'

'It's just because he said he loved you, isn't it?'

'You were the one who said that would put me off, remember? And you were right. It has. I can't abide that soppy oul shite.'

'But you said you loved him.'

'Not to his face I didn't. I wouldn't. I'm not that pathetic. Anyway, I was telling the girls yesterday: I'm gonna break it off with him on Wednesday.'

The girls start sniggering.

'What's so funny, youse two?' Lesley asks.

'You,' Orla says. 'You've more lovers than Elizabeth Taylor.'

'Huh! And so I should have: I'm much better-looking. Aren't I, Frances?'

'Yeah. I think so anyway.'

Jackie bursts out laughing.

'Jealousy will get you nowhere,' Lesley says, flinging her butt on to the wet grass. 'Come on, Frances. Thank God I've one true friend.'

I can't stop myself from smiling the whole way up the avenue. I'm thrilled that Lesley is over Johnny. At last, things will go back to the way they were between me and Lesley before he came along and turned her head. Now, she'll have more time for me. No one mentions anything about what I was supposed to be looking for in the mirror.

During our first class, Maths, Lesley passes a note over to me saying: *I missed you like crazy. XXX.*

Because of our giddiness in the past, we're not allowed to sit together. When I look over at her, she has her head down pretending to be looking at her Maths book, but she's peeping out from underneath her hands at me.

I missed you too. XXX. I scrawl at the bottom of her note and pass it back.

She winks over at me when she reads and starts writing again.

How much? she writes.

Tucks, I reply.

Good, cos you're the one I fancy more than GBM. I have to read it twice. Jesus, is she serious? I can feel the heat on my face. I look up at her again. There's a glint in her eye. It's impossible not to get carried away. The note is written on such a tiny scrap of paper, I have to tear a piece from the back of my copy.

QUIT MESSING!!!! I write.

I'm not messing, I swear.

I don't know what to think. I do love Lesley, but am I in love with her? Am I? I look across at her again. Yes. There's no doubt about it. I'm in love with her.

Good. I feel the same way. My heart is racing as I write it.

Tell me what you want to do to me. It's written on the bottom of the same piece of paper.

'What are you giggling at, Miss Fall?' the teacher says. 'Perhaps you'd like to share the joke with the rest of the class.'

'Nothing. Sorry, Miss.'

After a minute, when I haven't replied to Lesley's note, she starts making eyes at me and squiggling her pen a few inches above her book, indicating to me to reply to her last message. I nod towards the teacher, letting her know that she's keeping an eye on me. But Lesley doesn't give up. She wants an answer. 'Go on,' she mouths. The other girls are watching us. When the teacher turns to write an equation on the blackboard, I tear off another strip of paper from the back page of my copy.

I want to see you naked. I want to kiss your lips. XXX.

'This is the last one,' the girl beside me whispers when I fold the note and hand it to her to pass on.

I watch a beautiful smile spread across Lesley's face as she reads it.

After class, she comes over and sits on my desk. She leans across and cups her hands around my ear.

'See you later,' she whispers, and then, for a couple of seconds, holds my earlobe between her teeth, making my skin tingle with pleasure.

Before I get the chance to draw a reactional breath, she's down off the desk and flouncing across the classroom, picking up her Art books on her way out. Feeling flustered, I look around the classroom to see if any of the girls are watching me, but no one is. They're all busy chatting or rummaging through their schoolbags. Having different classes to attend, Lesley and I don't see each other again until lunchtime.

It's a cold, crispy January afternoon. The sky is still and pale.

'Will we go for a walk?' she says.

'Yeah.' I smile at her.

We're both wearing scarves and fingerless gloves. No jackets. We stroll down the tree-lined path towards the orchard, puffing condensation from our speechless mouths. There are still the remnants of autumn leaves on the ground. My heart is pounding and my lips have gone dry. Without saying a word, she slips her hand in mine. I gasp and look behind me.

'Relax, will you?' she says. 'No one is going to see us. It's always deserted down here in the winter.'

'OK,' I say, squeezing her hand gently. 'OK.'

'Where did you put the notes I wrote you?'

'Here.' I open my skirt pocket and take them out. 'You must have the others.'

'I tore them up and flushed them down the bog after Art class,' she says, taking the pieces of paper from me and burning them with her lighter. 'Always get rid of the evidence, that's what I say.'

'Yeah, I suppose. Can you imagine the gossip if anyone found out?'

'I couldn't give a fuck about gossip, could you?'

'No, but –'

'But nothing. You're ashamed of how you feel, aren't you?'

'No.'

'Yes you are. And you're ashamed of me,' she says, stomping on ahead of me.

I run to catch up with her. 'I'm not ashamed, Lesley,' I tell her, laying my hand on her shoulder.

She shrugs it off and turns to me with watery eyes. 'Really?'

'Really.'

Raising her face to the pale sky, she bites her lip and sighs. 'OK, I believe you.'

'It's just when you said about getting rid of the evidence, I thought *you* didn't want anyone to know.'

'I couldn't give a flying shite what other people think; I just didn't want to get you into trouble. I care about you.'

'I know. And I'm sorry if I offended you.'

'Mmm,' she says, looking at me with a playful grin. 'I suppose I'll forgive you.'

We stop at the orchard gate for a smoke.

'So what do we do now?' she says, looking into my eyes with an intensity I've never seen in her before. She tilts her head and starts playing with her hair.

'I . . . eh . . . I don't know,' I blurt.

Backing up against the orchard wall, she pulls off her scarf and opens the top two buttons of her blouse. 'Go on,' she says, closing her eyes, 'feel me.'

I reach over and skim my fingers across her glossed lips, down her chin and elongated neck, and into the softness of her bosom, hesitating when I get as far as her bra. My hand is trembling.

'What's wrong?' she asks, opening her eyes.

'Nothing.'

She leans towards me, almost touching my lips with hers. Her hair is tickling my cheeks. 'You want to kiss me, don't you?'

I nod and press my mouth against her parted lips.

'Sick bitch,' she screams, pulling back and slapping me hard across both cheeks.

'What . . . why . . . ?' I gulp, trying to steady myself and at the same time catch my breath, but she has already turned on her heels and is walking away. 'What did I do wrong?'

She ignores me, marching on indignantly with her nose in the air. I sit down on the grassy bank that surrounds the orchard wall, nursing my face in my hands.

'Come back,' I cry out helplessly, as she disappears round the corner. 'I'm sorry.'

With the end of my scarf, I mop up the tears that are streaming down my cheeks. It's not the pain that's making me cry, or even the humiliation I'm feeling – they will pass in time; it's the realization that Lesley and I are history. It's over. I'm sure of it. Hanging my head, I blubber my way through a string of Hail Marys, beseeching Her to soften Lesley's heart. For reinforcement, I pray to Aunty Lily, asking her to have a word in Mary's ear. They're the first prayers I've said in over a year. Then, with a heavy heart, I pick myself up and walk back down the path through a confetti of snowflakes.

I sit alone in the classroom until the bell rings. Dreading what Lesley might say to me in front of the others, I keep my head down as the other girls start drifting into the room in twos and threes. Someone passing behind me kicks the leg of my chair. I don't bother to react until she does it again, harder this time. When I look up, Jackie is leering down at me.

'Dirty lezzer,' she jeers. 'I always said you were a fucking weirdo.'

I have to swallow hard to stop the tears from flowing again. Our Religion teacher, Sister Helena, saves the moment by breezing in and telling everyone to sit down and be quiet.

'Where's Lesley?' she asks.

'At the principal's office,' Jackie says.

What's she doing there, I wonder.

Half-way through the class, someone knocks on the door. When the girl sitting nearest to it opens it, PMT breezes in past her and whispers something to Sister Helena.

'Jackie Doherty and Orla Corcoran,' PMT says, looking down at the girls. 'Could you both come to my office, please?'

They must have been caught smoking with Lesley is all I can think of.

A few minutes later, Jackie and Orla arrive back. Jackie walks straight to her desk. Orla goes up to Sister Helena and says something to her.

'Frances Fall,' Sister Helena says, 'Sister Marie-Therese would like to see you in her office.'

Orla smirks at me as I pass her on my way to the door. They must have squealed on me and said I was smoking too. My mother will have a fit when she hears about this. Outside PMT's office, Lesley is sitting on a chair with red, swollen eyes. My heart goes out to her.

'Are you OK?'

'Stay away from me,' she screeches.

PMT opens the door of the office and summons me in.

'Sit down.' Her tone is horribly grave.

I sit on my hands to hide the nicotine stains on my fingers.

'I've had a complaint from Lesley that you made inappropriate advances towards her today during the lunch break.'

For a few seconds, I'm not able to speak.

'Have you anything to say?'

'No, Sister. I mean yes, Sister. I didn't do anything.'

'Where did you go at lunchtime?'

'For a walk, Sister, and then I came back to the classroom.'

'Where did you go for the walk?'

'Down towards the orchard.'

'With whom?'

'Lesley, Sister.'

'And what happened during this walk?'

'Nothing.'

'Nothing!'

'We just talked.'

'Did you walk back together?'

'No, Sister.'

'Why not?'

'I don't know. She just ran off on me.'

'So you were walking down the path and all of a sudden she ran away from you?'

'We went as far as the orchard and we were talking and then she ran off. I don't know why, honest.'

'How would you describe your relationship with Lesley, Frances?'

'We're friends.'

'Best friends?'

'Yes.'

'So why would your best friend suddenly run away from you for no good reason?'

'I told you, Sister, I don't know.'

'You don't know! I must say, I find that rather hard to

believe.' Clearing her throat, she leans across the desk, psyching me out with an impatient stare. 'Did you at any stage instigate any physical contact with Lesley during this walk?'

'No.'

'You never touched?' Her eyes broaden.

'No. Yes. We held hands, but that's all.'

'Are you sure about that?'

'Yes, Sister.'

'How would you describe your feelings for Lesley?'

'As I said, she's my best friend. I care about her.'

'Do you have a crush on her?'

'Of course not.'

'I'll ask you again, Frances. Do you have a crush on her?'

'No, Sister.'

She sits back, opens the top drawer of her desk, takes out a piece of paper and puts it down in front of me.

'Is that your handwriting?'

I want to see you naked. I want to kiss your lips. XXX.

My God!

'I said, is that your handwriting?'

'I-eh-I . . .'

'I'll ask you one more time,' she says, hammering the note with an accusatory finger: 'Is that your handwriting?'

'Yes, Sister.' I start to weep.

'Did you try to kiss Lesley while ye were out walking at lunchtime?'

'No, Sister.' I look up at her, willing her to believe me.

'Frances, stop lying, for heaven's sake.'

'But I didn't.'

'You were seen. Jackie and Orla were walking a short distance behind you. They saw you.'

'But she went to kiss me first.'

'That's not what they saw, Frances.'

'But –'

'Stop it, will you?' she snaps.

Someone starts talking outside in the corridor and then there's a knock on the door. She walks out from behind her desk to answer it.

'Thanks for coming, Missus Kelly,' she says, going out to talk to Lesley's mother.

All I manage to pick up from their conversation is that Lesley is taking the rest of the day off. When she comes back into the office, PMT tells me that I must learn to control these urges I'm having.

'They're not natural,' she says; 'they're sinful.'

She's going to transfer me from all the classes I share with Lesley. I must keep my distance from her and never engage her in conversation again. If I try to communicate with her by any means, I'll be suspended.

'Do I make myself crystal clear, Frances?'

'Yes, Sister.'

25 November 1999 (morning)

I've just posted the letter to my father. I swing from feeling angry with him one day to feeling sorry for him the next. Today I just miss him.

27 November 1999 (afternoon)

My father will have received his post by now. Whatever he decides to do, he won't make a spur of the moment decision. He likes to weigh things up, consider the consequences. My mother will be his biggest deterrent. He won't want to let her down; the way I let her down.

In the family way

The truth about what happened between myself and Lesley doesn't stand a chance. Everyone wants to hear *her* version of events. The morning after, I watch them flock around her at the school gates, in the cloakroom, in the mall. Even girls she wouldn't normally bid the time of day to are hovering around her with timid faces, twiddling their earrings and waiting for her to acknowledge their presence, which she does because she wants to turn everyone against me. They pay for her attention with their loyalty. Afterwards, I hear two of them talking in the toilets as if they're her long-lost friends.

'Did you hear about poor Lesley?'

'Yeah, I was chatting to her this morning. She told me the whole story.'

'I've just been talking to her myself. She's in bits over it.'

'Would you blame her? Imagine finding out that your best friend was trying to get into your knickers. Jaysus, I'd run a mile.'

'She says she still can't believe it, that she never suspected a thing, but that now, looking back on it, she should have seen it coming.'

'Sure, it's not her fault. She shouldn't be blaming herself, poor thing.'

'I know; that's what I said to her.'

'And what did she say?'

'She thanked me; told me I made her feel a whole lot better.'

'Ah, she's really nice, isn't she?'

'Yeah, she's dead on.'

'I'll tell you one thing: I'll be keeping my distance from Frances Fall. Even the thought of her gives me the creeps.'

I swallow the truth and the sadness.

During class I avoid eye contact with my classmates in case any of them gets the wrong idea. I don't want to be caught looking at their legs or boobs so, as far as I can, I keep my nose in my books.

On the Wednesday afternoon, I find a mousetrap in my schoolbag. Later, on the school bus, I put my hand in my gabardine pocket and pull out a page torn from a porn magazine of two naked women kissing. During Maths class, the next day, I come across a note between the pages of my textbook. It's done out in letters cut from a newspaper, reading *Watch your back*. As I'm walking down the avenue on Friday, a girl from second year, whom I know to be a neighbour of Lesley's, catches up with me and asks me if I realize that the short for Frances is Fanny. When I tell her to get stuffed, she skips away laughing. Even though I manage not to cry, inside I'm crumbling.

It's not enough for my mother that I'm staying in over the weekend, and apparently studying; she wants to know why. Or, more to the point, why now.

'You've taken a fierce sudden interest in your schoolbooks

this past couple of weeks,' she says, putting my dinner on the table. 'Though it's a bit late in the day, as far as I'm concerned.'

'Aye, well, better late than never,' my father says, winking at me. 'It's good to see you knuckling down.'

'Thanks, Daddy.'

'So, why the sudden change of heart?' my mother asks, managing to pour her gravy without taking her eye off me.

'I don't want to fail, do I?'

'Mmm.' She swallows a mouthful of food and pats both sides of her mouth with her napkin. 'So, it's nothing to do with the fact that the phone hasn't rung once for you in nearly two weeks?'

'No!'

'There's no need to snap.'

'I didn't.'

'Yes you did, didn't she, Joe?'

'Ah, I'm sure she didn't mean —'

'It's OK, Daddy, I know she's only trying to rise me.'

'By asking you a simple question,' my mother sneers. 'It doesn't take much so, unless of course I've hit a nerve.'

'Just leave me alone, will you?'

As I push away my plate, my knife and fork slip off the table, clattering on the tiled floor. When I bend down to pick them up, I'm tempted to dig the fork into my mother's leg. Straightening up, I bang my head on the table.

'Fuck it,' I shout, flinging the cutlery into the sink.

'Oh, that's lovely language,' my mother says as I storm out the door.

In the privacy of my bedroom, I call her every crude name I can think of, before kneeling down and praying for her death.

As soon as I wake up on the Monday morning, I need to

dash to the loo. I've been having bouts of diarrhoea for several days now and my body feels drained. I don't know how I'm going to face another day at school.

On the school bus, I end up sitting beside the wildest of the lads from the village. When he asks me if the rumour is true about me being a lesbian, I tell him it's not.

'Prove it,' he says, grabbing my hand and putting it on his crotch.

'Would you ever fuck off,' I shout, pulling back my hand.

'If you don't like that,' he says, 'you are a lezzie.'

'Shag off, you bollocks.'

'Jaysus, I'd give anything to see two girls snogging. I'm getting a fucking horn just thinking about it.'

Everyone starts laughing. Don't cry, I think, don't cry, don't cry, don't cry, don't cry. I tell myself that they're laughing at him, and not me. He's the joke, he's the fool. Go away, tears. I start to count the oncoming cars: one, two, three, four – they're still laughing – five, six – how could you do this to me, Lesley? – seven, eight – stop thinking about her – nine, ten, eleven – they've stopped.

When I don't see Lesley, Jackie or Orla hanging around the school gates, I assume that the town bus is running late and I hurry up the avenue alone, hoping to be away from the cloakroom before they get there.

'Lock up your cheese sandwiches, girls,' Jackie shouts as I walk in the door. 'There's a mangy mouse on the loose.'

'Ah Jaysus,' some girl yelps, climbing up on to a bench.

'You mean, lock up your fannies,' Lesley roars.

Even the first years are sniggering into their hands.

'Don't cry, Frances,' Jackie says, slapping my back, 'we're only slagging you.'

Everyone I meet as I walk down the corridor and up the

stairs to my new classroom is looking at me and giggling. I can't take much more. On my way to the science lab after the eleven o'clock break, someone touches my sleeve. When I look round, the third-year girl whom Lesley had teased a few weeks earlier about her prominent teeth hands me a piece of paper.

'This was stuck to your back,' she says. 'That's what they're all laughing at.'

It reads: FANNY FALL FANCIES YOU ALL *(Told you to watch your back)*

I look at the girl through glazed eyes. 'It's not true what they're saying about me, you know.'

'I know.'

'Thanks.'

She smiles and walks away.

On the Friday afternoon, the word spreads like wildfire: Lesley has been expelled. She was standing at the lectern in the convent chapel giving a sacrilegious sermon to a handful of naive first years who were trying to fit in the Stations of the Cross during their break, a chalice full of wine in one hand, a lit fag in the other. Jackie and Orla were trying to coax her away when PMT came flapping up the centre aisle in a rage.

I should be relieved, but I'm not. I'm heartbroken.

Living without Lesley is like living without a cause. Everything seems pointless. I fall asleep crying and wake up in a black hole. I skip breakfast, feed my lunch to the birds and struggle over a bowl of soup at dinnertime. Nancy says I look like the divil and that maybe a good tonic would help. She knows a pharmacist who makes up his own special concoction. Anyone who's taken it swears by it. She brings it round the following day. Before I get the spoon to my mouth, I start gagging, spilling the medicine all over the floor.

'This time, just hold your nose and knock it back,' Nancy says, pouring another spoonful. 'It'll do you a power of good.'

It feels like warm blood trickling down my throat. I gag again, but manage to keep it down.

A few weeks later, my mother arrives home after attending evening Mass with Nancy in Castleowen cathedral. My father and I are watching *The Good Life*.

'I was talking to Kitty Devine after Mass,' she says, pulling off her gloves and warming her hands at the fire. 'Nancy gave her a lift home.'

Kitty is the wife of Seamie Devine, a retired postman. They live in the same estate as Lesley.

'How's Seamie keeping?' my father says.

'No complaints, she says. He's doing a bit of taxiing at the weekends.'

'Ah, good man, Seamie. And how's Kitty herself?'

'Full of news, as it happens.'

'Aye, typical. As Seamie used to say when he'd spin a yarn in the office: that's the gossip according to Kitty.'

'Turn that down, Frances,' my mother says, nodding at the TV.

I know rightly what's coming next.

'You never told us your friend Lesley got expelled.'

'Mmm.' I keep my eye on the screen.

'My God,' my father says. 'She didn't, did she?'

'Yeah,' I say flatly.

'Why?'

'For smoking in the chapel and drinking altar wine, the

brazen so and so,' my mother tells him. 'I always said that one was a rare piece of work.'

'Is that right, Frances?'

'Yeah.'

'God, that's a terra. Such a thing to do! Has she no respect at all at all?'

'Respect!' my mother says, throwing her eyes to heaven. 'Obviously not, because she's expecting as well.'

The following Wednesday, I hang around the courtyard waiting for Johnny. I need to know what's going on: if he's been talking to her, if it's his, if he knows, whether or not they're still together, if she's OK. I need something, any little scrap of news. I feel cut off. I want to be her friend again. She needs me.

Around one o'clock, I hear the van coming and my heart starts galloping. I haven't seen him since the day we had sex. What if he ignores me or tells me to get lost? What if he starts flirting with me again? I look the other way as he drives past me and pulls up by the refectory door. Taking a deep breath, I start walking towards the van. I need to talk to him before Sister Bernadine comes on the scene and starts getting suspicious. The driver's door swings open and a dark-haired, moustached man in his forties jumps out.

'Howaya?'

'Hello,' I say, stalling for a moment, then walking on, unsure of what I should do next.

I hear the back door swing open. Feck it, I think, I'll just have to find out what I can from this man.

'Excuse me,' I say, turning to face him.

'Yes, love?'

'Is Johnny off today?'

'He is, and every other day from now on. He quit a fortnight ago.'

'Oh.'

'You didn't know?'

'No.'

'A friend of yours, is he?'

'Not really. More a friend of a friend.'

'Not that wee lassie he got pregnant?'

'Yeah.'

'Between you and me, love, I think she's better off without him. He's a bit of wanderer, the same boy.'

'So he knows about my friend being . . . you know.'

'He should do. Her brothers got in touch with the boss man, looking for his address. They were none too happy about not getting it; they wanted to knock seven bells out of him. They're hardy bucks from what I hear. Do you know them?'

'Just a bit. Not very well.'

'Ah, I wouldn't blame them, I suppose,' he says, stepping up into the back of the van. 'They've every right to be annoyed. What is it about you young lassies at all? Youse always fall for the bad boys.'

My father is off on annual leave during Easter week. He doesn't like to miss the services. Over the previous year, my parents have taken to attending Mass more often in Castle-owen than they do in Crosslea. My mother says she's sick of running into Mrs Jones and Mrs O'Grady, who are always talking about their sons and daughters at college and asking her what I intend studying after the Leaving.

'They know full well,' she grumbles to my father, 'that Frances has no intention of furthering her education. If she was going on to do medicine, mark my words, that pair of oul doses wouldn't speak to me at all.'

On Good Friday, my father finds me in tears.

'I thought I heard you crying,' he says, opening my bedroom door. 'What's wrong?'

'Nothing.'

'Nobody cries for nothing.' He sits down beside me on the bed. 'There must be something bothering you.'

'No, there isn't, honest. I'm tired, that's all.'

When he reaches out to touch my face, I turn away and wipe my eyes. I don't want him thinking I'm going soft.

'I'm gonna lie down for a while,' I say. 'I'll be OK then.'

There's no point in telling him that Lesley is making me ill; he wouldn't understand. How could he? I don't understand it myself, and I have no control over it.

While my parents attend the Passion, I stay in my room, listening to love songs on my radio: 'Reunited' by Peaches and Herb, 'I Can't Stop Loving You' by Leo Sayer, 'Please Don't Go' by KC and the Sunshine Band. Holding a pocket-sized photograph of myself and Lesley to my chest, I wallow in the grief that engulfs me, wailing unashamedly.

After a listless evening sprawled across the sofa watching TV, I climb the stairs for bed around half nine.

'What are you looking for?' I ask my mother, finding her on her hunkers, rummaging through the bottom drawer of my dressing-table.

'Have you something to tell me?' she says, standing up and closing the drawer with her foot.

'What?'

'I said: have you something to tell me?'

'Like what?'

'Never mind,' she says, brushing by me and heading down-stairs.

'What do you mean? What were you looking for?'

The bitch won't even answer me.

The following morning my mother says it's time we got to the bottom of my problem: I'm still not eating properly. We have to wait an hour and a half in an overcrowded and stuffy waiting room before seeing Dr Harte. She insists on accompanying me into his office. I haven't the will to argue with her.

He goes through all the usual tests – taking my blood pressure, a blood test, my temperature, examining my ears, listening to my breathing, feeling my glands, weighing me.

'She must have lost the best part of a stone,' my mother says, as I step off the scales.

'How's your appetite, Frances?'

'Bad. I only eat because I have to. I never actually feel like it.'

'What about your periods?'

My face starts to tingle. I can't talk to a man about my periods.

'When was your last one?'

'Eh.' I can sense my mother's eyes boring into me. 'I don't know. About a month, or maybe a bit more. I can't remember.'

My mother gasps when he says he needs a urine sample. 'I thought as much,' she peeps, putting her hand to her mouth.

God, she must think there's something seriously wrong with me.

'Let's just wait and see,' Dr Harte says.

My legs are trembling as I try to wee into the sample cup. What *is* wrong with me? Why is my mother so worried? What is she thinking? Then it dawns on me. Cancer. Bloody cancer. Just like Aunty Lily. Just like my grandmother. That's why I've been feeling so weak; I'm going to die. They'll both be sorry now – Lesley and my mother.

The doctor dips a stick into the urine. My mother has her handkerchief wound as tight as a piece of rope. The doctor looks up at her and nods sombrely.

'It's positive, I'm afraid,' he says. 'I'm sorry.'

'Oh my God,' my mother whispers, standing up and pacing across the office. 'I knew it. I knew this would happen.'

The doctor is looking at her sympathetically.

'When?' she asks.

'Well, if her last period was in February, September or October, I think.'

I start counting the months in my head: only five or six.

'What are you blubbering about, you little tramp?' my mother flashes.

'I don't want to die.'

'You're not going to die,' Dr Harte says. 'You're going to have a baby.'

A baby! No, I couldn't be. Jesus! I can't take it in. It's shocking.

1 December 1999 (afternoon)

Pregnant! I couldn't believe it. The thought hadn't once crossed my mind. I was going to be a mother.

Frances Fall, the mother.

Not Frances Fall, the childless cunt, as the horrible woman in Mountjoy prison called me.

I wanted to scream in her face: I AM A MOTHER.

Mountjoy

Within the first few minutes of my arrival at the prison, I can sense the underlying threat as heads turn and menacing eyes tail me with a funereal silence the length of two corridors to my cell. I've about as much chance of making myself inconspicuous among these women as a lone deer would have of wandering unnoticed among a pack of lions.

My cell is like any small hotel room except for the bars on the window. In the middle of the prison officer telling me where everything is and how things work, I burst into tears.

'I shouldn't be here,' I cry.

'That's what they all say,' she says, closing the door behind her.

When I've cried myself out, I switch on the television, lie on the bed and gaze at the screen. There's a snooker match on. It's easy viewing. It requires no thought – the ball either goes into the pocket or it doesn't. I don't look at the players, only the balls; all different colours rolling in every direction. After a while, I close my eyes and just listen to the balls – clunk clunk clunk. Clunk. Clap. Clunk.

Eventually I fall asleep.

'Fucking baby-snatcher,' someone shouts, kicking my door. She has an accent like one of the street traders on Moore Street.

'Leave her for now, Sharon; here comes Hatchet Face. We'll get the cunt when the time is right.'

A few minutes later, I stand at the dining-room door looking in at the other sixty or seventy prisoners, wondering which two of them are Sharon and her friend.

'Go on in,' an officer says, urging me through the door with her hand on my back.

Within seconds, the murmur of chatter fades away as I make my way shakily towards the food counter. I don't look to the right or left. At the end of the counter, I grab a tray and slide it along the stand, lifting a tub of yoghurt and a bottle of water as I go.

'Can I have a cuppa tea?' I ask, holding out an empty cup to the sullen woman standing behind the counter.

'Wha?'

'A cuppa tea, please.'

'Wha? I can't hear ya. Speak up.'

'Just tea, please.'

'Does any of yis understand this one's language?' she shouts. 'Where's she from? Pigs Head? Or Muckamaddy?'

'Oinksville,' someone shouts and everyone starts to snort.

'That's enough, girls,' one of the officers shouts.

'Crosshagging.'

'Culchie-cathair.'

'Killbumpkin.'

'Killbumpkin.' Clap clap clap. 'Killbumpkin.'

Others join in. 'Killbumpkin.' Clap clap clap. 'Kilbumpkin.'

'Oy,' an officer roars, 'cut it out.'

I drop the cup on the floor and run out the door. I can still hear them chanting as I turn the corner at the end of the corridor.

One of the officers follows me back to my room.

'Come on back,' she says,' and don't let that shower get to you.'

'I don't want to go back,' I snivel. 'I'm not hungry now anyway.'

'It's a long time until breakfast.'

259

'I don't care.'

'Suit yourself. At least you've broken the ice, I suppose.'

I spend the next three hours, until lock-up, sitting on the edge of my bed, my eyes fixed firmly on the door lock, waiting for the women who were jeering to burst in and batter me.

The following morning, I'm standing by the window looking out on to the courtyard, wondering how I'm going to get through the day, when someone knocks on my slightly open door.

When I turn around, a prune-faced woman in her fifties pokes her head in.

'I'm from next door. You can walk down to breakfast with me if you like.'

'Thanks.' I pull a tissue from my sleeve and wipe my eyes.

'Don't let dat lot see you crying, love. You have to show dem dat you're not boddered by what dey say.'

'OK.'

'I lost tree of mine.'

'Pardon?'

'I read your story in de paper. I know your baby died, love. And I'm just saying, I lost tree of mine.'

'It was in the paper about my baby?'

'Yes, love.'

'But how did they know? Sergeant Hennessy said no one would know until after the court hearing.'

'You can't rely on dat shower of wankers to keep der gobs shut. I wouldn't trust dem as far as I'd trow dem. Anyway, alls I'm trying to tell you is dat I know how it feels to lose a child. I'm Veronica, by de way.'

During breakfast, I tell Veronica about the woman called Sharon who had kicked my door the evening before.

'Oh, it must've been Sharon Pepper. Don't look now, but she's sitting at de table underneat de clock. She's de one with de bruise on her face.'

'What happened to her?' I ask, keeping my head down.

'She got in a fight. She's a bit of a Rottweiler, de same one. If she ever axes you for a fag or money, just give it to her, all right?'

'But I don't smoke. I gave them up years ago.'

'If I were you, I'd buy a couple of packets. Dey might buy you your way out of trouble.'

'OK. Thanks.'

In the late afternoon, I have a doctor's appointment. As soon as I step into his office, I burst out crying. I think it's because I've been putting on a brave face and bottling up my fear since early morning, and now that I feel safe, I cannot hold back.

He hands me a tablet and a glass of water. 'It'll help you to relax.'

It's not long until I feel the tension drain from my body. Where does it all go?

The doctor thinks that, in the short term, I could do with a mild sedative to get me through the next week or so. I'm willing to try anything that will help me cope with this hostile hellhole.

On my way back to my room, Sharon Pepper comes walking towards me wearing a pernicious smile. Before we meet, I move to the right out of her path, but she sidesteps with me, walking directly towards me. When I step to the left, the same thing happens.

'Excuse me, please,' I say, moving out of her way as we meet.

Denise Sewell

'Look at me when you're fucking talking to me,' she says, grabbing my chin and levelling my face with hers.

She has pockmarked skin, a mean mouth and the sly, merciless eyes of a tiger. Some women hurry past us, pretending not to notice the confrontation. Others egg her on.

'Give her a good hiding, Sharon. Go on, girl, go for it! We'll keep an eye out for the screws.'

At that, a male officer comes round the corner.

'Oy, Pepper, keep moving,' he shouts.

She points at my face, then turns her finger sideways and rubs it slowly across her neck.

'I'll get you,' she says, shouldering me as she struts on, laughing to herself.

The next two days pass without any serious incident. There are still jibes, dirty looks and hissing, but at least no one lays a hand on me. Veronica calls to my room before mealtimes and sits with me in the dining-room. She babbles on about her life and her extended family as if I should know, by their Christian names alone, who is who. She even goes as far as to tell me where each relative lives – all Dublin addresses – expecting me to be familiar with these places. I'm far too self-absorbed either to concentrate or to care. All I know is that it seems strange to me that someone so harmless should be behind bars. I don't know why she's ended up in jail. That's the one thing she doesn't talk about.

On my final evening, after nagging me for the best part of an hour, Veronica finally persuades me to go out for a walk with her. I hadn't risked venturing outdoors before for fear of being set upon. But having seen my solicitor earlier on in the day, I'm in reasonably good spirits. He said that after reading the psychiatrist's report, he thought I had a very good chance of avoiding a jail sentence, provided I agreed to a specified period of therapy under supervision. I feel relieved. It's probably my last night in prison and I've managed to survive it, albeit with the help of Veronica and the tablets.

Before we leave the room, I open my drawer, take ten pounds out of my purse and hand it to Veronica.

'Here,' I say, smiling at her. 'To buy yourself out of trouble.'

'Ah Jaysus, tanks, love.'

'You're welcome.'

'Are you sure you'll not be needing it yourself?'

'I can get more if I'm stuck.'

'You're very good,' she says, plonking herself down on my bed.

'What about the walk?'

'On seconds toughts, let's stay where we are and have an oul natter. You don't seem dat pushed on going out.'

'No, it's OK; I feel like going now. I've been cooped up for far too long. I could do with the fresh air.'

'Well, if you're sure,' she sighs, standing up reluctantly.

Her mood has suddenly changed. She's quiet and edgy.

'How long are you in here for?' I ask, as we stroll along the path.

'Wha?' She's scanning the courtyard, as though she's looking out for someone.

'Are you OK?'

'Yeah, I'm fine. What were you saying?' She pulls a cigarette from her pocket and lights it.

'Hey, Veronica,' someone shouts. 'Would ya be so bleedin' understanding if it'd been one of your kids she'd nicked?'

'Let's go back inside, love,' Veronica says, doing a U-turn. 'You don't need dis aggro on your last evening.'

When I turn to follow her, someone grabs my hair from behind and starts pulling me backwards. I have to run to stay on my feet. I call out after Veronica, but she keeps on walking as if she hasn't heard me. I know she has.

'Gotya now, you childless cunt,' Sharon Pepper hisses as she drags me backwards around a corner and throws me against a wall where there are several others waiting.

'Did you really think we were going to let you get away with it?' she says, striking me hard across the face. 'Tuck in, girls, and teach the bitch a lesson.'

I put my hand to my cheek, but the others grab me and hold back my arms while Sharon continues to batter my face, blow after blow. When I lower my head to protect my face, my hair is pulled in opposite directions and someone starts kicking my legs. I make a feeble attempt to call out for help, but I can barely breathe, let alone scream. A sharp pang pierces my ankle and my legs go from under me. As I fall, I'm sure I hear my scalp tear.

Someone blows a whistle.

'Come on, Sharon, let's go,' one of them says, and suddenly I'm released from their grasp.

They all scatter, except Sharon, who gets down on her hunkers, grabs my hair and holds up my head.

'You can thank Veronica for that. All it cost us was a packet of fags to get her to lure you into the trap,' she sneers. 'That's all you were worth to her, you piece of farmyard shite.'

'What's going on, Pepper?' one of the male prison officers asks, coming around the corner.

'Dunno. I found her like this. Obviously someone decided to give her a good hiding.'

'And you just happened to be passing by, I suppose?'

'You got it in one there, sir,' she says. 'It was bound to

happen though: you know that, sir. People don't take too kindly to baby-snatchers. Especially mothers, and there are plenty of them in here.'

'Who did this to you, Frances?'

'I dunno,' I sob. 'I didn't see their faces.'

Veronica calls to say goodbye the following morning.

'Here,' she says, holding out the ten-pound note. 'I can't take dis, not after what I done.'

When I don't take it from her, she tiptoes by me and puts it on the bedside table.

'Are you still sore?' she asks, standing with her back to me.

I want to shout at her that my feelings are a lot more bruised than my face and that I feel worse today – the day I'm leaving – than I felt on the day I arrived. But what's the point? She doesn't care.

'I'm a bit busy,' I say, walking into the toilet and closing the door.

I put down the toilet seat and sit on it. At least, in here, she won't see me crying.

'I didn't do it for de fags, you know,' she shouts. 'I did it because I'm a bloody coward. No one says no to Sharon Pepper. If I hadn't agreed, de bitch would've made my life a misery . . . long after you were gone. Are you listening to me, love?'

I wish she'd go away. I want to be on my own.

'Dat was why I changed my mind about going for de walk. But den you said you needed de fresh air and I hadn't de guts to tell you what was going on. You know, maybe we both would've been better off if I hadn't made friends with you in de first place.'

Maybe we would, I think.

'But on de other hand, love, I'm glad I met you because you're a lovely girl and I wish you de best of luck today.'

I tear off a wad of toilet roll and blow my nose.

'Goodbye, Frances, and well . . . I'm very sorry.'

2 December 1999 (evening)

Before I left prison, I put the tenner into an envelope and handed it to one of the prison officers to pass on to Veronica. I think I saw a piece of myself in this woman; that whatever wrong she'd done, there was no malice intended. She never meant to hurt me, just like I never meant to hurt Nathan or his parents. The only baby I ever wanted to hold was my own.

A baby girl

'Who's the father?' my mother shrills, slamming the sitting-room door behind her.

We're just in the door after my visit to the doctor.

My father steps in from the kitchen. 'What's going on?'

'Your daughter is pregnant,' she says, 'that's what's going on.'

'No!' He shakes his head. 'She couldn't be.'

'Huh! I don't know why you're so surprised, Joe Fall,' my mother says. 'You were the one who let her run wild, not me.'

My father turns to me and I know by his pleading eyes that he wants me to say she's lying.

'Sorry, Daddy,' I whisper, hanging my guilty head.

'Sorry!' my mother exclaims. 'A fat lot of good that will do you now.'

I sit on the sofa and start to cry.

'And it's a bit late in the day for whingeing too,' she says, untying her headscarf and stuffing it into her coat pocket. 'Now I'll ask you again: who's the father?'

Squeezing my eyes shut, I bite my lip. I don't want to tell them about the gingerbread man, because then they'd want to know when and where, and I can't tell them that.

'Answer your mother, Frances,' my father says, 'or God help me, I'll . . . I'll –'

'Is he from the village?' my mother asks, sitting straight-backed on the other end of the sofa.

'No.'

'Castleowen?' my father says.

'No.'

'Where then?' my mother asks. 'Where's this boy from?'

I look up at my father, who is now standing with his back to the fire.

'I don't know.'

'You don't know!' He bangs his fist on the mantelpiece. 'Are you telling me that you had sexual intercourse with a man you don't even know?'

'No.'

'So you do know him,' my mother says.

'Yes, but –'

'What's his name?' she asks.

'I can't tell you,' I sob. 'Anyway, what does it matter? You don't know him and I won't be seeing him ever again.'

'Damn right you won't!' my father shouts.

'Does he know you're pregnant?' my mother asks.

'No! How would he? I didn't know myself until today.'

'So you say.'

'I didn't, I swear.'

'You had intercourse. You missed your monthlies. For heaven's sake, how could you not know, you stupid girl?'

'I don't know; I just didn't.'

'So you're a hundred per cent certain he knows nothing about your condition?' my father asks.

'Yes.'

'When did you last see him?'

'A couple of months ago.'

'Hah!' my mother sneers, throwing back her head. 'He hasn't bothered with you since he had his wicked way with you, has he?'

'No.'

'Fool,' she shouts, leaning her face towards mine.

'Stop.' Putting my hands over my ears, I crouch down and start rocking. 'Stop stop stop stop stop stop stop.'

'Pull yourself together,' she says, shaking me, 'and stop your silly nonsense.'

'I'm not a fool. I'm not a fool.'

Over the next few days, my father won't even look at me. The atmosphere in the house is as laden with blame and shame as it was in the days and weeks after Aunty Lily died nine years earlier. This time I know whose fault it is.

'It's imperative that you don't breathe a word about this to anyone,' my mother says.

'OK.'

'If you do, I'll throw you out on the street.'

'I won't.'

'On Monday morning, you'll go back to school, get stuck into your books and act like normal while I figure out what to do. There'll be no more pocket money and there'll be no more gallivanting.'

*

On school mornings, my mother stands over me while I struggle to swallow several teaspoons of milky porridge.

'The baby deserves to be properly nourished,' she says, 'no matter what sin its mother has committed.'

Before I leave to get the bus, she pats powder puff on my face and pinches my cheeks to take the gaunt look off me. In my precarious frame of mind, I feel powerless to do anything about her re-established dominance over my life. My father, having done a Pontius Pilate on me, ignores my pitiful efforts to regain his respect.

Night after night my parents stay up talking into the small hours of the morning, while I lie in my bed daydreaming about an impossible future. I see Lesley and myself up in Dublin sharing a flat together with our new babies. On summer days, we put white floppy hats on their downy heads and take them to the beach, where we sit on a rug and watch the waves. Afterwards, we stroll along the promenade, pushing our buggies, smoking cigarettes and licking ninety-nines. We ride home on a double-decker bus, each of us nursing our sleeping infants. Lesley is tired too and is leaning her head on my shoulder. I can feel her breath on my neck, her hair on my skin, the warmth of her sun-kissed limbs next to mine. I don't want to open my eyes to the materiality of my bedroom, my safe box, my hiding place.

I drive myself scatty trying to predict how Lesley would react if she knew that I too was pregnant by the gingerbread man. On a couple of occasions when I find myself alone in the house, I pick up the telephone and dial her number. The first time her mother answers, having to clear her throat before she says hello.

'Is that you, Frances?' she says, when I ask to speak to Lesley.

Despite the croakiness of her voice, there's a softness about the way she speaks to me. As my lips part to say yes, I hear Lesley shout out, 'If it is, tell her to stop stalking me or I'll ring the Guards.'

'I'm sorry, love,' her mother says.

'It's OK.'

I hang up. Why is Lesley doing this to me? Why won't she at least listen to what I have to say? It doesn't have to be this way between us. I know we could work it out. With that in mind, I try again a couple of weeks later. This time, Lesley herself answers the phone.

'It's me,' I say as soon as she says hello.

'Stop ringing my house, you fucking space cadet.'

'Don't call me that,' I say, raising my voice.

She sighs down the line.

'I need to talk to you,' I say. 'I've something to tell you. It's important.'

'Important! You and important don't exactly fit in the same sentence. You're a mouse, remember.'

'It's about the gingerbread man.' I won't let her insults put me off.

'You can tell me over the phone.'

'I can't.'

'Why not?'

'Because I need to see you.'

'N. O.'

'Please.'

'Are you deaf?'

'Please, Lesley!'

'Say pretty please.'

'Lesley!'

'You want to meet me, don't you?'

'You know I do.'

'Then say pretty please.'

'Pretty please.'

'Say pretty pretty please.'

'Stop.'

'If you don't say it, I won't meet you.'

'Why are you doing this?'

'Fine, don't bother. See ya.'

'Pretty pretty please. Jesus!'

'Again. Nicely this time.'

'Pretty pretty please.' My voice is shaking with anger.

'I said nicely. Say it nicely.'

'I did.'

'You can do better than that.'

Gulping down my pride, I say it again. 'Pretty pretty please.'

'Is that what you said to Johnny in the bread van?'

'What?'

'Oh, please ride me, Johnny,' she squeaks, 'pretty pretty please. I want to be just like Lesley.'

'No!'

'Yeah, right! So, let's have it one more time – Will you meet me, Lesley, pretty pretty please?'

Outside I hear my father's car pull up.

'What's wrong, Mousy? Cat got your tongue?'

I'm ready to burst into tears. I know she's being a hurtful cow and that she doesn't give a damn about me, but I still don't want to accept it.

'Bye, Lesley,' I say, hanging up and hurrying into the living-room before my parents catch me on the phone.

Underneath my clothes, my body is changing. I'm too embar-rassed to ask my mother to buy me a bigger bra, even though the one I'm wearing is digging into me and leaving a red ring around my back. My tummy, though not yet protruding, feels solid and sensitive to touch. No matter how often I brush my teeth, I cannot dispel the acidy taste. A cigarette I scrounge from one of the boys on the school bus leaves my head swimming and my stomach full of gas.

Early in May, I wake up in the middle of the night to the first stirring of the secret life that is growing inside me. Just below my navel, it seems as if a baby bird has tried to flutter its wings for the first time. The feebleness of it fills my lungs with a gasp of maternal love.

The following morning, I feel a great urgency to speak to my mother about my baby's future. I find her in the garden hanging sheets on the clothesline.

'Can I keep my baby?' I ask, standing facing her.

She takes a dangling peg from her mouth. 'What are you doing outside in your nightdress?'

'Can I keep my baby?'

'Don't be stupid.'

'I'm not being stupid. I want to keep it.'

'You can't,' she says, picking up another sheet from the linen basket. 'You're not a married woman.'

'I'd be a good mother,' I tell her, as she drapes the sheet over the line.

'No child deserves to be raised a bastard,' she says, pegging it down. 'Luckily for you, Father Vincent is already in the process of making arrangements.'

'What sort of arrangements?'

'I'll tell you when they're finalized,' she says, plucking a pillowcase from the linen basket.

'No,' I say, grabbing it from her and flinging it on the grass. 'Tell me now.'

She sits me down at the kitchen table and places a glass of milk in front of me.

'I don't want that.'

'Drink it. The baby needs it.'

'It tastes sour,' I tell her, after taking a sip.

'It couldn't be; it's this morning's milk.'

'Just tell me what's going on, will you?'

She tells me that Father Vincent has handpicked adoptive parents for my baby. They're a childless couple in their early thirties, devout Catholics and not short of a bob or two.

'That's all you need to know,' she says.

'I'm not giving my baby away,' I say, shaking my head. 'I don't care what anyone says; I'm keeping it.'

'Don't talk soft.'

'I'm not. I know I've done wrong, Mammy, and I'm really sorry, but it's *my* baby,' I say, laying my hand on my tummy, 'and I love it already.'

Her shoulders slacken and for a split second she looks sad.

'I felt it kick last night,' I say in tears, reaching out and touching her shoulder. 'It was lovely.'

'Stop it,' she says, pulling back. 'Stop that snivelling at once.'

'But –'

'But nothing. Now, pull yourself together and stop your nonsense.'

'You've no heart, Mammy, do you know that? You're dead cold. Why can't you be more like Aunty Lily was? If she was alive, she'd be on my side.'

The colour drains from her face and her eyes bloat with fury. 'Don't you try and tell me about Aunty Lily, you ungrateful yoke. You know nothing about her.'

'I know she loved me, which is more than I can say about you.'

'Get out.' She points to the door. 'Get out of my sight now, Frances, before I say something I'll regret.'

'I'm gonna keep my baby,' I sob, getting up and heading for the door. 'You'll see.'

'If that's your intention,' she shouts, 'you may leave right now.'

We both know I can't leave – I've no one to turn to – but I don't give up either. Over the following few days, I beg my parents, together and in turn, to reconsider. I even suggest that my mother pretend the baby is hers. Mrs Galvin, a farmer's wife from the locality, had a baby a couple of weeks earlier and she's nearly fifty, which is older than my mother. No one would ever know.

'That's out of the question,' my mother says.

'Daddy?'

'You heard your mother.'

They keep telling me to forget about the baby and get on with my schoolwork. A decent future is dependent on a semi-respectable Leaving Certificate and not on an illegitimate child.

I'm a ball of sensitivity. Every time someone raises their voice to me, or brushes by me in the schoolyard, or sings a sad song, I cry.

'If she doesn't stop blubbering,' my mother tells my father, 'she'll give the game away.'

The following evening Nancy knocks on my bedroom door.

'You're at the books, I see,' she says, smiling.

'Yeah.'

'Good lassie. Can I come in for a minute?'

I nod.

She treads lightly across the floor and sits down on my bed.

'You look a bit peaky,' she says, 'but I suppose that's to be expected.'

'I'm just tired.'

'Your mother says you're very weepy these days. She's really worried about how the whole thing will affect your exams.'

'She says I have to give the baby up for adoption.'

'And you don't want to.' She doesn't sound the least bit surprised.

'No.' At last, I think, someone who understands how I'm feeling.

'Sit down here,' she says, patting the eiderdown.

Before I get to her, the tears are flowing again.

'It's OK, love,' she says, putting her arms around me. 'You have a good cry.'

'I don't want them to take my baby away,' I sob.

'I know it's hard, Frances,' she says, rubbing my arm. 'In my line of work, I've come across dozens of girls in your situation over the years and they've all felt the very same way you're feeling now. No mother finds it easy to part with her baby, but, under the circumstances, it's the best thing to do, especially for the child's sake.'

'Loads of girls are keeping their babies nowadays.'

'Aye, and more's the pity. What kind of society will that lead to ten or twenty years down the line? Think about it, love.'

'I don't care about that. I just want my baby.'

'Are you still hankering after the father, hoping that keeping this baby might bring youse back together?'

'No, it's not like that at all. It's nothing to do with him.'

'You're sure?'

'Positive.'

'OK, OK.'

'I'm seventeen, for God's sake. In fact, I'll be eighteen by the time the baby is born. It's due on the fifth of October.'

'Yes, so your mother was telling me.'

'Why can't she accept that I'm old enough to make my own decisions?'

'Well, if you are, you're old enough to take responsibility for your actions and do the right thing – the unselfish thing – which is putting your baby's needs before your own.'

'I can give it everything it needs.'

'You can't give it a father.'

'Daddy grew up without his *mother* and he turned out OK.'

'Speaking of your father, what about the shame you'd be bringing on him and your mother by keeping this baby? Have you thought of that?'

'Of course I have.'

'And?'

'I'm sorry for what I've done, but that doesn't change how I feel. If they don't let me keep it, Nancy, I'll just move out and get a flat.'

'Now you're talking nonsense. How could you afford that, and you at home all day with a newborn baby?'

'I'd get money from Social Welfare, wouldn't I?'

'Aye, a pittance. It wouldn't keep you in nappies.'

'I don't care.'

'Off the top of my head, I can think of three . . . no, four women from this locality who have given up babies for adoption. Each of them has gone on to get married and have kids with their husbands. If they'd kept their babies, as sure as eggs are eggs, they'd still be on their own and they'd never have had more children. You need to think about the whole thing on a long-term basis. A year from now, you could be away at college and doing the things that girls of your age should be doing, not stuck in some poky flat with a baby.'

'I don't want to go to college.'

'What do you want to do with the rest of your life?'

'I don't know. I haven't thought about it.'

'You're six weeks away from finishing your secondary education and you haven't even thought about it?'

'I was planning on going to Dublin to get a job, but all I can think about now is keeping my baby. Please help me, Nancy. Talk to my mother; she listens to you. Just ask her to think about it!'

'I don't see that there's any point.'

'Then I'm not doing my Leaving.'

'Don't be so foolish. You have to do it.'

'Why? I know I'm going to fail. How can I possibly study when all I can think about is them giving my baby away to strangers?'

For a moment, she looks thoughtful.

'OK,' she says, getting up and walking over to the window, 'let's say I do decide to have a chat with your mother, will you promise to concentrate on your schoolwork and do your best in your exams?'

'Yes.'

'And will you continue to keep your pregnancy a secret for as long as your mother wants you to?'

'I will.'

She pulls back the net curtains and looks out on to the street.

'Because even if she does change her mind, it won't happen overnight.'

'Yeah, I know.'

'So, you'll stay calm and go along with her wishes for now?'

'OK.'

'Then I'll have a word with her,' she says. 'Not today or tomorrow, mind you, but whenever I think the time is right.'

'Thanks, Nancy.'

'Merciful hour, is that the angelus I hear already?' she says, checking her watch. 'I'd better be off.'

'You know, I'm really sorry for the trouble I've caused,' I say as she heads for the door.

She mutters something under her breath. I can't be certain, but it sounded like 'You girls always are.'

I'm the only student in the examination hall wearing a cardigan. My mother has warned me not to take it off because it conceals my now suspicious protrusion. My armpits are seeping and my blouse is cleaving to my skin. I can't stop scratching myself. Since my chat with Nancy a few weeks earlier, I haven't discussed my baby's future with either of my parents, but if the number of times my mother has visited Nancy's house recently is anything to go by, then the matter is being discussed at length, which I'm taking as a good sign. Half-way through my Maths paper, my mind drifts. I can't help imagining Lesley's reaction when she hears I'm having a baby too. If nothing else, it will make her see that she'll have to stop gossiping about me being a lesbian. And who knows, she might even be glad of a friend who's in the same boat as herself.

The Sunday after I finish my exams, my mother tells me I have an appointment at the hospital the following day.

'OK,' I say, opening my jeans button to sit down.

'It's in Enniskillen.'

'Enniskillen!'

'Yes, that's what I said.'

'Why there? I thought you hated the North.'

'I do, but that's where you'll be delivering the baby.'

'Why will I be going there? What's wrong with Castleowen hospital?'

'What do you think is wrong with it? If you have it there, all and sundry will know about it.'

'But I'm keeping it: they'll know anyway.'

'What do you mean you're keeping it? You're doing no such thing.'

'But Nancy said she'd –'

'Nancy is of the same opinion as I am. The best option . . . no, no, the *only* option is adoption.'

'But she said she'd talk to you about me keeping the baby.' My lips are trembling.

'Yes, and she did. She thought it was a ridiculous idea, if you must know.'

'She said she understood,' I cry, cradling my tummy.

'Look,' my mother says with a sigh, 'no matter how *you* feel, you have to do the right thing by your baby.'

'Nancy led me to believe that there was a chance you'd change your mind.'

'Because she wanted you to be able to get through your exams. We all did.'

'So she lied to me.'

'She was only trying to help you.'

'She's worse than Lesley.'

'Lesley! Don't talk to me about that trollop. It was hanging around with that madam that got you into this mess in the first place,' she says, walking through to the kitchen.

'At least she had good reason to betray me.'

I hear her rooting in a cupboard, then filling a glass with water and popping in two aspirin.

I get up and stand in the doorway between the two rooms.

'How would you have felt if someone had taken me away from you after I was born?'

She looks down into her fizzing remedy. 'I . . . I . . .'

'Oh, Mammy, if you have to think about it . . .'

'You should be counting your blessings that there's a nice, good-living young couple out there, willing to raise your child as their own.'

'That doesn't answer my question, Mammy. I want to know how you'd have felt if –'

'No matter how I'd have felt, I couldn't or wouldn't have kept you if I hadn't been married. It wouldn't have been right.'

'It wouldn't have been right for whom?'

'Either of us.'

'So, you'd have handed me over to a stranger . . . just like that.'

'The woman who's adopting your baby is barren. Can you imagine how happy she'll be to get this baby?'

'I don't a give a damn about her! She's not having *my* child.'

She turns her back to me. 'Stop torturing yourself, Frances,' she quavers. 'Just accept that you have to give it up. It's for the best.'

By early July, I can't hide it any longer; even in my baggy sweatshirts I look pregnant. Father Vincent rings my mother to tell her that I'm welcome to stay in a convent in Enniskillen until the baby is born.

'Everyone will be wondering where she is,' she says to my

father. 'If it was only for a couple of weeks, grand, but from July until October, how do you explain that?'

'It's up to you,' my father says. 'Whatever you think yourself.'

'I think it's best to wait until September.'

My father's indifference is killing me. Sometimes I feel like lifting up my T-shirt and saying, Look, Daddy, it's your grandchild, but then I know that he'd pretend not to see me or hear me, or even feel for me.

I'm not allowed out. The only fresh air I get is in the back garden. Any time the doorbell rings, I'm shooed upstairs out of sight. One Sunday early in August, my mother arrives home after attending Mass in the village.

'I've told everyone that you have shingles,' she says. 'They're highly contagious, so they'll understand why they don't see you out and about.'

When Nuddy Neary hears of my plight, he arrives at the front door with the name of a man who has the cure. I listen in amusement from my bedroom door.

'He lives up in the Cooley Mountains,' he tells my mother. 'Everyone swears by him.'

'Really. Well, thanks very much. I'll think about it.'

'It's an odious tricky spot to find,' he says, 'but if youse like, I'll accompany youse on the journey and be your navigator, so to speak.'

'I don't think so.'

'He'd have her right as rain in no time. They travel from all over the country to see him. He's dynamite altogether.'

Inside my tummy, the baby stretches its limbs. I'd swear that's a foot pressing down on my hipbone. I lift my T-shirt and watch the contortions underneath my skin.

'Don't worry,' I whisper, touching my tummy. 'I'll never sign those papers.'

After an afternoon nap, I wake up with pins and needles in my feet. Across the landing, I can hear my mother humming. As I hobble towards the top of the stairs, I catch sight of her standing facing the mirror on the inside of her wardrobe door. She doesn't normally leave her bedroom door open. Standing with my back to the landing wall, I stop to listen. It's only then I recognize the song she's humming – 'The Mocking Bird'. Peeping round the corner, I see that she's holding something to her cheek and swaying her upper body. There's a white ball of wool, stabbed with knitting needles, lying on her bedside table.

'How long have you been watching me?' she says, swinging round and stuffing something into a drawer.

'You want this baby as much as I do, don't you?' I say, stepping into her room.

'Don't talk nonsense.'

'Let me see.' As I walk towards the drawer, she stands with her back to it.

'Go away,' she says. 'Get out of my bedroom right now.'

'I'm not going anywhere until I see what's in that drawer.'

'It's none of your business.'

'If you don't let me see, I'll go downstairs, open the front door and walk up and down the street until everyone witnesses this,' I say, pointing at my stomach.

'If you do, my girl, you won't get back in.'

'I don't give a monkey's. I'm sure someone will take pity on me.'

'For God's sake, Frances, it's just something I knitted for the baby.'

'I want to see it.'

'Why?'

'I just do. What's wrong with that?'

With eyes downcast, she steps to one side. As I reach out to open the drawer, she says, 'It'll be cold in October,' then turns on her heel and walks away.

Inside the drawer I find three matinee coats in white, yellow and pale green, three little hats and mitts to match, and two pairs of bootees in yellow and green. One by one, I spread them on the eiderdown. Three little sets: all that's missing are the white bootees. They're the sweetest things I've ever seen. Picking up the white matinee coat, I sit down on the bed and lay it across my tummy. The mere thought of being separated from my baby sends me into floods of tears.

'Getting yourself into a state is no good for the baby,' my mother says.

I hadn't heard her come back into the room.

'I love the little pearl buttons,' I snivel, fingering them.

'Here,' she says, handing me a handkerchief.

'We could always raise it together.'

'No,' she says, shaking her head.

'What does it matter what other people think or say?'

'It mightn't matter to you, but it matters to me and it'll matter to that child.'

'Times have changed.'

'Oh, don't kid yourself, Frances. Children born out of wedlock will always be considered bastards. That's what they were a hundred years ago, that's what they are now, and that's what they'll be a hundred years from now.'

Nancy gives me a quick examination. I've been complaining about pains in my back all day.

'Likely it's the lack of exercise,' she says. 'You're bound to be stiff and you sitting about all day.'

'That's probably all it is,' my mother says. 'Sure, she's not due for six weeks yet.'

During the night the pain grows stronger. It feels as if an iron claw is crushing my back. I don't want to disturb my mother. She's already said that all pregnant women get aches and pains. When it eases, I try to sleep, but each time I'm about to drift off, it comes back – fiercer, sharper, longer. Around three o'clock, when the pain becomes unbearable, I roll out of the bed and crawl across the room and on to the landing.

'Daddy,' I cry out. 'Daddy! Daddy!'

My mother comes to me first and tries to pick me up off the floor. She's shouting at my father to get up and ring Nancy at once. I'm clutching the carpet pile and moaning with pain. My father's bare feet hurry past me and thud down the stairs.

'Offer it up,' my mother says, getting down on her knees and rubbing my back. 'Think of it as penance and offer it up.'

'Nancy's on her way,' my father pants, dashing up the stairs.

Taking an arm each, they help me back into the bedroom and lay me down on my bed.

'Can you feel the baby moving at all?' my mother asks.

'No,' I cry, as another spasm seizes me.

When Nancy arrives, my father leaves the room and the two women start to strip me.

'She's definitely in labour,' Nancy tells my mother, as she removes my panties. 'She's had a show. You'll have to take her straight to Castleowen hospital.'

'Castleowen!' my mother says.

'Yes. Youse mightn't make it to Enniskillen.'

'We will.'

'Youse mightn't, Rita.'

'Joe!' my mother shouts. 'Get dressed quickly.'

'You get ready too,' Nancy tells her. 'I'll stay with her.'

'Oh, the pain,' I cry. 'Make it stop.'

'You're all right, love; just take deep breaths,' Nancy says over and over as she dresses me. 'There's no need to panic.' But her voice is shaking, her hands are fumbling and her eyes are taut with fear.

Outside I hear the car's engine running. My mother sends Nancy out first to make sure there's no one around; then they both help me into the back seat. All the time, I'm groaning and crying and begging them to take the pain away.

'Keep going, Joe,' my mother says, as we head into Castleowen. 'Enniskillen is only thirty miles away. We'll get there.'

'No,' I howl, as he turns left to follow her instructions.

Nancy is sitting in the back with me holding my hand.

'Her contractions are getting worse, Rita,' she says. 'My advice is to turn back. What do you say, Joe?'

'It's up to Rita,' he says.

'If she delivers it in Castleowen,' my mother says, 'town and country will be gossiping about her by morning and then where will we be?'

The pain spreads across my stomach and down into my groin. Every mile we travel seems longer and bumpier than the one before. Nancy tells my father that I'm sweating buckets and asks him to turn down the heat, but he can't; he needs to keep the windscreen clear. While I cry and curse and dig my fingers into the back of my father's seat, my parents say a frantic rosary and Nancy says, 'Take deep breaths, Frances. Come on now. Calm down, deep breaths.'

'Aaaah, help me,' I scream. My lower body feels as if it's being torn apart. I'm sure I'm going to hear my pelvis snap.

'Keep her quiet,' my father says, 'we're coming up to a checkpoint.'

'But the baby's coming,' I sob. 'The baby's coming.'

'Don't push yet whatever you do,' Nancy says. 'We're nearly there now.'

'We have a young lassie in labour,' my father tells the policeman and we're immediately waved on.

In the next couple of minutes, the pain becomes so intense that I start to lose consciousness. Nancy is looking at me and her lips are moving, but I can't hear a word she's saying. It feels as if my ears are bleeding.

What happens after that is hazy. I remember the cold night air, the vibration of the trolley as I'm rushed down a corridor. I can still hear the huff of my own breath inside the mask over my mouth and nose, the jangle of medical instruments. I don't know if the blinding light that makes me squint is real or just a figment of my imagination, but I do know that the living, breathing baby I see, all dressed in white with rosy lips, is just that.

'They did everything they could for her,' my mother whispers before I even manage to raise my post-sedative eyelids.

She and Nancy say I shouldn't see her, but I know that if I don't, I'll lose my mind. A kind nurse takes me to her and lays her in my arms. I look down on her tininess and cry on top of her.

'I was right to want to keep her, wasn't I?' I sob, stroking her cheek with the back of my forefinger.

'Of course you were,' the nurse says.

'She's my flesh and blood after all.'

'Yes, she is.'

'My little girl.'

'Yes.'

'My disgrace.'

'No, Frances,' she says, putting her arm around me.

'Yes,' I say, lowering my head and kissing her cold lips. 'My beautiful disgrace.'

5 December 1999 (evening)

I saw my therapist today.

'I'm very sorry about your daughter, Frances.'

'Thank you,' I said, wiping the condensation from the window. 'You're the first person to say that to me.'

'Were you told why she died?'

'Yes.' I sat down and touched my throat. 'The umbilical cord was tangled around her neck.'

In the long sad silence that followed, I tried to remember her perfect little face, but I couldn't picture it. It was like waking up from a dream, still feeling absorbed by its atmosphere and charged with its emotions, but unable to grasp its physical existence. In frustration, I began to cry.

'Does she have a name?' he asked, passing me the box of tissues.

'No,' I sobbed, 'just Baby Fall. My mother and Nancy told me there was no point in giving her a name. She was a stillborn, not a child. Stillborns didn't get names.'

'Do you mind me asking, where was she laid to rest?'

'With Aunty Lily.' I began to twiddle her wedding ring on

the chain round my neck. 'I suppose I should be grateful for small mercies – she couldn't be in better company.'

'That must have been a difficult day for you.'

'It took place sometime after dark, but I wasn't there. My father and Father Vincent buried her before I was discharged from the hospital. It was all very hush hush.'

'Do you visit the grave?'

I shook my head. 'I could never face it.'

'Do you think you could face it now?'

'Maybe . . . some day. When the time is right. When I'm ready to let her go.'

'Only from this life, Frances. She'll always be in your heart, where she belongs.'

Placing my hand on my chest, I inhaled a languishing breath. 'God, how I'd have loved her.'

'You still do and you always will.'

'Remember I told you about the three knitted sets I found in my mother's drawer, and that all that was missing was the white bootees?'

'Yes.'

'The day my father drove me home from hospital, I made him stop outside a drapery shop and I went in and bought her white bootees. I still have them. I carry them around in my pocket on her birthday.'

'That's good. It's comforting to have something to hold on to.'

'Imagine if she'd lived, Lesley's son Simon would have a sister only five or six weeks younger than himself.'

'Did you ever see Lesley again after she had her baby?'

'No. I thought about writing to her a while back, but I've changed my mind.'

'Why?'

'Because I have to move on. If our paths are meant to cross again, then they will.'

'*Che sera, sera.*'

'Yes,' I smiled, 'according to Aunty Lily.'

Epilogue

4 February 2000

It's Friday evening and I'm just over my second week at college. I'm doing a six-month course in gardening and landscaping. I do believe I've finally found my niche.

After I left hospital early last month, I moved to Salthill in Galway and rented a one-bed-roomed apartment not far from the sea. And yes, I have a room with a view. It was daunting at first, setting up home in a strange town, but I'm beginning to feel a little more at ease in my new surroundings, especially since I started my course. Apart from the fact that it's keeping me busy, I'm enjoying the company of the other pupils, who are mature students like myself. The weekends, however, are still pretty lonely.

Once a month, I travel to Dublin to see my therapist. We talk less now about the past, and more about the future.

A couple of weeks ago, I jotted down my new address on a scrap of paper, slipped it into an envelope and sent it to my father, just to leave the line of communication open. I miss him dreadfully. When I picked up my post from the front doormat an hour ago, I saw his handwriting on one of the envelopes and I'm just about to open it. My hands are shaking.

Later

The final piece of the jigsaw:

1 Feb. 2000
Crosslea

Dear Frances

I've been doing a lot of thinking these past few weeks about all them questions you want answering, and to be quite frank, I'm not sure that any good will come out of it. If your mother were alive, she certainly wouldn't approve. She sincerely believed that the truth could only ever hurt you. All I can do is hope and pray that she was wrong in her thinking.

For what you're about to read, I am heartily sorry.

You were indeed born just three months after your mother and I got married, but as I said to you before, your mother wasn't in the family way: she wasn't that kind of girl. Your Aunty Lily was your birth mother.

The man who spoke to you at her funeral was a schoolteacher and her one-time fiancé, Emmet O'Sullivan. The engagement lasted only a couple of weeks, however, because Emmet soon became aware that Lily was concealing a pregnancy. When your grandfather heard that Emmet had reneged on his promise, he stormed around to his digs and demanded an explanation. Under duress, Emmet told him that Lily was expecting and that he, never having interfered with her in that way, was not the father.

That night your grandfather gave poor Lily the mother of all beatings and threw her out. Your mother, disgusted by her father's brutality, packed both their belongings and left with Lily. Having nowhere else to go, they arrived on our doorstep. My father insisted that both girls move into our guest bedroom until arrangements could be made for Lily to go away to have her baby. Lily, however, had other ideas, as I discovered about a week later when I found your mother on her knees by the bed, sobbing and clutching her rosary beads. She told me that Lily was planning to go to England to have an abortion. The poor woman was devastated. All she kept saying was – We can't let her do it, Joe.

Secretly, I had my own worries over an incident that had occurred one night the previous January. Around half past ten your mother turned up on my doorstep in flitters. Your grandfather, she said, was on the rampage, looking for Lily, who was supposed to have been home two hours earlier. Knowing what would happen to her younger sister if her father caught up with her, she begged me to go out and look for Lily, which I did without any hesitation. A fella I met in the street told me that he'd seen Lily earlier that day knocking about with Sadie Sweeney, undesirable company by anyone's standards, so I drove straight out to Sadie's cottage to see if Lily was there. I could hardly believe my eyes when I got out of the car and saw the pair of them in through the kitchen window dancing around the floor in nothing more than their slips. I went inside and told Lily to cover herself up and to get into the car at once. It was only then I realized they were both blind drunk.

While Lily was picking up her clothes off the floor, the other dirty tramp was pawing at me and trying to get me to kiss her. It was woefully embarrassing. Lily wasn't even fit to tie her own shoelaces, so I bent down and tied them for her. Then I linked her arm and took her out to the car. As soon as I started the engine, she began to sob. She didn't want to go home to face her father, she said. She was very distressed. Despite her reckless behaviour, it was impossible not to feel sorry for the lassie. When I pulled up half-way down the lane, all I ever intended doing was comforting her. But she hadn't buttoned up her coat, and she smelled of perfume and she asked to be held. I don't know if her lips rose to

mine or mine descended on hers, or they met somewhere in the
middle, but one way or another I lost all control of myself.
Afterwards, I wept bitter tears.

When I discovered Lily was pregnant, I hoped and prayed that
she would come and tell me that I wasn't responsible, but she
didn't and I, to my shame, was too much of a coward to ask her. I
didn't want to lose your mother, Frances. That woman meant the
world to me. I had the height of respect for her. A man could go
home after a night out with your mother with a clear conscience.
She was a clean-living lassie, and a devout Catholic. She begged
and pleaded with Lily not to go through with the abortion, offering
to raise the baby for her. Eventually, after many long and
emotional exchanges between the two women, Lily agreed to go
to Dublin to a Mother and Baby Home, run by nuns, to have her
baby. There were, however, three conditions she insisted upon:
one, that she enter the home under your mother's name – she
wanted no hand or part in the child's life, even down to having her
name on the birth certificate; two, that I would be named as father
of the baby and not Emmet; and three, that after the birth I would
give her a couple of hundred pounds, enough to allow her to start a
new life in England.

Although the night before Lily left for the home, I tried, when I
found her alone in the scullery, to broach the subject of whether or
not I was, in fact, the baby's (your) father, she never gave me a
straight answer, saying only that I would be, and wasn't that all
that mattered?

Your mother, either not realizing or refusing to question the
extent of Lily's experience with men, insisted that Emmet had to
be the father, backing up her conclusion with one question – Sure,
who else's could it be?

If only Lily had left things as they were, instead of confessing all
to Xavier in a letter before she died. It was only then that I knew

*for sure that you were my flesh and blood. I'll never forget the look
on your mother's face when she read that letter. It ruined
everything: our relationship with Xavier, my relationship with
your mother, but most of all, your mother's relationship with you.*

*She never forgave me, you know. I begged her to, even on her
deathbed. But all she said was, Tell Frances I forgive her, and then
she drew her last breath.*

As I said, Frances: I'm heartily sorry.

Daddy

*P. S. Your grandfather Murphy died just ten years ago in an old
folks' home down in Cork. As far as your mother was concerned,
her father had died the night he beat the pregnant Lily, and she
did not attend the funeral. You see, she was the kind of woman
who found it hard to forgive. I suppose you were the lucky one.*

Acknowledgements

Special thanks to Patricia Deevy, Michael McLoughlin and everyone at Penguin Ireland. To my editor, Alison Walsh, for your expertise, your advice and your encouragement; I am very grateful.

Thanks to my parents, my sisters and my extended family – especially, my aunt, Vera McGrath – who are constantly supportive and interested – cheers: I hope I do you proud.

To the people who supported me locally, Joe McCabe, Michael McDonnell, Donagh McKeown, Michelle and Philip in Keegan's bookshop, Carrickmacross and Ann and John in Crannóg bookshop, Cavan.

For their comments and support, thanks to Sue Leonard, the members of bibliofemme.com, Mary Gallagher of the Irish World in London and Lucille Redmond.

For their help in my research, thanks to my brother-in-law, Sergeant Pasty Baldwin and Teresa Mansfield.

Part of this novel is about the highs and lows of teenage friendship. I couldn't help looking back on my own teenage years while writing this book and thinking how blessed I am to have shared this sensitive and exhilarating period with my lifelong friend, Deirdre O'Donoghue. So, to you, Deidre, thanks for your loyalty, your strength and, above all, the crack.

A huge thanks to my agent, Jonathan Williams. Along the way, your encouragement has inspired me to do better.

And, finally, to Eamonn, Kevin and Olivia: for making me feel like a success, every day of my life.

DENISE SEWELL

SOME GIRLS WILL

'This could be how *Angela's Ashes* would have read, had Frank McCourt grown up in the 1980s' *Irish Independent*

Marcella and Teresa. Niece and aunt. Two sides of the same coin: smart, funny, feisty – and on a collision course.

By turns, funny, sexy and heart-breaking, *Some Girls Will* is the story of a fateful year in the lives of two irrepressible women. A year when their loyalty to each other is tested beyond endurance and they discover the real meaning of family, friendship and love.

'Astonishing ... echoes of [Roddy] Doyle's earlier work ... her characters also bounce off the page' *Woman's Way*

'In the style of TV's *Shameless*, the Buckleys may be going through the roughest of rough patches, but there is knockabout comedy in their commonsense wit' *Irish Examiner*

'Brilliantly written ... achingly honest ... captivating' *Bibliofemme.com*

He just wanted a decent book to read ...

Not too much to ask, is it? It was in 1935 when Allen Lane, Managing Director of Bodley Head Publishers, stood on a platform at Exeter railway station looking for something good to read on his journey back to London. His choice was limited to popular magazines and poor-quality paperbacks – the same choice faced every day by the vast majority of readers, few of whom could afford hardbacks. Lane's disappointment and subsequent anger at the range of books generally available led him to found a company – and change the world.

'We believed in the existence in this country of a vast reading public for intelligent books at a low price, and staked everything on it'
Sir Allen Lane, 1902–1970, founder of Penguin Books

The quality paperback had arrived – and not just in bookshops. Lane was adamant that his Penguins should appear in chain stores and tobacconists, and should cost no more than a packet of cigarettes.

Reading habits (and cigarette prices) have changed since 1935, but Penguin still believes in publishing the best books for everybody to enjoy. We still believe that good design costs no more than bad design, and we still believe that quality books published passionately and responsibly make the world a better place.

So wherever you see the little bird – whether it's on a piece of prize-winning literary fiction or a celebrity autobiography, political tour de force or historical masterpiece, a serial-killer thriller, reference book, world classic or a piece of pure escapism – you can bet that it represents the very best that the genre has to offer.

Whatever you like to read – trust Penguin.